ONCE UPON a DREAM

ALL THAT GLITTERS

Also by Barbara Jean Hicks
in Large Print:

An Unlikely Prince
China Doll

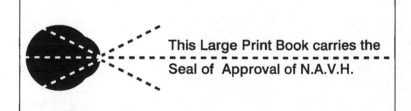

This Large Print Book carries the
Seal of Approval of N.A.V.H.

ONCE UPON a DREAM

ALL THAT GLITTERS

BARBARA JEAN HICKS

Thorndike Press • Waterville, Maine

The characters and events in this book are fictional, and any resemblance to actual persons or events is coincidental.

Published in 2003 by arrangement with WaterBrook Press, a division of Random House, Inc.

Thorndike Press® Large Print Candlelight Series.

The tree indicium is a trademark of Thorndike Press.

The text of this Large Print edition is unabridged. Other aspects of the book may vary from the original edition.

Set in 16 pt. Plantin by Myrna S. Raven.

Printed in the United States on permanent paper.

Library of Congress Cataloging-in-Publication Data

Hicks, Barbara Jean.
    All that glitters : a romantic comedy / by Barbara Jean Hicks.
        p. cm. (Once upon a dream)
    ISBN 0-7862-5078-X (lg. print : hc : alk. paper)
    1. Triangles (Interpersonal relations) — Fiction.
2. Women fashion designers — Fiction. 3. Washington (State) — Fiction. 4. Large type books. I. Title.
PS3558.I22976 A78 2003
  813'.54—dc21   2002043059

To Michael,
whose sense of humor
and sense of delight in the world
constantly renew my own.

Acknowledgments

Thanks again to Grace Witwer Housholder for permission to use stories from her delightful volumes *The Funny Things Kids Say Can Brighten Any Day.*

Thanks also to Rachelle Atlas, Donna Davis, Lori Hinkle, Carolyn Schultz, and Annelie Thurin-Mullen for insight into the world of apparel design and apparel manufacturing. Your ideas and information took me on wild flights of fancy!

Finally, thanks to my brother Bill and his wife, Denise, for sharing their expertise in carpentry and nursing. Cindy wouldn't have been the same without you.

1

"I'm surprised Filene hasn't married you off yet, Franklin."

Franklin Cameron Fitz III threw a startled glance at his rearview mirror, where his eyes met the sharp, bright eyes of his passenger. "Married me off?" he said weakly.

The vintage limousine — a 1949 Packard Custom that Franklin drove as often as he could wrestle the keys away from its equally vintage chauffeur — suddenly hit a bump, sending Miniver Macready's reflection flying and Franklin's eyes jumping back to the road.

He gripped the wheel more firmly. A half mile of tricky curves and potholes lay between his aunt's house on the hill overlooking Bellingrath Bay and the interstate below.

"Toad Mountain Road is *never* this warty when I ride with Eustace, Franklin," Miniver complained from the backseat. "If you were my chauffeur — well, you wouldn't be for long, that's all. And yes — married you off. You don't think she's

7

going to leave it to chance, now, do you?"

"Really, Aunt Min! *You* don't think she'd go so far as to arrange my marriage!"

"To keep you from choosing 'imprudently,' as she would say? I most certainly do."

For a moment, Franklin was silent. It was true that in his stepmother's eyes, impropriety was practically the unforgivable sin. And Filene had very definite ideas about what was "proper."

"She *is* always going on about the daughter of this friend at the tennis club, or the niece of that friend on the opera board, or the granddaughter of some university president," he admitted.

"I'm sure she is."

Franklin thought it wise not to tell his aunt about the episode with Aubrey du Puy and her mother in Seattle last weekend. "We were in the neighborhood and thought we'd drop by," Mrs. du Puy had said at the time. Even then, Franklin had wondered. Something about the knowing glances the women had tossed each other.

To his relief, the glamorous Aubrey had made it clear from the moment she set foot in the historic Fitz family mansion in Washington Park that she was more interested in the newly redecorated French Renaissance drawing room than she was in Franklin. She "adored" the Louis XVI furniture and the antique Aubusson rug and the Sevres and Meissen porcelain. Noting that Franklin didn't share her enthusiasm, she'd directed her comments to Filene, who of course found her enchanting.

And why wouldn't she? They were cut from the same high-society-maven mold, Filene and Aubrey. Two peas in a pod. Practically clones.

"You might have made yourself a little more charming," Filene had rebuked him after what seemed the longest hour of tea and chitchat he'd ever endured. "It's time you started thinking seriously about a suitable match, Franklin. Aubrey du Puy has brains, beauty, money, and social status. What more could you ask for?"

Originality, he would have answered if he'd thought Filene was really interested. *Warmth. A sense of humor. A kind and caring heart.*

"I won't let her do it, Aunt Min," Franklin now said firmly. "I'm not the least bit interested in her cookie-cutter socialites."

"Of course you're not! And the best defense is a good offense, Franklin."

"I beg your pardon?"

"If you don't want Filene arranging your love life," Aunt Min said, "you'd better see to arranging it yourself."

He sighed. As Aunt Min knew, he hadn't had much luck in the romance department. The trouble was, not many women appealed to him. The trouble was, no woman had ever captured his interest for longer than two or three dates.

The trouble was, he wanted to feel about a woman the way his father had felt about his mother: As if his happiness depended on her smile, Franklin Cameron Fitz Jr. used to say about Molly Macready Fitz. As if his very life depended on her being there. As if they shared one heart.

If that was love, so far Franklin hadn't felt anything close to it.

"If you need some help . . ." Aunt Min paused, clearly inviting Franklin's eager acceptance of her assistance.

"Oh no," he groaned. "Don't tell me — you know a girl."

Her face in the mirror looked peeved. "Yes, I do know a girl," she huffed. "And it just so happens she would be perfect for you." The annoyance in her voice increased as she muttered, "If only she weren't so besotted with that boyfriend of hers . . ."

Besotted or not, the girl in question, at the moment, had only one thing on her mind: how to get Gordie Wyatt out from under the table before the lunch rush started at the Kitsch 'n' Caboodle Café. The pint-size redhead hadn't taken well to his mother's scolding; all he'd wanted to do was give his baby brother a hug.

Or was Cindy Reilly being generous about the little rapscallion's motives?

Life was rarely dull in the Kitsch 'n' Caboodle, where Cindy worked, in the little town of Pilchuck, Washington — a dozen miles north of Miniver Macready's Bellingrath home. And it was *never* dull when Gordie Wyatt was around.

Cindy could only sympathize with his mother, Priscilla; the carrot-haired, freckle-faced four-year-old was every inch an imp.

On the other hand, it had to be hard after almost five years as the center of attention to have a squalling, red-faced monkey suddenly upstaging him at every turn. Cindy had been seven, already past the "cute" stage, when the twins were born; seventeen years later, she still remembered how it felt to play second fiddle.

"Hey, Gordie," she said in a stage whisper. She was on her hands and knees, her head poked between the stainless-steel legs of a chair.

"Hey, Cindy-relly!" Gordie whispered back. His sudden grin was right off the cover of *Mad* magazine. "Is my mom after you *too?!*"

Cindy laughed. "Not exactly," she said, grinning back. "I just wanted to see what was so interesting down here."

"Gum." Gordie opened his hand, proudly displaying several pieces of dried, chewed gum, obviously peeled from the underside of the table.

"Ee-yew! You haven't put any of that stuff in your mouth, have you?!"

"It's *yucky*," he said, making a face.

Cindy shuddered. "Come on out and we'll get you a fresh piece from the gumball machine," she coaxed.

"My mom won't let me."

"I think she will this time."

Priscilla Wyatt sighed as her son crawled out from under the table. "You've earned your tip a hundredfold today, Cindy," she said. "If the twins have half your golden touch, KinderKottage is in good hands."

Cindy's sisters, newly graduated from Pilchuck High School, were helping out at KinderKottage Preschool and Day Care Center for the summer.

Cindy pulled a penny out of her pocket and scooted Gordie off to the gumball machine. She poked a finger at the infant in the carrier on the table, smiling when he grabbed it and held on. "Hello, Baby Gregor," she cooed. Then, to Priscilla: "Robin and Rosie are having the time of their lives at KinderKottage. And so is Olga Pfefferkuchen, if I read her right. Doesn't that beat all!"

"Suzie's doings," Priscilla said. "Certainly not mine."

"The good Lord's doings," a voice corrected the redhead from over Cindy's shoulder. Suzie Wyatt — no, make that Suzie Wyatt *Hunt* — slipped into the booth across from her sister-in-law and plunked down a white satin photo album on the table.

"Hi, Cindy. Sorry I'm late, Pris," Suzie said. "I stopped by the Foto-Mat to pick up our honeymoon pictures and got stuck behind Carl Peabody." Carl, editor of the *Pilchuck Post*, was also the local weekly's chief photographer. "And then they weren't even ready."

"Murphy's Law," said Cindy.

"Murphy's Law," Suzie agreed. "Anyway — Olga Pfefferkuchen. The good Lord's doings. After all the fuss she made last fall about closing down KinderKottage, whoever would have guessed she'd volunteer to step in for me so Harrison and I could have a honeymoon? And for Pris until she's ready to come back to work?"

"Not me," Priscilla said, shaking her head.

"Like I said — the good Lord's doings."

A sudden clatter from the direction of the front door interrupted their conversation. "Gordon Randall Wyatt!" Priscilla shrieked as bright-colored gumballs bounced across the black-and-white tiled floor and Gordie scrambled after them like — well, like a kid after candy.

"Tell Biddy to send me the bill for the gumball machine, Cindy," Priscilla said, her voice resigned. She slid from the booth and headed for Gordie.

"Stuff and nonsense!" A plump, energetic woman in her fifties hurried from behind the counter with an empty bucket. Biddy Barton, along with her husband Buster, was Kitsch 'n' Caboodle's owner and Cindy's boss. Her bouffant hairdo and rhinestone-studded cat's-eye glasses were right out of a fifties high-school yearbook, and her cotton-print shirtwaist looked like something the Beaver's mother might have worn.

"The little mite just hit the jackpot, is all," Biddy said cheerfully. "The durned thing does that once in a while." She knelt to set the plastic container on the floor next to Gordie. "A penny for every gumball you get in the bucket, boy-o. After 'em, now!" Then, glancing up: "Cindy, I was just about to make rounds with the coffeepot —"

"I've got it," Cindy said, hurrying around the counter. Harley Burns, retired county extension agent, lifted his cup along with his bushy eyebrows as she rounded the corner. Harley was a stickler for service. There could have been an earthquake shaking the pictures off the wall, and Harley would want his coffee cup filled the instant it hit empty.

When Gordie started popping gumballs in his mouth instead of the bucket, an exasperated Priscilla gave up on the whole idea of lunch. She told Suzie she'd catch her another time — possibly after Gordie was twenty-one — grabbed her baby carrier, her diaper bag, and her chipmunk-cheeked imp of a kid, and was out the door, looking none too happy.

"Join us at the counter, Suzie," Jonas Muncey urged the petite brunette who'd been abandoned in her booth. Jonas was a Saturday morning Kitsch 'n' Caboodle regular who owned Strip Joint Furniture Refinishing and Drive-Through Espresso at the edge of town.

Suzie did, hauling along her coffee cup and photo album.

Cindy leaned her elbows on the counter. "That wouldn't be your wedding pictures?" she asked, not hiding her eagerness.

"The very same," said Suzie, smiling. "Featuring a certain gown designed by the very-soon-to-be famous Cindy Reilly."

Cindy blushed. But she was already reaching for the book.

Franklin Fitz, meanwhile, was getting an earful about Cindy Reilly. Whether he wanted to hear it or not. He sighed. When Aunt Min got a bee in her bonnet, she couldn't be stopped.

"It's a shame she's waiting tables," his aunt was saying now. "With *her* talent. But it couldn't be helped, her father dying just when she was set to go off to design school. Not that she needed schooling,

16

mind you. That girl's a natural. A wonder, Franklin. A whiz!"

Franklin slowed the limo as he approached the stop sign at the bottom of the hill. "Oh?" he asked absently. "What kind of a whiz?"

"Didn't I just say she was set to go off to design school when her father died?" Aunt Min said irritably. "A design whiz, of course."

Franklin sighed. His aunt was never exactly sweet as honey, but this was ridiculous. It was that silly diet she put herself on every summer. Diets made her so *snappish*.

Besides, she was built the way she was built, and no diet on earth was going to change that. In fact, she regularly occupied the backseat of the limousine not for the sake of propriety — which meant less than nothing to Aunt Min — but because her ample hips and sturdy piano legs required more room than the front seat afforded. It was unfortunate, but that's the way it was.

"I'm sure she's very talented," he soothed.

"Of course she is! And such a love, Franklin. It really *is* too bad she's so besotted with that boyfriend of hers."

"Aunt Min — please! You don't think one matchmaker in my life is enough?"

"I'm not Filene," she snapped. "And believe me, Cindy Reilly's no cookie-cutter socialite."

He sighed again. A good thing he was so easygoing, he told himself, or he'd be snapping right back at her. But he'd had plenty of practice dealing with snappishness, living with Filene for twenty-two years. By now, it was water off a duck's back.

"I'm sure she's not, Aunt Min."

She didn't say anything until he'd reached the interstate and safely merged into traffic on the freeway. When she did, her question was so unexpected he nearly lost his grip on the steering wheel.

"Are you happy, Franklin?"

He could literally feel his stomach sinking. "Happy? What do you mean?"

"What do you mean, what do I mean?" she snapped. "Are you happy with your life, or aren't you?"

"Happy," Franklin repeated helplessly. "It isn't something I sit around thinking about, Aunt Min."

"Well maybe you should, Franklin. Molly and Fitzy, God rest their souls, would certainly want you to be happy."

Molly and Fitzy. Aunt Min's sister and brother-in-law, Franklin's mother and father. So he wasn't the only one who had

18

them on his mind today. If things had worked out differently, it would have been their twenty-seventh wedding anniversary.

"Do you think they could have lived happily ever after, Aunt Min?"

He didn't especially want to talk about his parents, today of all days; just thinking about them brought a lump to his throat. But talking about them was better than talking about whether or not he was happy. Where in the world did his aunt come up with these things?

"Or would they have ended up barely tolerating each other?" he prompted. "Like Father and Filene?"

"Molly was as different from Filene as a ladybug is from a black widow spider," Aunt Min said emphatically. "And as far as 'happily ever after' goes, I'd say your parents had a better chance than most. It was something rare and wonderful, Franklin, what the two of 'em had."

"Then what*ever* possessed Father to marry Filene?"

"Filene may have her faults," Aunt Min said. Then, correcting herself: "Filene *does* have her faults. But stupidity isn't one of them, Franklin. After your mother died — well, she took advantage of your father's grief, to put it plainly. Fitzy's broken heart wanted mending, and Filene was on the spot, duct tape in hand." She sighed extravagantly. "I expect she thought she had a right, being Fitzy's ex-fiancée."

"What?" Franklin's startled gaze once again met Miniver's in the rearview mirror. "You mean before he married Mother? Father and Filene were *engaged?*"

"They were. And when Filene saw her second chance at Fitzdom after Molly died, she grabbed it in a heartbeat, I can tell you."

Franklin shook his head in disbelief.

"I wouldn't find it in me to forgive her," Aunt Min added, "except that in a way I do believe she saved your father's life. Which needed saving" — her voice went suddenly and unexpectedly soft — "as he had a precious son who needed saving too."

Franklin squirmed in his seat. *Precious* was Aunt Min's adjective of choice for her nephew, a fact that caused him no end of mortification. Such sentimental talk was by no means typical of his aunt either. She seemed to reserve it just for him.

"Have you met my precious Franklin?" she would say to introduce him. Or meeting *his* friends for the first time, "So you're a friend of Franklin's. Isn't he just *precious?!*" Linking her arm in his, or even, unbelievably — when she happened to catch him off guard — grabbing his cheeks and shaking his face like an old lady fussing over a baby.

The very thought made him tug self-consciously at the bill of Eustace Phillips's chauffeur's cap. There wasn't a soul on earth he adored the way he did Aunt Min — except for Cookie, of course — but he was twenty-six years old, for crying out loud!

And Aunt Min might complain from time to time that she was over the hill — but an old lady? Hardly.

So her hair was gray — it had been for as long as Franklin could remember. Besides, it was a stunning shade of gray. More silver, really, and falling in shiny waves to her shoulders in a very *un*-old-ladyish way. Her skin was smooth, and her dark eyes, framed by a pair of equally dark eyebrows, snapped with energy and didn't miss anything.

"You deserve to be happy, Franklin," she was saying now.

He sighed. How could he disagree?

The problem was, as far as he could tell, happily-ever-after wasn't the easiest trick to pull off.

21

2

Pushing aside the bluebird-of-happiness salt-and-pepper shakers, the glass-slipper sugar caddy, and the Minnie Mouse napkin holder on the counter, Cindy Reilly opened Suzie's wedding album to the portrait on the first page.

Her brown eyes went immediately misty. Suzie and Harrison Hunt positively glowed with happiness as they gazed at each other. Harrison looked dashing in his cutaway and satin-striped trousers and bowler hat. And Suzie — well, Suzie was a fairy-tale princess. No other description would do.

"You and your mother outdid yourselves on that wedding gown, Cindy," Biddy's voice came from over her shoulder.

"You did," Suzie fervently agreed. "I've never felt so beautiful in all my life."

Cindy felt her face flush with satisfaction. *We did,* she thought. *We really did.*

Cait Reilly had brought her daughter's design to life in winter white silk peau de soie with pink and mocha ribbon-embroidery and tiny ribbon-rose appliqués that trailed across the fitted bodice, down the length, and around the hem of the full, floor-length skirt. It was even more beautiful than Cindy had imagined it.

Creating Suzie's wedding gown wasn't the first time Cindy and her mother had collaborated. They made a great team, Cindy and Cait Reilly. Demand for their joint creations continued to grow.

Cait was already something of a legend in Tillicum County. After all, she could look at a drawing or photograph of a dress, a suit, a coat, or a formal gown and reproduce it exactly, down to the last hook and eye.

And Cindy — well, Cindy intended to be a legend even beyond Tillicum County. Someday.

"Happy Chic!" the fashion magazine headlines would blare. "Designer Cindy Reilly Brings Smiles to the Runway with Glad Raggs Line! Angst Is Out, Fun Is In!"

Yes, someday she was going to see her designs hanging on the racks of Bergdorf Goodman, Saks Fifth Avenue, Strawbridge & Fitz. She knew there was a market for her fanciful Glad Raggs party dresses — part Todd Oldham–whimsical, part Bob Mackie–outrageous, part Karl Lagerfeld–soigné, yet still one hundred percent Cindy Reilly–original.

If only she could find some way to increase production! Selling her designs one dress at a time through Nadine's Not-Your-Basic-Black-Dress Shop in the county seat at Bellingrath simply wasn't going to make her name.

Everything Cindy knew about fabric and draping and pattern-making and tailoring — the backbone of an apparel designer's education — she'd learned from her mother. And a good thing, too, since her coveted scholarship to design school had had to go unused. The summer after high school was the summer her father died. The twins had been only ten. Her mother had needed her.

So here she was, seven years later, still in Pilchuck and still working what was supposed to have been a one-summer job. Still dreaming and sketching and sewing. Waiting tables, biding time . . .

Not that she minded waiting tables while she bided her time. Biddy and Buster, not to mention the Kitsch 'n' Caboodle regulars who came in every day, were practically family by now. But seven years was still a long time to wait. And a very long time to wait tables.

She leaned over Suzie's album, her elbows on the counter, studying the wedding portrait dreamily. A wreath woven of roses, ribbon, and baby's breath circled the bride's head, while additional ribbons in pink, mocha, and white satin cascaded down her back. The overall effect was both playful, like Suzie, and deliciously romantic.

"A fairy-tale princess," Cindy repeated aloud, her expression rapturous.

Suzie laughed. "I'll go along with the fairy-tale part," she said wryly. "Complete with seven dwarfs!" Leaning over the counter, she flipped several pages over to a picture of herself and Harrison surrounded by children. The girls wore pretty dresses with lace collars; the boys, miniature tuxedos.

Suzie's day-care charges — including her nephew Gordie. Cindy knew the band of rug rats well; Kitsch 'n' Caboodle was a once-a-month lunchtime field trip for the KinderKottage crew.

"Life was a little *too* much like a fairy tale for a while there," Suzie added, "what with Olga Pfefferkuchen standing in for the wicked witch and Harrison for the poisoned apple."

Cindy knew the story, of course. In a little town like Pilchuck, word got around. In fact, the Kitsch 'n' Caboodle Café was the second-best spot within the city limits to get the scoop on what was going on in Pilchuck: who did what to whom, and where and when, and mostly what everyone else was saying about it. Cindy never got all the details that True Marie Weatherby, down at the Belle o' the Ball Beauty Salon, picked up, but a waitress in a busy diner overheard a lot in the course of a day. A *lot*.

By this time — the middle of June — the romance between Suzie Wyatt and Harrison Hunt was practically Pilchuck legend. Everybody knew how one-time sourpuss Olga Pfefferkuchen had set out to close down Suzie's preschool; how Harrison had fallen in love with Suzie and tried to hide the fact he'd been in on the plot to put her out of business; how Suzie, in an awe-inspiring display of temper right in the middle of Main Street, had reamed him up and down for his betrayal.

But they'd worked it out. And here they were, home from their honeymoon, and Suzie as radiant as anyone had ever seen her.

It was all so delectably romantic . . .

Cindy Reilly sighed. Despite the sorrows and setbacks she'd experienced already in her twenty-four years, she believed wholeheartedly in fairy tales. After all, she had a name about as close to Cinderella as a name could get. And while she didn't have a wicked stepmother and two wicked stepsisters who forced her to wait on them hand and foot, waiting tables during a busy lunch rush could feel an awful lot like it. More than once she'd wanted to snap at someone, "I'm your *server*, not your *servant!*"

Her name and job aside, the number-one reason Cindy believed in fairy tales was the fact that she had her very own fairy-tale prince.

And he was perfect.

She clasped her hands to her chest, unconsciously fingering the simple promise ring she'd been wearing almost forever. She and Jonathan had been sweethearts since their junior year at Pilchuck High School. Eight years!

She'd never forget the moment when Jonathan Crum — captain of the football team, president of the junior class, founder of the Pilchuck High School Sword of the Spirit Club, straight-A student, and star of every girl's dreams — sat down next to her in the school cafeteria and told her she was the prettiest, smartest, most interesting girl in Pilchuck and would she go to the homecoming dance with him?

They'd been inseparable ever since. Well, as inseparable as a couple could be when one of them lived in Pilchuck and the other a hundred miles and a world away in Seattle.

It hadn't been easy on either of them, Cindy staying behind in Pilchuck while Jonathan pursued his undergraduate and law degrees at Duwamish University. He came home on the weekends, of course. As often as he could — which hadn't been often enough the last few months while he finished up his schooling.

"Speaking of fairy tales," Suzie said, as if reading Cindy's mind, "how's Jonathan?"

"Oh, Suzie, he has just one more class this summer to get ready for the bar exam, and he's all done!"

Cindy was counting the days, too, because when Jonathan passed the Washington bar, he was coming home to Pilchuck to hang his shingle. And to marry her! No, she didn't have a diamond yet, but it was understood between them. More than understood. They'd been talking about it for years.

It would be just like Jonathan to officially propose on her birthday — just a month away, in mid-July. Jonathan Crum

28

was a master of the romantic moment.

They wouldn't want a long engagement, after all the waiting they'd already done. Maybe they would marry at Christmas — Cindy did love Christmas. Then they'd move into a little house together, a place of their very own. Maybe one of those charming Tudor-style cottages on Hokan-vander Street. The perfect setting for the rest of her personal fairy tale to unfold.

It only got better, the farther into the future Cindy looked. When Jonathan's practice got off the ground, she'd finally be able to quit her job at the Kitsch 'n' Caboodle and concentrate all her energies on Glad Raggs. Someday in the foreseeable future her gowns would be parading down New York runways, draping elegant mannequins in upscale department stores, gliding effortlessly across dance floors at charity balls . . .

And then when the time was right, after they had their respective careers off the ground, she and Jonathan would have a pair of beautiful, talented, well-behaved children. A boy first, and then a girl.

And, of course, they'd all live happily ever after.

Franklin absently pulled the Packard

around a semi lumbering up the hill at the north end of Bellingrath, his mind in the past. When he hadn't responded to Aunt Min's last comment, she'd lapsed into silence, which was just as well, the mood she was in.

His father's relationship with his stepmother had always been a puzzle to Franklin. And how odd he'd never heard about that pre-Molly engagement!

Then again, maybe not so odd . . .

Filene, after all, would never tell a story that reflected badly on herself. And for a woman who still unabashedly believed in class distinctions, what could possibly reflect more poorly than being thrown over for a common shop girl?

Pretty, perky Molly Macready, Miniver's younger sister, had bought a one-way ticket out of Tillicum County the day after high-school graduation. Tillicum County wasn't big enough for either of the Macready girls. By that time Miniver was studying piano on full scholarship at Julliard, getting ready to take on the world.

Molly's aspirations were more modest than her sister's; she'd stepped off the bus ninety miles south of Bellingrath in Seattle, where she found a job as a men's shoe clerk at the flagship Strawbridge & Fitz department store downtown.

Franklin Cameron Fitz Jr. — "Fitzy" to those who knew him best — had been her last customer on her first day of work. She'd sold him a pair of Florsheim tan-and-oxblood saddle shoes, a pair of Sperry Topsiders, and one of the very first pairs of Birkenstocks ever made — not a pair of which he ever would have bought on his own. The rest, as they say, was history.

At least, that was the story Franklin Cameron Fitz III remembered his mother telling him more than once in his first four years. The last time was the night of his parents' five-year anniversary — their last anniversary, twenty-two years ago today. The fact that it was the last time he ever saw his mother alive made it the bedtime story he would never forget.

By the time he was six years old, it was Filene tucking him into bed. Or, more likely, Cookie Simms, before she made her way across the garden to the cottage she shared with her husband, Clement, who ran the grounds of the Fitz estate as efficiently as Cookie ran the kitchen. Cookie had been more of a mother to Franklin than Filene had ever been.

His father was as unlikely to have told Franklin about his history with Filene as was Filene herself. His father simply hadn't talked about his second wife. He *had* talked about Molly, though, once in a while, when he and Franklin were alone. Enough for Franklin to know that what his parents had had between them was, as Aunt Min said, "something rare and wonderful." Enough to ruin Franklin for a merely satisfactory relationship with a merely adequate mate.

The only other thing Franklin could remember his father ever talking about was business. Pro forma projections, break-even analyses, inventory turnover, profit margins. And, of course, how proud he was of Franklin's business aptitude. How much he counted on him. How pleased he was to have a son to carry on the Strawbridge & Fitz commitment to quality when he was gone.

Whoever would have guessed how soon that would be?

Before he could congratulate his son for graduating with honors from Duwamish University's Graduate School of Finance and Business Administration.

Before he could see Franklin settled into his very own cubicle in the accounting department at Strawbridge & Fitz, analyzing operating decisions, preparing financial statements, gaining a thorough under-standing of the company's bottom line. Preparing himself to take his place on the company's board of directors and lead it confidently into the twenty-first century.

But not before Franklin had made the mistake of telling his father he had his own dream.

Out of the blue, as if she knew exactly what he was thinking, Aunt Min once again broke into the silence:

"So tell me, Franklin — how's work?"

He swallowed. He was beginning to feel sorry he'd swiped the keys from Eustace this morning. Aunt Min was hitting every nerve.

Maybe it wasn't just her, he told himself. Maybe sharing his aunt's diet fare this morning had made him overly sensitive. Cabbage soup and raw vegetables wasn't exactly his stomach's idea of a good time, especially for breakfast. If he'd known she'd started her summer regimen, he'd have stopped off at a grocery store on his way from Seattle to pick up a box of Rice Krispies and a quart of milk.

"Work is work, Aunt Min," he answered her question. "I'm doing my part to carry on the business, just the way Father wanted me to."

"Harrumph. Strawbridge & Fitz wouldn't go under without you, you know."

He sighed, wishing, not for the first time, that he could make her understand. Aunt Min had always lived by her own rules. She was just too free a spirit to comprehend his sense of obligation to the Fitz family business — a duty even more weighty now that his father was gone.

After all, the Fitzes who'd preceded Franklin III had made Strawbridge & Fitz a name that *meant* something. Quality, style, value, service. It was up to him to make sure the business continued to live up to its name. His father had certainly made that clear enough. Why, the last words Franklin had heard from his father's lips were, *I depend on you, Son.*

Sometimes he did envy Aunt Min's independence though.

"Duty is as duty does, Franklin. You really do deserve to be happy."

He stifled a groan. She was worse than a dog with a bone! "Did I tell you I got out my sousaphone last week?" he asked a little too brightly. *Happy!* A man had to do what a man had to do; "happy" didn't come into it.

"Your sousaphone!" Aunt Min cried, clearly delighted.

Good — he'd derailed her!

"Didn't sound half bad either," he said. "At least, according to Cookie."

"And what was the occasion?"

"Believe it or not, Cookie's talked me into joining the Leschi Senior Center John Philip Sousa Memorial Concert Band."

"A band!"

"They lost their sousaphone player not long ago," he added.

Imagine — Sousa without a sousaphone! had been Cookie's actual words. *We might as well cash the whole thing in, Biscuit. Unless you could see your way to helping us out. At least for the summer.*

Biscuit, Franklin thought, tugging once again at the bill of Eustace's cap. Between Cookie's "Biscuit" and Aunt Min's "Precious," anyone who didn't know better would think he was a babe in arms!

But then, compared to the other members of the John Philip Sousa Memorial Concert Band, he was. A good two dozen musicians, and not a one of them under sixty-five. "We have a gig at the senior center on the Fourth of July," he said, "and a couple more in August during Seafair. In the food court at Seattle Center, of all places."

Aunt Min clapped her hands. "What fun!"

"Those old-timers do know how to have fun," Franklin agreed, grinning as an image of Avery Farnsworth going wild on the snare drums flickered across his mind.

"Speaking of old-timers," Miniver said as Franklin crested the last hill before the Pilchuck exit, "you'll find an interesting collection at the Kitsch 'n' Caboodle Café in town. Eustace fits in at the Kitsch 'n' Caboodle like a penguin at a nuns' convention."

Anywhere Eustace Phillips fit in was bound to be interesting. Aunt Min's chauffeur was almost as eccentric as Aunt Min. An old flame of Miniver Macready's mother, he'd lost his chance with his sweetheart when he'd gone to work as a long-haul truck driver; she'd wanted hearth and home, he'd needed the open road.

Eustace never had married, and he still loved to drive. Chauffeuring for the daughter of the woman he'd loved almost as much as he'd loved driving gave meaning to his sunset years, he said. He lived in the basement apartment of Aunt Min's house, took care of the place the nine months out of twelve she was away on her concert tours, and catered to her every whim in the summer, when she was home.

It was a most agreeable arrangement all around.

Miniver pointed out the Kitsch 'n' Caboodle Café as they passed it on their way through town. Franklin did a double take; a giant, inflatable Betty Boop was tethered to the roof.

"The coffee's Pretty Darn Good," Aunt Min said.

A local brand that lived up to its name, if Franklin remembered right.

"And Buster Barton's a pretty darn good cook," she added. "You might want to have yourself some lunch while I'm about my business at the Reillys', Franklin. Unless you're up for cabbage soup again."

Franklin's stomach growled loudly, as if on cue. "I'll take your word on the cook," he said. "I don't think I can do cabbage soup two meals in a row, Aunt Min. You're a braver soul than I am."

He followed her directions to a street of small, well-kept houses of the Victorian working-class style. "The one with the gingerbread," she said.

They all had gingerbread, but there was no mistaking which house Aunt Min meant. The siding was beige, but the gingerbread was detailed in no less than half a dozen colors: pink, raspberry, lilac, chartreuse, and two different shades of blue. It shouldn't have worked, but somehow, it did.

"Wow." Franklin stopped the car at the curb and stared. *The Reillys,* a painted sign over the front porch read. "You didn't tell me your dressmaker was the Sugarplum Fairy."

Aunt Min laughed in delight. "Isn't it splendid?"

"It's highly original," Franklin said. A compliment — he liked original almost more than anything.

"I'll look you up at the Kitsch 'n' Caboodle when I'm through," she said.

"You're sure? I have my cell phone, if you want to call."

Aunt Min shook her head. "The exercise will do me good. And I'll want to say hello to Cindy."

Cindy again. "If she's the whiz you say she is, why's she waiting tables?"

"Didn't I say it couldn't be helped?" Aunt Min answered peevishly.

Franklin sighed. And here he thought he'd worked her into a better mood.

"It's that silly *duty* thing," she said as Franklin opened the trunk of the Packard and she began to unload its contents into his arms. "Though I must say hers isn't so displaced as yours is, Franklin."

Water off a duck's back, Franklin reminded himself, breathing deeply.

"And it's the money, too, of course," Aunt Min went on, adding the last bolt of fabric onto the pile in his arms.

"Of course," he answered automatically.

"If I could put my hands on the money, I'd set her up in business myself, Franklin. I have that much confidence in Cindy Reilly." She slammed the trunk as if to emphasize her words.

Franklin kept his mouth shut. He'd never liked the idea that Miniver's business agent had all her savings tied up in a trust annuity, but frankly, without it, she probably *would* spend all her money willy-nilly on things she knew nothing about. Like, for instance, setting up the Cindy Reillys of the world in business.

"She's such a love, Franklin!"

"I'm sure she is, Aunt Min," he answered carefully.

"And no cookie-cutter socialite either."

"I'm sure she's not, Aunt Min." He followed her up the steps to the front porch of the colorful Victorian.

"You get yourself some lunch at the Kitsch 'n' Caboodle," she said as she punched the doorbell, "and we'll stop at the market on the way back to Bellingrath for meat and potatoes for your supper. Cabbage soup's no diet for a growing boy."

"I don't want to be a bother, Aunt Min."

She turned around, her dark eyes gleaming. "You're never a bother, dear boy." Before he could guess what she was going to do, she grabbed his cheeks in either hand and gently shook his face. With his arms piled high with bolts of cloth, he was helpless as a baby to stop her.

The door opened.

"Oh, hello, Cait," Miniver said gaily, dropping her hands. "I don't believe you've ever met my nephew, Franklin. Isn't he *precious?*"

3

"Was that your fairy godmother's limo I saw go by a few minutes ago?"

"I didn't see it, but most likely," Cindy answered Biddy, as if the question wasn't the least bit out of the ordinary. "You don't see too many cars like Mini Mac's around, and she does have an appointment with Mom today."

"Guess we'll know for sure if Eustace shows up in the next five minutes," Suzie put in.

"Eustace wouldn't miss coffee at the Kitsch 'n' Caboodle," Cindy agreed.

It was Cait who'd first christened Miniver Macready the Reilly family fairy godmother. "What is she, if not a fairy godmother?" Cait inquired of her three daughters — not expecting an answer — the year after Cindy's father died. "An angel? A *godsend,* that's for certain. An indisputable answer to prayer. We'd be paupers without her, girls, plain and simple. We'd be destitute."

Cindy's mother tended to overdramatize. Life hadn't been easy for the Reillys since

Joe-Joe's tragic death, it was true. But between Cindy's job and the dressmaking business, they'd always managed to get by. Why, practically every wedding in the county — not to mention the annual Tillicum County Blossomtime Festival in Bellingrath — featured a Cait Reilly production or two. And as often as not these days, the gowns were Cindy's designs, which upped the ante.

Still, Miniver Macready — a world-class concert pianist and Tillicum County's resident celebrity — was their single most important client. Unfortunately for Mini Mac and fortunately for the Reillys, she was nearly six feet tall and built from the waist down somewhat like the instrument she played, while from the waist up she resembled a metronome. Nowhere on the racks of any dress shop or department store in the *universe* was she going to find ready-to-wear to fit her frame.

Enter Cindy and Cait Reilly.

Beyond her everyday wardrobe, Mini Mac had a perpetual need for magnificent concert gowns that "minimize here and maximize there and camouflage a multitude of evils," in her words. She marveled at the way Cindy's made-to-order designs accomplished that very thing. "You're a miracle worker, my dear," Mini Mac had told her on more than one occasion. "A wonder. A whiz!"

Cindy picked up the coffeepot and absently refilled the cups along the counter. She was grateful for more than just the business Mini Mac brought the Reillys, she told herself. The beautiful, brilliant scraps left over from the pianist's concert gowns, after all, had been the inspiration for Cindy's pieced-fabric Glad Raggs designs — and still provided their substance on occasion. She had a strong suspicion, in fact, that Mini Mac purposely bought more fabric than she needed just so Cindy would have more of it to play with.

How she'd managed to leave out so loyal, benevolent, and eccentric a patron as Miniver Macready while flipping through the fairy-tale features of her life, Cindy couldn't imagine. Mini Mac was as close to a fairy godmother as any real, live, actual person could get.

"How was Alaska, Suzie?"

Jonas Muncey called his question down the counter, interrupting Cindy's ruminations. Everyone sitting between Jonas and Suzie swung their heads to hear her answer.

"Incredible," Suzie said, smiling down

the line. "If you've never taken that Inside Passage cruise — do it."

"Taken my boat up as far as Princess Luisa Inlet," said Harley. "Prettiest place on God's green earth."

Alf Mayer begged to differ. "Prettiest place on God's green earth is right here in Tillicum County," he said.

"The good Lord outdid himself in both places, is my opinion," said Biddy, clearly trying to avert a hopeless argument.

"I don't doubt that one little bit," said Jonas.

The bell over the front door jangled. Cindy, along with everyone sitting at the counter, turned her head. The citizens of Pilchuck — at least the ones who frequented the Kitsch 'n' Caboodle Café — were nothing if not curious.

For an instant, the man in the doorway was no more than a dark silhouette against the morning light behind him, but all Cindy needed to see was his gold-trimmed cap and the graceful swan hood ornament on the vintage limousine at the curb out front to know it was Eustace Phillips.

Then he stepped forward hesitantly. Cindy's eyes widened. Eustace, who'd worked for Mini Mac as long as Mini Mac had been coming to the Reillys for her wardrobe, was an ageless little man with a ready smile, a twinkle in his eyes, and enormous ears that stuck out at right angles to his head. The man in the doorway was fifty years younger, at least, and definitely didn't have the ears. Or the smile. In fact, he looked a little dazed.

"You don't suppose something's happened to Eustace?" Biddy whispered worriedly.

"I'll find out," Cindy whispered back. She grabbed a menu and headed for the door.

The name of the restaurant, pulsating in pink and green neon in the window, and even the larger-than-life inflatable Betty Boop on the roof, staring across Main Street at the Apple Basket Market with her googly eyes, wasn't enough to prepare Franklin for the Kitsch 'n' Caboodle Café.

He felt, in fact, when he opened the door and crossed the threshold, automatically removing Eustace's chauffeur's cap from his head, as if he were entering into an alternate universe. A universe entirely without taste — which, despite his aunt's recommendation, wasn't a good sign when he was looking for lunch and a decent cup of coffee.

Every item on display in the Kitsch 'n' Caboodle begged for Franklin's attention. No — *screamed* for it:

The velvet Elvis, which held a position of obvious honor directly across from the doorway. The paint-by-number *Mona Lisa* and the crewel-embroidered Van Gogh *Sunflowers* that flanked the King. The series of Japanese geisha prints, burned around the edges and glued to thick slabs of highly varnished scrap wood, interspersed with studio shots of old movie stars and gaudy memorabilia from the 1962 Seattle World's Fair.

A lava lamp stood on one table and a Venus de Milo lamp with a garish Victorian-bordello-red-velvet shade on another. The coat rack inside the door was a wrought-iron replica of the Space Needle. The light fixture in the center of the room was crafted from deer antlers. If *crafted* was a word that even applied.

It went on and on, the glaring, blaring, incredibly tacky *stuff.* The effect was utterly mind-boggling. Franklin actually closed his eyes to get his bearings.

When he opened them again and saw a prototype for the All-American-Girl-Next-Door-Hometown-Sweetheart walking directly toward him, a dazzling smile lighting her face, her spun-gold ponytail swinging from side to side behind her, the glaring, blaring, incredibly tacky surroundings disappeared. Zip. Zap. Gone. Just like that.

There was only the girl, and her golden hair, and the smile that invited him to wonderful places he'd dreamed of but never visited.

He wondered suddenly how his father had felt the first time he'd set eyes on Molly Macready. Had the shoe department at Strawbridge & Fitz simply faded away around her? Had he felt himself beckoned, welcomed, invited in, like a weary traveler come home?

"One for lunch?" she asked brightly.

The question confused him. He gave his head a shake. "One — one *what?*"

She cocked her head, her brown eyes widening as she considered him curiously. No, not brown eyes; *cinnamon,* he thought. Her expression reminded him suddenly and unexpectedly of Cookie's beloved pair of Welsh corgis: earnest, alert, inquisitive. Friendly.

Not that she was in the least like a corgi in any other way. "Lean and long-legged" did *not* describe Zollie and Zelda.

"One — well, one *person,* I suppose," she said. "No one's ever asked before."

"Oh!" *Pull yourself together, man!* he admonished himself. *She's just a woman. That's all.* "One person. Yes. For lunch. Please." He twirled his cap nervously on one finger.

She turned away to lead him to a booth, and without the bewildering distraction of her gaze, the Kitsch 'n' Caboodle Café crashed into place around him.

He slid across the clear plastic that protected the red cut-velvet upholstery of the booth, setting his cap and newspaper on the table. A dour farmer and his equally dour wife — Grant Wood's *American Gothic* in jigsaw puzzle form — stared up at him from under the glass tabletop, while studio black-and-whites of Rock Hudson and Marilyn Monroe stared down at him from the knotty-pine paneling. A lamp shaped like the Statue of Liberty's hand holding an ice cream cone shared table space with a Campbell's soup kid napkin holder and pink poodle salt-and-pepper shakers.

Franklin looked up at the All-American-Girl-Next-Door-Hometown-Sweetheart to keep his head from spinning.

As if *that* would help.

She was as fresh and unspoiled as — he hated to say it even to himself, it seemed so trite — as fresh and unspoiled as a daisy, and dressed right out of a fifties TV show: a white, short-sleeved shirt tucked into bubblegum-pink cotton pants hemmed just below the knees, and pink ankle socks with tennis shoes. The dish towel wrapped around her hips was clean and white. A pink-and-green print scarf held back her curly golden ponytail. *Cindy,* her nametag read.

Ah. So this was Aunt Min's Cindy Reilly. The dressmaker's daughter. The one who would be perfect for him . . .

She smiled again as she handed him a menu. A wide, welcoming, generous smile. *Come in,* her cinnamon eyes seemed to say.

Without warning, Franklin heard Miniver's voice in his head: *Too bad she's so besotted with that boyfriend of hers.*

He didn't realize he was frowning till Cindy responded in kind. "What?" she asked.

He felt his face grow hot. Here he was, not only staring, but *scowling* at her! He smoothed his expression and blurted the first thing that came to mind. "Those pants," he said, gesturing. "I was just trying to think . . . what are those pants called? Bike pedalers or something?"

Cindy's frown cleared. Once again she

regarded him with curiosity. "Pedal pushers," she said. "I'm surprised you came as close as you did. Most people call them clam diggers these days."

"Oh."

"They're awkward for riding bicycles though. They tend to bunch up at the knees."

"Oh," he said again, not knowing what else to say.

"Lycra bike shorts are a better idea. For bicycling," she added. "Probably not for clam digging. And I wouldn't want to wear them waiting tables."

"Of course not," he said, feeling quite helpless to come up with anything more intelligent.

Cindy's no cookie-cutter socialite, Aunt Min's voice declared in his head.

He dropped his eyes to the menu, more to hide his confusion than anything else. The entire episode felt surreal: the surroundings, the woman, the conversation.

Cindy reached across the table and fiddled with the poodle salt-and-pepper shakers. "Nothing wrong with Eustace, is there?"

Her voice reflected genuine concern. At least, Franklin presumed it was genuine. He couldn't imagine anyone who looked as fresh and innocent as Cindy Reilly being anything but genuine.

"Eustace is fine," he said, peering at her over the top of the menu. My, but she appealed! And what was so bad about surreal, anyhow?

Her nametag came into focus once again. *Cindy,* he repeated to himself, and felt suddenly grounded. *Cindy.* A fine, all-purpose, no-nonsense, old-fashioned name, without pretensions. He liked it.

"In fact," he added, suddenly wanting to prolong the conversation, "I had to wrestle the keys away from Eustace to get him to let me drive."

She laughed. A low, throaty sort of laugh that made the breath catch in the back of Franklin's throat. "I hope you didn't hurt him," she said.

"Eustace can take care of himself," he managed around the catch.

She shoved her hands in the pockets of her pants and rocked back on her heels, smiling her generous, welcoming smile. "Eustace has been old and wrinkled and wizened since I first met him, but you're right. I'd never call him helpless."

Wizened, Franklin thought, delighted. It was the perfect word for Eustace. He gave himself up to Cindy's smile, relaxed into it, returned it in kind. "Eustace is a gnome," he said. "Gnomes know how to take care of themselves."

"A gnome! He is, isn't he?"

They smiled at each other, as if sharing some inside joke.

"Coffee while you're looking over the menu?" she offered.

"Please."

He watched her turn on her heel, her ponytail flouncing. *Oh my,* he thought as she walked away. *Oh my!* She was as lovely going as she was coming.

And as different from Filene's protégé Aubrey as a corgi was from a French-cut poodle. Not that there was anything *wrong* with French-cut poodles, he told himself; he simply preferred Cookie's wonderful, whimsical little dogs.

Cindy was back in a flash with a steaming mug of coffee. "How's Miniver?" she asked as she set it in front of him.

He smiled again. Smiling was so easy around her. "As full of vinegar as ever. Even jet lag doesn't take it out of her." Aunt Min was only a week back from an Asian concert tour.

Cindy looked at him curiously. "As ever? You've known her awhile, then?"

"Awhile." Then, thrusting out a hand:

"I'm Franklin. Miniver's my aunt," he confessed.

Cindy's brown eyes widened as she extended her own hand. "Your aunt! How — who — she's never said a word about a nephew!"

She'd never said a word about Cindy Reilly, either, until today. He wished he'd been paying more attention. If only he'd known . . .

Cindy Reilly has a boyfriend, he reminded himself an instant before their hands connected and a sudden jolt of static electricity leapt between them.

"Oh!" they both exclaimed in unison, jerking their hands away.

"I've been doing that all morning," Cindy said, shaking her hand as if it were afire. She smiled. "Biddy says it's my electric personality."

Franklin had no idea who Biddy was, but who was he to disagree?

"And you — I've been assuming — *are* Cindy Reilly," he said, rubbing away the lingering tingle in his hand.

She nodded. "You must have met my mother when you dropped off your aunt. Isn't hard to tell we're from the same gene pool. But where do *you* fit in with the Macreadys?"

It was an Aunt Min kind of question: unexpectedly forthright. It took him by surprise — so many people weren't straightforward these days. Franklin liked directness, even when it disconcerted him. He was, after all, Miniver Macready's nephew. He liked it that Cindy's forthrightness had taken him by surprise.

"My mother was Miniver's younger sister," he explained. "Molly Macready. She died when I was four. I don't suppose Aunt Min has much occasion to talk about her. Or about me either."

He wished she had. He wished with all his heart that Aunt Min had told Cindy Reilly years ago she had a wonderful nephew who would be just perfect for her.

He was sure he would be.

"I'm sorry," Cindy said in response to his disclosure. Her voice was sympathetic. "I lost my father seven years ago. I know how it feels."

Franklin was glad when the bell on the front door jangled just then. It would have been hard to say anything around the lump in his throat.

"Excuse me a moment," Cindy murmured, and hurried toward the dignified elderly woman who stood in the doorway.

"Mrs. Pfefferkuchen!" she greeted the

newcomer with enthusiasm. "Hello!"

Franklin knew from the dowager's pleased expression that Cindy Reilly was smiling her hundred-watt, welcoming, "I'm-so-glad-to-see-you!" smile.

For just the briefest of moments he felt a surprising pang of jealousy.

4

"Did I hear him say he was Mini Mac's *nephew?*" Biddy whispered to Cindy when she hurried behind the counter for Olga Pfefferkuchen's tea setup. "I never heard she had a nephew."

"Miniver's sister Molly's son," Cindy whispered back. "Molly died a long time ago. When Franklin was four."

"Molly . . . ," Biddy said thoughtfully. Then, shaking her head, "But never mind that. What about Eustace?"

Cindy smiled. "Eustace is a gnome."

"A gnome!" Biddy blinked at Cindy behind her cat's-eye glasses.

"That's what Franklin says." Cindy poured hot water into a tiny teapot shaped like a fat black-and-white cat in a pink tutu. Mrs. Pfefferkuchen loved cats. "It's kind of a joke, Biddy. Eustace is fine."

"A gnome!" Biddy muttered. She shook her head again. "All the same, when Miniver stops in, I believe I'll give her a dish of apple betty to take to Eustace." Eustace had a notorious weakness for Biddy's apple betty.

"Would it be too much for a man to get a refill on his coffee?" Harley Burns called loudly from down the counter, waving his coffee cup. Biddy glared at him, which took Harley so aback he thumped the mug down on the counter and added meekly, "When you've got a minute."

By the time Cindy set the teapot down in front of Olga Pfefferkuchen, Suzie Wyatt Hunt had relocated, coffee cup and wedding album in tow, from the counter to the booth where her ex-nemesis sat.

Suzie's idea that the good Lord was responsible for the remarkable turnaround in Mrs. Pfefferkuchen over the last nine months made perfect sense to Cindy, who'd always taken her relationship with the Most High seriously. It was true that after her father died she'd wrestled with her faith for a season, but now she knew she'd never have survived her questions and her grief without the Almighty's shoulder to lean on and his loving arms to cling to.

And who but the Almighty could have engineered the change from Olga Pfefferkuchen, town shrew, to Olga Pfefferkuchen, enlightened citizen? Not that the old woman wasn't still a busybody, but at least now her causes had Pilchuck's interests at heart instead of merely her own.

At the moment, Olga was poring over Suzie's wedding album, oohing and ahhing and tossing out compliments like confetti. Suzie, for her part — and much to Cindy's surprise — was sitting quietly with her chin resting on her hands, gazing over the old woman's shoulder at Mini Mac's nephew, her expression thoughtful.

She glanced up, caught Cindy's eye, tilted her head toward Franklin, and mouthed, *Cute!*

"Suzie!" Cindy whispered, shocked. "You're a married woman!"

"Not for me, silly," Suzie said in a low voice. "I was thinking of Robin and Rosie."

Mrs. Pfefferkuchen shifted in her seat and craned her neck to peer behind her.

"Too serious," she pronounced in a confidential tone when she turned around again.

"But then, so was Harrison," Suzie reminded her. "I think in the hands of the right woman —"

"Suzie!" Cindy said again. "They're seventeen years *old!*"

Suzie sighed. "Okay, okay, maybe I'm getting a little ahead of myself. I just hate to see something like *that*" — she inclined her head — "go to waste."

Cindy glanced over at Franklin, who had set his menu aside and was working the crossword puzzle in the *Bellingrath Daily News*. Until now, she hadn't even registered his physical appearance. Good grief, she barely even registered the looks of movie stars anymore. Jonathan Crum was so incredibly, unbelievably, drop-dead gorgeous, most movie stars paled in comparison.

Mini Mac's nephew was pleasant enough looking, she supposed. Not *outstanding* in any way, but not unappealing.

He was of medium height and medium build, with a face, she decided, more interesting than handsome — his nose a little large, his lips a trifle thin, his haircut just a tad conservative. She did like his eyebrows — thick, but nicely arched, and a shade darker than his sandy brown hair. And his ears — he did have quite attractive ears, she mused. Small, well-shaped, flat against his head . . .

Franklin glanced up at that moment and caught her staring. She looked away quickly, but not before she saw his startled expression.

She flushed. A plague on Suzie! And now she had to walk over there and take his order, her face as red as a tropical sunburn!

Taking a determined breath, she sidled over to his table. "Ready to order?" she asked, avoiding his eyes.

"Tell me about the specials," he said.

Was it her imagination, or did he sound amused? Was he having fun at her expense?

She braved a quick glance and instantly relaxed. He looked friendly, she decided. But he wasn't laughing at her. The thought flashed through her mind that he wasn't the kind who would have fun at someone else's expense.

"Hot Dogs and Sauerkraut with French Fries," she answered his query. "Or Moroccan Cornish Game Hens with Garlic Smashed Potatoes and Mustard-Dressed Asparagus."

He raised his eyebrows, and Cindy shrugged. What could she say? Biddy and Buster liked variety.

"What makes the Cornish game hens Moroccan?" Franklin wanted to know.

His eyes, she noted somewhere in the back of her mind as she tried to explain the taste of cardamom, cumin, and coriander, were — she had to admit — quite beautiful. Pale, intriguing, gray-green-golden eyes with a darker ring around the outer rim. Hazel, she supposed most people would call them; khaki was the word that came to her own mind. The color of summer: summer clothes, the summer sand at Heron Bay, the summer hills in eastern Washington where, when she was younger, Joe-Joe Reilly had always taken the family camping.

She put in his order and once again made the rounds of the diner with the coffeepot, ending at Franklin's table. He was probably ten years older than the twins, she thought as she filled his cup, but ten years wasn't all that much. Or wouldn't be when he was seventy and they were sixty. He did seem awfully nice — and he did have those beautiful eyes. And those lovely ears.

Of course, there was only one of him, and two of the twins — an inconvenience Rosie and Robin hadn't yet worked out when it came to boyfriends. The problem was they always liked the same boy, and whatever boy it was, he could never decide between them. On top of which, he usually couldn't even tell which twin was which — which didn't go over particularly well with either of them.

"Were my sisters home when you

dropped off Mini Mac?" she asked.

He looked confused. "Mini Mac? Oh! You mean Aunt Min! I don't know — I only met your mother."

She placed the coffeepot on his table, ready to settle in for a talk. One nice thing about the Kitsch 'n' Caboodle, as compared to other county restaurants where Cindy might have worked for better tips: Biddy actually encouraged conversation with the customers.

"Remember — we're not just sellin' food," her employer reminded her trio of waitresses on a regular basis. "We're sellin' atmosphere. Kitsch and conversation keep the customers comin' back as much as Buster's cookin' does. Give 'em what they want. That's my rule of thumb."

Cindy was always more than happy to do her part.

Mini Mac. Franklin hid his smile behind his coffee cup.

"So . . . ," the All-American-Girl-Next-Door-Hometown-Sweetheart said, her head tilted like an inquisitive gold-feathered bird. "Are you going to be around for a while? At Mini Mac's, I mean?"

"Just for the weekend. But I do see Aunt

Min as often as possible over the summer while she's home. I'm only an hour and a half away in Seattle." He tilted his head in opposition to hers. "Does she know you call her Mini Mac?"

Cindy looked surprised. "Well, of course she does! I wouldn't call her anything behind her back I wouldn't call her to her face." She looked suddenly anxious. "You don't think she takes it as disrespectful?"

"If she did, you would have heard about it by now."

"True." Cindy tugged thoughtfully at her lower lip with her teeth. Franklin struggled not to stare. *Mercy!* as Cookie would say. Did she even know how utterly enchanting she was?

"I know Miniver well enough by now," she recalled his attention, "to know she's not afraid to call a spade a spade."

"Nor a wonder a wonder," he said. "Which is what she calls *you*, Cindy Reilly."

Cindy's lilting laughter nearly did Franklin in. She really ought to register that laugh as a deadly weapon, he told himself as reflex kicked in on his respiratory system and he started to breathe again.

"Mini Mac's my champion," Cindy declared.

I'll be your champion too, the words popped into his head. *If you'll be my lady . . .*

"Table ten!" a gruff voice bawled.

"That's your lunch. Be right back, Franklin."

He sighed audibly as he watched her stride across the restaurant, making quick work of it with her long legs.

The elderly woman who'd come in after him turned around in the booth next to his and peered at him over her shoulder, her dangly earrings swaying against her scrawny neck. Her hair was pink, her eyelids turquoise, and the expression on her face an odd mixture of asperity and compassion.

"She has a boyfriend," Lady Pink Hair said.

Before he could react — before he could even *think* of reacting — she turned her back on him.

To say Franklin was astonished was to put it mildly. Stupefied, perhaps. Flabbergasted. Dumbfounded. He found himself staring at the back of Lady Pink Hair's head with his eyebrows raised and his mouth open and not a sound coming out of it. One little sigh — behind her back yet — and the old woman had known exactly what he was thinking!

"Moroccan Cornish Game Hen," Cindy announced, appearing out of nowhere to set a dinner plate before him. A veritable bouquet of exotic and tantalizing aromas rose from the steaming chicken, potatoes, and asparagus.

He lowered his brows, snapped his mouth shut, and mumbled a "thank you," not daring to look at her. Just in case Lady Pink Hair wasn't the only mind reader in the Kitsch 'n' Caboodle Café.

The front door opened, and a noisy group of guests poured in. Cindy strode off to greet them, snagging a stack of menus from the end of the counter on her way. Franklin gulped for air; he couldn't seem to get enough when she was near.

He stared after her for a moment, then stared down at the miniature chicken, sizzling on his plate, as if he had no idea what to do with it.

Pick up your knife and fork, some part of his brain told another. *Lunch is here. You're starved, man. You had cabbage soup for breakfast, for Pete's sake!*

He picked up his knife and fork and began to carve the little hen, but his mind was still on Cindy. On the way he was reacting to Cindy.

He knew exactly what this was all about.

It was his parents' anniversary that had him going. It was thinking about their romance, talking about it to Aunt Min, remembering how his father had adored his mother.

It wasn't Cindy Reilly who had his heart missing beats and his lungs forgetting they were part of an involuntary system. It really had nothing to do with her at all.

Why was everyone so intent on telling him she had a boyfriend anyhow? And just who *was* this boyfriend? The local enforcer? A goon? Was Franklin's life in danger because he'd made pleasant conversation with an attractive woman?

Besides, if she had a boyfriend, what was she doing giving *Franklin* the "glad eye," as Cookie called it? He hadn't imagined *that*. Or the color in her cheeks when she'd taken his order. *He* wasn't the one who'd set the coffeepot on *her* table and quizzed her about *her* availability!

He took a bite of chicken. The cardamom-coriander-cumin combination exploded in his mouth. His outrage melted away. Delicious! Whoever would have guessed he'd have a genuine gourmet experience in a place called —

"So . . ." Once again Cindy Reilly appeared out of nowhere. "Do you have a girlfriend?"

Franklin choked. And this time, he really did stop breathing.

Cindy stood frozen for a moment that felt like forever as Franklin clutched at his throat. His face was rapidly turning blue.

"Franklin!"

He stumbled out of the booth, wild-eyed, pounding on the back of his neck with the flat of one hand.

Cindy grabbed his arm. "Are you okay? Can you breathe?"

He shook his head frantically. He was making a horrible, strangled, gurgling noise.

Cindy's adrenaline suddenly kicked in. "Somebody — call 911!" she shouted. "I'm here, Franklin. I'm going to help you." Pilchuck's resident RN, Lily Johansen, had just given the Kitsch 'n' Caboodle employees a first-aid refresher course last week — including rescue breathing and the Heimlich maneuver.

Quickly! Get behind him! She didn't know if it was the Almighty, Lily Johansen, or her gut talking, but she didn't hesitate to follow directions.

Brace yourself.

In a matter of seconds she had her hip braced against him and one of her legs planted solidly between his.

Make a fist.

In a lightning flash she had her fist against his abdomen, thumb first, just above his navel, and covered with her other hand.

Elbows out. Sharp. Quick.

She jerked her fist inward and upward. One! Two! Three! Four!

Please, God!

Five! Six!

The next few seconds passed in excruciating slow motion:

Franklin coughed, choked, coughed again. Violently.

Something flew out of his mouth with such force he fell backward, still coughing — right into Cindy.

They went down together, a tangle of arms and legs and coughing, like a barking beetle on its back.

Whatever it was the coughing had ejected from Franklin's throat hit Mrs. Pfefferkuchen's coffee cup and rebounded, landing on the floor in the middle of the restaurant.

Cindy and Franklin untangled themselves and sat up, Cindy automatically reaching out to snag the offending object. A good waitress never left a cluttered floor.

She opened her hand. They both stared down at it.

A tiny chicken bone. The wishbone, in fact. Still in one piece.

"Come back next week when it's dried out," Cindy wheezed — a wheeze being all she could manage at the moment. "We'll make a wish on it."

Franklin politely declined.

By the time the ambulance arrived from Bellingrath, its siren wailing, he was sitting on a stool at the counter, head in hands, eyes closed, trying to relax as Cindy hovered over him inquiring anxiously if he was really, truly all right.

"Really," he groaned. "Truly."

Though if he hadn't been so grateful to be alive, he'd have been absolutely mortified.

The EMTs, disappointed not to have found an emergency after all, accepted coffee and apple betty to go and went their way.

"Well, I guess I owe you my life," Franklin said to Cindy as he sipped at a soothing brew Buster Barton had concocted for him after he'd assured Biddy Barton that no, the Moroccan game hen *wasn't* too spicy, and yes, it *was* just one of those things, and no, he *wasn't* planning to sue the Bartons or the Kitsch 'n' Caboodle Café.

He pulled his wallet from his jeans and opened it. "If there's ever anything I can do for you, please call me, Cindy," he told her, digging out a business card and laying it on the counter. "I mean *anything*."

"Don't be silly," she said cheerfully. "Saving people from chicken bones is in my job description." By now she'd stopped hovering and was rounding the end of the counter to enter the server aisle. Backlit from the front window, the strands of golden hair shone around her face like a halo.

She moved away from the window and the effect was lost. But Franklin wasn't fooled. Cindy Reilly *was* an angel. His very own guardian angel.

Get serious, Fitz, a voice protested in his head. *If she hadn't startled you with that question, you wouldn't have choked in the first place!*

"Please," he said, ignoring the voice and pushing the business card toward her. "And by the way" — he tapped his fingers nervously against the counter — "no, I don't have a girlfriend."

He very much liked the way her face lit up at the information. Until she asked hopefully, "Any chance you'd want to meet my sisters?"

5

Franklin didn't seem too hungry after his brush with death, Cindy noted. And no wonder, seeing as how it was food that had nearly done him in. She hoped the incident hadn't ruined him for cardamom, cumin, and coriander. Or Cornish game hens, for that matter. She couldn't imagine how he'd gotten an entire wishbone stuck in his throat, even if it was a miniature.

The aftermath of the bone-choking incident was almost as exciting as the incident itself. In the camaraderie that comes of sharing danger — even though Franklin was the only one who'd actually *been* in danger — he was instantly accepted into the Pilchuck brotherhood by the Kitsch 'n' Caboodle regulars present at the occasion. And as for Cindy — Cindy was a hero.

"Never saw the like," Alf Mayer, who owned the local feed and seed, told her with admiration as he pumped her hand across the counter. "A skinny little gal like you a-grabbin' and a-pushin' like one o' them TV wrestlers! Tony'll be hearin' about this one, little lady. Wouldn't su'prise me there was an official commendation comin'." Alf's son Tony was Pilchuck's longtime mayor, and issuing official commendations was a major function of his job.

"Hear, hear!" Harley Burns lifted his coffee cup. The rest of the customers raised their mugs to join him in a toast. Buster Barton, meanwhile, got on the horn to Carl Peabody at the offices of the *Pilchuck Post* and told him to grab his camera and get on over to the Kitsch 'n' Caboodle for "news so fresh it'll bite your behind."

Buster didn't miss a beggar's chance for free publicity. It didn't seem to occur to him that news about someone nearly choking to death in his restaurant might not be good for business.

The regulars, after their toast to Cindy, actually got up off their stools and filed by Franklin one by one to introduce themselves and share their own life-threatening experiences — of which there seemed an exceptional number, Cindy thought, for so small a group.

Biddy, for her part, bustled about the diner with the coffeepot, looking enormously pleased. To Biddy, the Kitsch 'n' Caboodle was as much a social club as it was a restaurant and kitsch museum. Just now, things were feeling very much like a party.

Of course it wasn't long before everyone in the place knew that Franklin-the-Chicken-Bone-Survivor and Franklin-Mini-Mac's-Nephew was also Franklin Cameron Fitz III, heir to the Strawbridge & Fitz department-store fortune. Biddy had caught the surname early on and poked Cindy in the ribs to whisper, "Fitz? Did you hear him say his name was Fitz?"

Cindy, frowning, pulled his business card from the pocket where she'd stashed it earlier. Even that didn't tell all: *Franklin Fitz, Department Manager, General Accounting Division, Strawbridge & Fitz, Inc.*

"Might be a coincidence," Cindy whispered back. "Like Jimmy Smith working at Smith Appliances." But in the next instant Jonas Muncey, who kept up with such things, blurted outright, "Would that be Franklin Cameron Fitz the Third of the Strawbridge & Fitz department-store Fitzes?"

The diner fell suddenly silent and every eye rested on Franklin, who looked uncomfortable but nodded that yes, indeed, it would be.

In the excited buzz that followed, Biddy

nudged Cindy and murmured, "Strawbridge & Fitz, Cindy! Glad Raggs! Didn't he say he owed you his life? Maybe he'll get your evening gowns into his stores!"

Cindy shook her head, sighing. "A big department store doesn't buy one-of-a-kinds, Biddy. I can't even *think* about Strawbridge & Fitz without having some way to mass produce my dresses."

Despite her recent elevation to hero status, she felt let down. The perfect chance to advance her career, and not a thing she could do to take advantage of it.

Well, maybe it just wasn't time. *To every thing there is a season,* she reminded herself for probably the millionth time in the last seven years.

Somehow, at the moment, the thought didn't cheer her. She'd been waiting so long!

And she did mean long. She'd been drawing clothes since second grade, when her mother had brought home outdated pattern books from her job at the Fabric Faire in Bellingrath. She must have copied a thousand fashion sketches line for line — Butterick and Vogue were her favorites — before she started developing a style of her own. And a vision of her own.

At first that meant revising other designers' clothing — changing a seam here and a dart there, modifying a neckline or a waistline or a sleeve. But by sixth grade, Cindy had begun to sketch her own designs. And by the time she applied for the scholarship to Seattle's Beaux Arts School of Design, she'd already developed her unique line of pieced-fabric party dresses — including the one she wore to her own Spring Fling with Jonathan that year.

And then Joe-Joe had died, and design school was out of the question, and so was ever moving away from Pilchuck to work her way up in a design firm — of which Tillicum County, not surprisingly, was sadly lacking. So she'd picked her mother's brain, and read every book on apparel design she could get her hands on, and kept up with the world of fashion on the pages of *Vogue* and *W* and *Women's Wear Daily*, which Ina Rafferty, the town librarian, ordered especially for Cindy.

She knew what she was doing. But the only way she was ever going to make a living doing what she knew and loved was to do it on her own — to somehow raise the capital to have her dresses manufactured. So far she hadn't been able to convince a banker she was good for the money. Not even Mr. Pickle at First National, where her parents had always banked and she'd had her savings account since she was thirteen years old.

Not that she hadn't made progress. Nadine's Not-Your-Basic-Black-Dress Shop in Bellingrath had carried Glad Raggs on consignment for two years now. And just in the last six weeks, Cindy's designs had been featured at three local very special occasions.

Suzie Wyatt's wedding, for one. Not only on the bride, but on the matron of honor and the mother of the bride. Both special challenges, as the matron of honor — Priscilla Wyatt — had been eight months pregnant at the time, and the mother of the bride had been in Papua New Guinea until three days before the wedding.

The Pilchuck High School Spring Fling, for another. Robin and Rosie, with a little help from their mother, had personally sewn their prom dresses from one of Cindy's patterns.

And Cait and Cindy's dressmaking and design skills had once again made a dramatic showing at the Tillicum County Blossomtime Festival coronation — on every last one of the seven junior Blossoms *and* Pilchuck's own Queen Bee, Olga

Pfefferkuchen, who was at the moment, Cindy noted, deep in conversation with Franklin Cameron Fitz III, holding one of his hands between her own and peering into his face with her sharp brown eyes.

Olga, eighty years old if she was a day, had looked not more than seventy-two or -three at the coronation, sashaying down the runway in her lovely evening dress of lilac-colored silk brocade and featherweight chiffon. Cindy found it particularly gratifying that since the festival, after years of wearing black and gray, Mrs. Pfefferkuchen had lately been seen around town sporting a rainbow of flattering colors. Like the dusty rose dress she wore today. If only she'd lose that turquoise eye shadow she wore with everything!

Cindy sighed. It was one thing to make a name for herself as a local designer of wedding dresses and special-occasion gowns. But she knew as well as anyone that it was a long way from Nadine's Not-Your-Basic-Black-Dress Shop to the racks of Strawbridge & Fitz.

She lifted a hand to knead the muscles of her neck, which seemed all at once to be a jumble of knots. It wasn't despair she felt exactly. But for a moment her fairy-tale vision of the future — the vision she'd counted on for so many years — wavered like the image of a desert mirage.

Destiny, Franklin told himself as he stared down at Cindy Reilly.

It was destiny, not Carl Peabody's instructions, that had him standing here in the Kitsch 'n' Caboodle Café next to Cindy, an arm around her shoulders. She was just the right height to fit comfortably under his arm.

"One, two, three, *cheese*," Carl said. The camera flashed. "One more, people! One, two, three, *cheese*." It flashed again. "Excellent! Now, if I could have you spell your names . . ."

Franklin Cameron Fitz III was in such a daze he hardly knew what he was doing as he slid onto a stool and tried to answer the newspaper editor's questions. He had never in all his life felt so utterly happy just to be alive. Or so utterly confident he was in the hands of God.

He was as certain the Lord of heaven had arranged this entire incredible episode in his life, in fact, as he was certain that Cookie Simms's arrival at the Fitz family estate, all those years ago, had been divinely ordained and ordered.

There was the timing, first of all: Filene's

getting after him lately about "making a good match" and Aunt Min's pestering him about whether or not he was happy. And that Cindy should have saved his life *today*, of all days — the anniversary of his mother's death! Of his parents' marriage!

Second, there were the circumstances: his spur-of-the-moment trip to Bellingrath last night, the cabbage-soup-and-raw-vegetable breakfast, Aunt Min's appointment in Pilchuck with Mrs. Reilly . . .

Finally, there was Cindy herself.

The woman he'd been waiting for.

The *feeling* he'd been waiting for.

As if your very life depended on her being there, his father had described it.

No "as if" about it, Franklin told himself — his very life *had* depended on Cindy's being there. How could the message be more clear?

The door to the Kitsch 'n' Caboodle burst open.

"Cindy!"

Franklin swung around on his stool. Too fast, apparently — or maybe his chicken-bone-choking experience had somehow affected his vision. He was seeing double.

He closed his eyes and shook his head to clear it, but when he opened them again, the girl in the doorway was still *two* girls.

Two startlingly pretty girls. Teenagers, with identical thick-lashed eyes and dimpled smiles. Wearing identical neon green T-shirts and baggy jeans — and identical buzz haircuts, dark brown with the ends bleached yellow.

"Robin! Rosie!" It was Cindy. "You've cut — you've bleached — you look — oh my!"

"We decided this morning," one of them said, pirouetting.

"We did it ourselves," said the second, pirouetting the other way round.

And then in unison, their identical arms around each other and their identical heads together: "So what do you think, Big Sister?"

Franklin swung his head to look at Cindy, who was, remarkably, smiling her hundred-watt smile. If he had to describe her expression, he'd call it proud.

"Dashing. Daring. Up to the minute." Her brow suddenly furrowed. "How's Mom?"

"How's Mom?" the girls repeated in one voice, their inflections identically puzzled.

"Yes — Mom." Cindy placed a hand on either hip and raised her eyebrows. "You mean to tell me she didn't have a cow?"

"She hasn't exactly seen us yet," said one twin.

"She doesn't exactly know what we were doing," said the other.

Cindy sighed. She looked at Franklin. "It's a good thing your aunt's here today," she told him. "Mom's never more mellow than after Mini Mac's been here. Maybe she'll only have a calf."

"That's why we did it today," the twins said together.

"Looks to me like ya stuck your finger in a socket," a grizzled old-timer down the counter said.

"Looks like ya had a run-in with a mower," said another.

"Or maybe a ghost," said Buster Barton, poking his head through the pass-through from the kitchen.

"Kids!" Lady Pink Hair's single word was as eloquent as any other comment she might have made. *Mrs. Pfefferkuchen,* he reminded himself. Mrs. Peppercookie. He'd felt inspired, on discovering her name, to tell her about his own Cookie, back in Seattle. The conversation seemed to have pleased her immeasurably.

"Speaking of Mini Mac . . ." Once again Cindy directed her comments to the twins. "There's someone here I'd like you to meet. Robin, Rosie," — she opened her hand toward Franklin — "this is Miniver

Macready's nephew, Franklin Fitz."

"Franklin Cameron Fitz the Third," Biddy Barton clarified.

"Of the Strawbridge & Fitz Fitzes," another voice volunteered.

"Cindy saved his life," Biddy said proudly, and with the help of the entire Kitsch 'n' Caboodle crew retold the story beginning to end.

"Wow," said Robin. At least, Franklin *thought* it was Robin.

"Double wow," said Rosie. "Did you know when you save someone's life you're, like, *bound* to him forever?"

"Forever and ever, amen," Robin agreed, her voice reverent. "Like, your spirits are knit together now, and there's nothing you can ever do to unknit them."

"Totally awesome," Rosie said.

Destiny, Franklin told himself again, gazing at Cindy.

Cindy laughed and shook her head. "Really, now! You're making too big a deal of it. All of you. I didn't do anything anyone else wouldn't have done."

"But you were the one who done it," an old-timer put in.

"Don't know how that boyfriend of yours is going to take to your spirit being knit together with Franklin's," Biddy said to Cindy, her tone teasing.

Franklin's heart plummeted. *The boy-friend.* How could he keep forgetting?

News traveled fast in Pilchuck. Not more than fifteen minutes after Carl Peabody's departure from the Kitsch 'n' Caboodle Café with his suitcase of cameras, Miniver Macready came barging into the restaurant, her silver hair flying. At nearly six feet, with her piano-esque frame, Aunt Min barging into anywhere was formidable.

"Franklin! Precious!" Aunt Min swept her nephew into an all-enveloping hug. "Are you really all right?"

When she loosened her hold enough so that he could breathe again, Franklin assured his aunt he was quite all right — and had the grace of God and Cindy Reilly to thank for it.

"I know, I know, I've heard all about it."

And she enveloped Cindy in a similar hug.

"Mini Mac, it's good to see you," Cindy wheezed when Miniver released her. "And will you be joining us for lunch today?"

"Oh, no, not today. Didn't Franklin tell you? I'm dieting. Very strict."

"Oh." Cindy looked disappointed. "I've

been waiting on pins and noodles to hear about your Asian tour."

"You've been waiting on pins and noodles to see the wonderful fabric I've brought back for my new concert gowns, is what *you've* been waiting for," Miniver said. "You'll think you've died and gone to heaven, my dear. I know *I* did. The silks! The satins! The jacquards and brocades!"

Cindy smiled. *Talk about died and gone to heaven,* Franklin thought, sighing to himself.

"You're right," she said. "I'm *itching* to get my hands on all that gorgeous stuff. And figure out what to do with it."

"Miracles, is what. As usual," Mini Mac said. "Do you know I wore the royal-purple silk shantung and velvet for a private concert in Bangkok, and when it was over, the wife of the Russian ambassador asked me how I stayed so slender? *Slender,* Cindy! Can you beat that!"

"See, Aunt Min?" Franklin cut in. "You don't need cabbage soup. You just need Cindy."

Cindy turned her smile on him. If she wasn't careful with that thing, she was going to blind someone, he told himself. But he didn't look away.

"Speaking of cabbage soup, we'd best get

to the grocery store," Aunt Min reminded him. "If I'd fed him a decent breakfast," she added to Cindy, "he'd never have ordered an entire chicken for lunch. It's all my fault. If he hadn't been so hungry —"

"Don't go blaming yourself, Aunt Min. It was a tiny chicken, and of course it wasn't your fault. I could have gone shopping. I could have gone out for breakfast. I could even have gone downstairs and begged bacon and eggs from Eustace."

A few minutes later, as he helped his aunt into the backseat of the Packard, Franklin said it again: "Really, Aunt Min — it wasn't your fault." He closed her door and hurried around to open his own. "Besides, the whole thing's given me a new perspective." He clapped Eustace's chauffeur's cap on his head and turned the key in the ignition. The engine purred to life.

"New perspective?" his aunt repeated doubtfully.

"I'm alive, Aunt Min! Alive! And with so much to be thankful for!"

He pulled away from the curb, not even aware he was whistling a cheerful tune he'd learned long ago in Sunday school and probably hadn't thought of since: *I'm so happy, I'm so happy, I'm so happy, happy, happy, happy, happy, happy, happy . . .*

"So —" Aunt Min leaned forward in her seat as Franklin stopped for the red light at the corner of Third and Main. "What do you think of Cindy Reilly?"

Franklin stopped whistling. "What do I think of Cindy Reilly!" he exclaimed. "She saved my life, Aunt Min. What do you *think* I think of Cindy Reilly?"

"No cookie cutter, is she?"

"No cookie cutter," Franklin agreed.

"An original. And such a love! Too bad she's so —"

"— besotted with that boyfriend of hers," Franklin finished with her. Then he added, casually, as if it didn't matter either way: "You're *certain* she's besotted?"

6

Franklin's renewed sense of the charm and beauty of life ran into a snag on Monday — a snag by the name of Filene Downing Fitz.

As Fitzy's heirs, Franklin and Filene each held an equal number of shares in the family business — 40 percent each, with management splitting the remaining 20. But that was on paper. Since Franklin's portion of the inheritance was being held in trust until he was thirty and Filene was the executor of her late husband's will, there was nothing equal about their current status.

Or about their say in how Strawbridge & Fitz was run. Not when Filene was voting his shares as well as her own.

The provisions of the will — especially the naming of Filene as executor — had been a shock to Franklin until he learned the papers had been drawn up in Filene and Fitzy's first year of marriage and never amended. Another way she'd taken advantage of his father's grief, Franklin told himself sourly as he stepped onto the elevator early Monday afternoon and punched the button up to the boardroom.

On the other hand — Fitzy had had plenty of opportunities to change his will over the seventeen years he and Filene were married. And two heart attacks prior to his fatal one to remind him such a course of action would be a very wise one. Why he hadn't — well, Franklin supposed no one would ever know. Maybe he hadn't meant to. Filene did have a good head for business, though Franklin didn't always like her methods.

The elevator lurched to a stop, and the doors opened into a beautifully appointed reception area. So different from the colorless, cramped claptrap of a cubicle one floor down where he sometimes thought he was going to drown in spreadsheets and sales figures.

"Good afternoon, Mr. Fitz," the receptionist greeted him formally. "How may we help you today?"

"I'm here for the board meeting, Evelyn. In for Walter Burgess. I'm sure you've heard he's gravely ill." The CFO had, in fact, been rushed to the hospital just last night. As Franklin had been helping his boss prepare the quarterly report from the finance and accounting department, he was the logical choice to present it at the meeting today.

"We've sent him flowers," Evelyn acknowledged.

Franklin felt a clap on his shoulder and turned to find Norman Meeks, VP of marketing and promotions, extending his hand. "Hello, Franklin! So you'll be joining us in the boardroom today!" He leaned closer and added confidentially, "Too bad you won't be in the chairman's seat."

Franklin grinned. "Or at least on the board," he said.

Norm was one of the old-line managers Franklin's father had counted on. The only one left, as Filene had arbitrarily replaced the other four senior vice presidents with her own cronies over the last three years. Apparently she recognized Norm's exceptional abilities, or she wouldn't have kept him around either.

"Someday," Norm encouraged Franklin as they fell into step and made their way to the boardroom.

"Someday," Franklin echoed.

Maybe his present position as a low-level manager in the accounting department wasn't the most exciting job in the world, he mused. Certainly not what Aunt Min would wish for him. After all, accounting was — well, accounting was accounting. What more could one say? Crunching numbers had never exactly been his idea of a good time, but, as everyone agreed, he did do it well.

And it was where his father had wanted him. "Get to know the bottom line, son," Fitzy had told him on numerous occasions. "That's what you'll need to know to run the business."

Four more years, and things would pick up, he told himself as he and Norm swung into the empty boardroom. Once he turned thirty and came into his inheritance, once he controlled his own shares in the company and actually had some say in how Strawbridge & Fitz was run . . .

A loud burst of laughter came from behind the closed door at the far end of the boardroom. Franklin recognized Filene's bray and shuddered. She had a Machiavellian sense of humor; her laughter could as likely mean somebody's head was about to roll as anything.

He sighed. The truth of the matter was, as long as Filene was chairman of the board, he'd *never* have a say in how the business was run. Even after he came into his inheritance, voting his shares against his stepmother wouldn't make a whit of difference when she already had half the board in her pocket and the CEO and CFO on leashes so short he was surprised they hadn't both choked to death by now. Though Walter, Franklin's boss, seemed to be working on it.

He didn't have the stomach for a power struggle with his stepmother. He hardly had the stomach to deal with the woman day to day. If it wasn't for Cookie — alone now since Clement had passed on — and the fact that Franklin had his own apartment over the carriage house and didn't have to see Filene except in passing — he'd have moved off the family estate long ago. And if it wasn't for his sense of loyalty to his father, he wouldn't be at Strawbridge & Fitz either.

"I'm pleased with the sales numbers you passed along for the June catalog," Norm was saying. "Especially the Retro line. It was about time for bell bottoms and platform shoes to be reprised."

"Maybe it was time for *fun* to be reprised," said Franklin as he took a seat at the oval table.

"You might as well join me over here, Franklin," Norm said, settling into a folding chair along the wall. "Since Filene had the private dining room put in and downsized the boardroom, only the board of directors sits at the table. We peons get the peanut gallery."

Franklin relocated, struggling not to roll his eyes. How could she treat her senior executives this way? But he held his tongue. "The numbers do look good, Norman," he said instead. "It looks as if that new model you used for the Retro line was a good bet."

"Fun and perky seems to be working for junior wear," the VP acknowledged.

Franklin had actually done a double take when he'd seen the cover of the June catalog, the model seemed so familiar. On a hunch, he'd dug out a box of old family photos Aunt Min had given him a number of years ago and discovered why: The girl kicking up her heels and holding down her hat on the catalog cover was a dead ringer for his mother as a teenager. They had the same energy too. And as the Retro line hearkened back to the seventies, they were even wearing the same styles.

A sudden beeping interrupted his musings. The alarm on Norm's wristwatch.

"I don't know why I bother to get here on time," the marketing director said, hitting the Off button. "No one else does. These things always start late." *Another way to keep us peons in our place,* his expression said.

In the next few minutes the folding chairs filled up with the other senior vice presidents. At twenty after the hour, the door from the private dining room finally opened. A dozen "suits" filed through and took their places around the table, barely glancing at the executives along the wall. Filene brought up the rear, moving like a jungle cat on the prowl, exuding danger and power.

Her hair was black. Her skin and her heavily shadowed eyes were pale. Her power suit was black, even to the silk shirt she wore under her black wool jacket. She never wore anything else – always black. It had nothing to do with being in mourning for Franklin's father either; she'd worn black for as long as Franklin could remember. "For dramatic effect," was Cookie's opinion.

She *was* dramatic, no question about it, he thought as she raked her eyes over the row of executives in the outer circle. When Filene was in a room, she made certain all eyes were on Filene.

She directed the meeting like a grandmaster playing both sides of a chess game. Franklin would have been fascinated if he hadn't been rehearsing his presentation in his head until the last minute before he gave it. He'd been to one board meeting since his father had died, to assist Walter Burgess with an ungainly set of visuals, but delivering a presentation on his own was an entirely different matter.

It apparently went off without a hitch. The board of directors paid close attention, and Filene had some searing questions, but he must have answered them to her satisfaction. In fact, her expression seemed almost pleased as he sat down. Could she actually be proud of him? He wasn't her son by blood, but they were, after all, bound together by more than business ties. In a sense, at least, they were family. And family connections certainly mattered to Filene, even if for all the wrong reasons.

Norman Meeks made the final and, at least in Franklin's mind, the best presentation of the afternoon.

Norm really is an asset to the company, Franklin was thinking as the marketing director closed with a description of his departmental goals for the third quarter. His marketing campaigns were always creative and, more important from a business standpoint, remarkably effective. Because part of Franklin's job involved tracking sales based on individual ad campaigns, he knew.

Which was why Filene's reaction to Norm's presentation was so unexpected and so shocking.

"That's all very nice, Mr. Meeks," she said when he finished.

Franklin's head snapped up at her tone of voice. *Cold.* So cold he could almost see icicles forming on her chin.

In contrast to Norm, whose forehead suddenly popped out in beads of sweat.

What was going on?

"Any questions, ladies and gentlemen?" Filene addressed her board.

There were a few, which Norm answered succinctly and knowledgeably.

"I have a question or two for you myself, Mr. Meeks," Filene announced in her Frigidaire voice.

How was it, Franklin wondered in fascination, that a voice so cold could produce such rivers of perspiration in the room? It wasn't just Norman Meeks anymore. Everyone in the room was sweating — silent and sweating. Filene hadn't bitten off anyone's head all afternoon, and clearly it was time.

But Norm? How could she possibly find fault with Norm?

Filene pushed back her chair and faced down her marketing director, arms crossed and expression stony. Her eyes gleamed with some emotion Franklin couldn't put his finger on — oddly, both malice and triumph came to mind. "Perhaps you would be so good as to explain to the board, Mr. Meeks, the standard operating procedure for developing an ad campaign."

What in the world was she up to? Franklin wondered as Norm explained — gingerly, as if creeping through a minefield — how ideas were generated, then how an idea became a catalog, a TV commercial, a series of newspaper ads.

He shouldn't have been surprised to find out how overinvolved Filene was in the process, he supposed. She had to have her fingers in every pie. Not the way Norm would have preferred it, Franklin was sure. Not the way any competent manager would have preferred it.

Approval for this, approval for that, approval for the other thing — Norm could hardly wipe his nose without getting Filene's approval, for Pete's sake. A much different approach than his father's — Fitzy had hired good people and let them run with the ball. They'd always done well by him too.

With Filene, it was a wonder any of the VPs ever got anything done.

"Then before the ad campaign launches," Norm finished, "Mrs. Fitz reviews the print and film ads and gives final approval."

"And this procedure is followed every time," Filene said frostily.

"As much as possible," Norm said quietly. "I'm very conscientious."

"Then how do you explain that until Mrs. Fitz got home from her vacation and found it in her mailbox" — Filene leaned over her chair and grabbed something up from the table — "Mrs. Fitz had never seen *this?*"

From the way she spat the word, Franklin expected something either horrendously ugly, in horrible taste, or at the very least, relentlessly run-of-the-mill.

None of the above, he saw with surprise. It was the retro-themed June catalog with the model who looked like his mother.

The model who looked like his mother. His heart sank.

"Correct me if I'm wrong," Norm stood up to her, "but I believe you approved the project before you left on your vacation."

"I did *not* approve this model."

"The model we wanted wasn't available

when we needed to shoot. This one was. And as you can see, she did an excellent job for us. We couldn't be happier."

"*You* couldn't be happier. I, on the other hand, could be a great deal happier, Mr. Meeks."

"I'm sorry, Mrs. Fitz. I did what in my judgment seemed best at the time."

"Ignoring protocol? Ignoring the chain of command? That, in your judgment, seemed best, did it?"

Norm sighed. "We had a window of opportunity, Mrs. Fitz. You'd been involved in the process up until the time you left for France; you'd given all the necessary approvals."

"But not final approval. Ever hear of e-mail, Mr. Meeks? Or a fax machine?"

"I thought you should hold the catalog in your hands," Norm said, breathing deeply. "I overnighted it to the address you left, but apparently you'd checked out without leaving a forwarding address."

"Are you criticizing me?" she demanded.

"I most certainly am not. What you do on vacation is of no interest to me."

She glared at him. *Uh-oh,* Franklin thought. Hardly a politic thing to say to Filene. She wouldn't understand anyone's being uninterested in any aspect of her life. "And when you didn't hear back from me?"

"I felt it expedient to send the catalog to press and get it in the mail."

"*You* felt it *expedient.*" Her voice was contemptuous.

"A decision borne out by the numbers," Norm patiently pointed out. "As I said earlier, sales from the June catalog have been exceptionally high."

"That's true," Franklin broke in. He usually wasn't one to make waves, but really, Filene was being ridiculous! "In the first three weeks —"

"Did I ask you, Mr. Fitz?"

"No ma'am, but —"

"Then kindly hold your tongue. Did you follow procedure, Mr. Meeks?"

"There wasn't time to follow procedure!"

"Did — you — follow — procedure?" She pronounced every word individually, as if she were talking to someone of limited intellectual capacity. Which Norman Meeks most assuredly was not.

Norm threw his arms up in the air, clearly exasperated. "No, I did not follow procedure! What do you want from me, Filene?"

"I want your office cleaned out, Mr. Meeks. *You're fired.*"

Franklin was so mad he hardly knew what to do with himself.

They were helpless in the face of Filene's despotic, tyrannical, utterly *capricious* will, he told himself as he pounded down the stairs, all the way from the top floor to street level. Seven floors, nonstop, and then he turned around and pounded back up the stairs, finally stopping on the landing outside the sixth floor where he worked, panting and gasping for breath.

Outrageous. She was *outrageous!*

He had half a mind to race on up another floor, march into Filene's office, and quit, right there on the spot.

Strawbridge & Fitz wouldn't go under without you, you know, he heard Aunt Min's voice in his mind.

Of all the stupid reasons to fire a valued, long-term employee, he raged inside his head. A senior vice president, for Pete's sake! Franklin Cameron Fitz Jr. must be rolling over in his grave!

I depend on you, son, his father's voice countered Aunt Min's.

And yet for all intents and purposes, he'd left Filene in charge of the company!

But had he really meant to?

Franklin leaned his head against the door leading from the stairwell onto the sixth floor and closed his eyes. Out of the blue, Cindy Reilly's smile popped into his head.

The Lord of heaven had spared his life last Saturday for *some* reason.

Was that reason duty? Or was it love?

The idea — as was the case with many ideas in Pilchuck — came out of an informal round-robin discussion at the Kitsch 'n' Caboodle Café.

Other than the regular sessions of the Pilchuck City Council, where the agenda was limited to those issues that in the opinion of the council members affected the community at large, the Kitsch 'n' Caboodle Café was Pilchuck's public forum of choice. There was the editorial page of the *Pilchuck Post*, of course, but as the paper was a weekly, the arguments and conversations tended to lag. Most citizens far preferred the café as a place to voice their opinions and air their concerns.

The Kitsch 'n' Caboodle regulars had developed the round-robin method of community discourse out of logistical necessity. Even if they'd all been able to fit within the walls of the little restaurant at any given time, at any given time they wouldn't all have been available. People worked, people had families, people had other obligations. Except perhaps for

Harley Burns, who was a fairly permanent fixture on "his" stool at the counter.

So it was that the Kitsch 'n' Caboodle had everyday regulars, every-other-day-regulars, and once-or-twice-a-week regulars. And breakfast, lunch, and dinner regulars, afternoon-coffee regulars, and late-night-dessert regulars. And then there were the crossover and irregular regulars — the regulars who either made multiple regular visits or regularly jumped around from day to day and from time to time.

Biddy and Buster — who might as well have lived at the diner, they were there so many hours of the day — were of course the primary movers in any Kitsch 'n' Caboodle round robin, having access as they did to every opinion, debate, and dialogue expressed, argued, and discussed within the confines of the café. With the Bartons, the crossover regulars, and the irregular regulars greasing the wheels, nearly any topic, within a week of initiation, could be thoroughly discussed — with input from every regular and usually an irregular or two.

Only on rare occasions did the Bartons themselves initiate a topic for round-robin review. Topics abounded and were allowed to emerge in the natural order.

This time, however, Biddy made an exception. Cindy Reilly had given Kitsch 'n' Caboodle seven years of her life. Cheerfully. Wholeheartedly. Never complaining that the work was beneath her. Never railing against the obstacles that stood between her and her dreams. Never losing hope that someday she would reach them. And now that Cindy had performed an act of heroism right there on the Kitsch 'n' Caboodle premises, Biddy said, it was time Kitsch 'n' Caboodle gave back something other than a minimum-wage paycheck and piddling small-town tips.

And so it was that within a week of her heroic deed, at the instigation of the Kitsch 'n' Caboodle regulars and armed with a crackerjack business plan, a brand-new genuine faux snakeskin portfolio case crammed with fashion sketches, and a slew of representative garment samples, Cindy Reilly was on her way to an appointment with Franklin Cameron Fitz III. It was his life, they reminded her, that she had saved. And it was he who had told her, in front of a crowd of witnesses, that if she ever needed anything, she had only to ask.

If anyone could provide the capital Cindy needed to get her business off the ground, they agreed, it was Franklin.

Cindy's head, by that time, was buzzing with phrases like *venture capital, silent partner,* and *investment opportunity,* introduced to her over the previous week by a bevy of local businessmen and bankers — including Mr. Pickle, who'd turned her down for a loan himself, he said, only because he "had a responsibility to First National's shareholders," not to mention to his wife and children, who depended on him for a paycheck.

As late as Thursday night — the day before her appointment — Cindy still wasn't keen on asking Franklin for money. No matter how many times her mentors explained the concept of venture capital, it felt a bit like begging to ask him to invest in Glad Raggs. One thing the Reillys had never done was beg.

"If you can convince him he'll make money," Mr. Pickle pointed out, "it isn't begging, Cindy."

Which wasn't very encouraging, seeing as how she hadn't been able to convince Mr. Pickle *he* would make money investing in Glad Raggs. It seemed to her that if Franklin agreed to finance her business venture, it would be only because he felt an obligation. Not because he believed in her — the way, for instance, Jonathan believed in her.

In the end, it had been the thought of Jonathan that led her to agree to the round-robin plan. What a wonderful gift to her fiancé — her soon-to-be fiancé — if she could enter the marriage with something more than her meager income from the Kitsch 'n' Caboodle Café!

Besides, a trip to Seattle meant she could see him. He hadn't been able to break away from his studies for more than two months. He called, of course, but talking over the phone wasn't the same as being with him.

Wouldn't he be astonished when she showed up on his doorstep with news that Glad Raggs was finally on its feet! If she could talk Franklin Fitz into investing, that is . . .

She purposely didn't tell Jonathan she was coming — only that he needed to be home by five o'clock on Friday for a "special delivery." He'd tried to talk her out of whatever it was she was sending: "You can't afford to be wasting money on me, Cindy."

It was so like Jonathan to be concerned about her needs, she told herself. So thoughtful!

But Jonathan did love surprises. And if

Franklin came through for her, what a wonderful surprise the news would be!

By Friday morning, Cindy had convinced herself that convincing Franklin to invest in her business venture was the most important thing in the world. It *wasn't* begging, she told herself. She was going to be successful. With all the coaching she'd been getting, she knew her business plan inside and out, upside and down, around and back again — and it was good. Franklin Cameron Fitz III would be a fool not to seize the opportunity!

Biddy, bless her soul, had made arrangements with Mini Mac to have Eustace drive her to Seattle in the Packard. That way, Cindy could spend her final hours going over her presentation instead of fighting traffic.

She did too. All the way through Tillicum, Snohomish, and Skagit counties, she practiced her sales pitch on Eustace — who wasn't an easy sell.

"Where would you like to stop for lunch, Miss Cindy?" he interrupted her spiel as they crossed the line into King County and approached the outskirts of Seattle.

"Oh! I don't think I can eat, Eustace. I'm too nervous."

"*You* may be. Ol' Eustace ain't," he said,

tugging at the bill of his cap. Eustace always spoke of himself in the third person.

"Oh!" she said again. "I'm sorry, Eustace. Of course you're not." She turned to look at him and thought immediately of Franklin's description. Did gnomes have white mustaches? Did they normally drive limousines? What did they eat? If anyone should know, she should; she'd waited on Eustace often enough at the Kitsch 'n' Caboodle.

"You're partial to seafood, if I remember right," she said.

His ears turned pink. She'd never known anyone else whose ears turned pink in quite the way Eustace's did when he was pleased.

"Yep, ol' Eustace likes his fish," he said, his smile lifting the corners of his mustache. "An' you're a right good girl to remember it."

"You know Seattle better than I do," she said. "Any ideas?"

In the seven years Jonathan had been attending school, Cindy had visited him in the city fewer than a dozen times. Biddy always needed her on Saturdays, and her fellow waitresses — Vestal and Louise, who both, remarkably, had been at the restaurant longer than she had — insisted on hours that made it difficult for Cindy to get two days off together. Her schedule made traveling inconvenient, to say the least.

Besides, Jonathan had always been eager to come home on the weekends. Until last quarter, that is, when his class load was just too much for him to justify the three-hour trip from Seattle to Pilchuck and back. Cindy could bear it only because she knew it meant his schooling was almost over and they'd be together for good. They'd both made sacrifices for their future. For their dreams . . .

"There's Ivar's on the waterfront," Eustace said.

"Ivar's it is then."

She did sip at a bowl of New England clam chowder at Ivar's Acres of Clams while Eustace devoured an enormous Captain's Plate.

"You've got no need for nerves around Master Franklin, Miss Cindy," he told her, wiping his mustache with his napkin. "Not after that Hemlock maneuverin' you done to save his life."

Cindy grinned.

"As fine a boy as you'll find, he is," he declared. "Takes time for a game of checkers with ol' Eustace each and ever' time he comes around Miss Miniver's."

"He seems nice enough, Eustace," said Cindy. "Everyone at the Kitsch 'n' Caboodle likes him. Olga Pfefferkuchen and Biddy especially."

"He's a right good boy."

"I tried to interest the twins," she said. "They think I'm nuts. 'Too old, too square, too status quo,' they told me." She sighed. What else could she have expected from seventeen-year-olds with tip-bleached buzz cuts?

"I'm surprised he doesn't have a girl-friend," she added.

"Says he's got a girl in mind," Eustace said. "Told me so just last weekend."

Cindy felt pleased. She liked Franklin. "Well, I'm glad to hear it, I have to say," she said. "There's nothing quite like being in love, Eustace."

He nodded sagely. "Nothin' but drivin', Miss Cindy. Nothin' but drivin' beats bein' in love."

She was early. She could have lingered longer at Ivar's or had Eustace drive her around till it was time, but all she could think about was selling Franklin on Glad Raggs. The sooner the better.

The corporate offices were on the sixth

and seventh floors above the flagship Strawbridge & Fitz department store near Westlake Center. She'd have taken the escalators as far up as she could, just to admire the opulence, if she hadn't been weighed down with her portfolio and the two clumsy garment bags. She took the elevator straight up to the seventh floor instead.

The front-desk receptionist, a middle-aged woman dressed in an understated oyster-colored linen suit right off the racks a few floors down, looked Cindy up and down in a way that made her squirm inside.

For a moment, in her khaki trousers, pumpkin-colored tank top, and yellow cardigan with its sleeves pushed to her elbows, she felt both woefully underdressed and horribly overstated. Nevertheless, she squared her shoulders, drew herself up to her full five feet eight inches, and met the woman's gaze without flinching.

The fact of the matter was, the outfit was one of her favorites — comfortable and colorful. And maybe her brightly painted wild-animal necklace couldn't compare with the other woman's pearls, but she loved it. Suzie's mother had brought it from Papua New Guinea when she came home for the wedding. It *meant* something to her.

If the receptionist could see what Cindy carried in her garment bags, she'd have a different look on her face, Cindy tried to reassure herself.

Or would she? If "understated" was the woman's style, the whimsical, lighthearted, fanciful, sometimes even outrageous Glad Raggs evening gowns wouldn't do a thing to warm her frosty expression.

Cindy shifted the burden slung over her shoulder and cleared her throat. "I have an appointment," she said. "Cindy Reilly for Franklin Fitz."

The woman's face contracted in a puzzled frown. "Franklin Fitz? In accounting?"

Cindy nodded, the receptionist shrugged and buzzed his office, and in another minute Cindy was on her way down to the floor below. He hadn't answered the buzz, but he was sure to be along soon, the woman said.

A maze of cubicles greeted her when the elevator doors opened. Cubicles created with the same kind of flimsy portable dividers, she noted with some surprise, that the Pilchuck Church of Saints and Sinners used to cordon off Sunday-school classrooms in the church fellowship hall. A far

112

cry from the elegant retail space on the floors below and the tasteful offices she'd glimpsed behind the reception area one floor up.

This workspace hadn't been redecorated for twenty years at least, if the color scheme was any indication. She gazed around at furniture and carpeting in harvest gold, burnt orange, avocado green — like her mother's kitchen before the Reilly women had taken on the task of remodeling as a way of working out their grief after Joe-Joe died.

At least Cindy's outfit coordinated with the colors.

She rested her portfolio against her legs and looked at the floor map the receptionist had given her. It seemed odd that she would have such easy access to the office of the heir to the Strawbridge & Fitz department-store fortune. And equally odd that the heir to the Strawbridge & Fitz department-store fortune would have only a cubicle for an office — and a cubicle straight out of the seventies.

Odd, but sort of nice. For all his money, Franklin certainly didn't put on airs. Good grief — last week at the Kitsch 'n' Caboodle she'd mistaken him for a substitute chauffeur!

She picked up the portfolio, once again shifted her garment bags, and resolutely set off through the maze of cubicles.

It was clearly still the lunch hour. Most of the cubicles she passed were empty, though a few hard-working souls pored over paperwork or clicked away at keyboards, every few minutes reaching blindly for the sandwiches on their desks.

No one sat at Franklin's desk — if it *was* his desk. She looked around the tiny office for a clue and, seeing a glossy portrait of Miniver Macready posted next to the computer with several other photos, decided she must be where she was supposed to be. She leaned the portfolio against a wall and glanced at her watch. Fifteen minutes before her appointment.

The full-length garment bags holding her evening gown samples were heavy and awkward. She looked around for a likely spot to lay them down and was about to drape them over a chair when an idea struck her. The tops of the partitions between the cubicles were narrow enough to hook a hanger over. If she took the dresses out and hung them around the room, Franklin would see from the moment he stepped into his office what Glad Raggs was all about. What *Cindy* was all about.

Her gowns were sensational, everyone told her. The fashion sketches in her portfolio were polished and professional. Her business plan was sound.

She was going to knock the socks off Franklin Cameron Fitz III.

"Show me where to sign," he'd say. And she'd show him.

Franklin wasn't certain what this meeting with Cindy Reilly was all about, but he did know he was thrilled at the thought of seeing her. He'd hardly thought about anything else since she'd called. In fact, he'd hardly thought about anything but Cindy for a week.

He pushed his way through the crowded cosmetic counters at the front of the store and toward the elevators along the back wall. What he'd tried *not* to think about since meeting Cindy was Cindy's boyfriend — with less than successful results, seeing as how he was thinking about Cindy's boyfriend even now.

Cindy's *possible* boyfriend. After all, he hadn't heard word one about a boyfriend from Cindy herself. As for Aunt Min and Mrs. Pfefferkuchen — what made them experts on the subject anyhow?

He stepped onto the elevator and

punched the button for his floor. The boyfriend — if there *was* a boyfriend — was really more a phantom than a flesh-and-blood man, he told himself. He had no form or substance in Franklin's mind. Why, he didn't even have a *name* attached to him! Really, the boyfriend wasn't an issue.

The boyfriend was so *not* an issue, in fact, that Franklin had confessed to both Eustace and Cookie that he'd "met a girl," though he didn't let on to Eustace that the girl was Cindy Reilly. Franklin had felt Cookie was safer to tell because she didn't know Cindy. Yet.

Which had brought him to the point of wondering how she ever *would* know Cindy, when Cindy lived a hundred miles away. The logistics of this romance weren't going to be easy.

He checked his watch as he stepped off the elevator on the sixth floor. Five minutes and he'd see her smile again. He could hardly wait.

He was ready to be dazzled.

Cindy stood in the center of Franklin's cubicle, turning slowly. The workspace looked more like Cinderella's closet than an accountant's office. She was pleased.

Pleased with the effect. Pleased with her dresses. Pleased that the Kitsch 'n' Caboodle crowd had pushed her into coming.

The five-foot walls were just a tad short for displaying her long gowns. She knelt to rearrange the hems where they bunched up at the floor along the hallway partition. The portable wall wobbled as she wrestled with the voluminous yardage. Rickety old thing! Really, hidden away from the public or not, the divider didn't fit the image of Strawbridge & Fitz. Franklin ought —

Her hand encountered an object on the floor beneath the fabric, sticking out into the room. Wouldn't want to get a hem caught —

She tried to pull it out, but it seemed to be stuck. This time she pushed, one way and then the other. Again. There! Whatever it was shifted beneath her hand. Now, if she could get it flush against the wall —

Not until the taffeta-lined skirt poufed up in front of her did Cindy realize what she had done. The mystery object she'd just rendered completely and utterly useless was the wooden foot that supported one end of the flimsy wall — the end weighed down with her gowns.

8

One minute Franklin was hurrying down the hallway to his cubicle, minding his own business. The next minute his office wall had collapsed without warning on top of him, knocking him flat on his back, and he found himself staring up into the face of an angel.

Cindy Reilly, that is. Looking very anxious.

"Franklin! Are you all right? I'm so sorry!"

By then, a crowd had gathered around him, everyone talking at once: "My *word!*" "Is he okay?" "These portable things are *ridiculous!*" "Get it off him!" "What's he doing with all those *dresses?*"

Dresses? Franklin wrinkled his forehead.

Someone heaved the wall off his legs and pushed it upright. "Darn foot got swiveled in somehow . . ." "He should have known that flimsy thing couldn't hold all those evening gowns!"

Evening gowns?

"Something you haven't been telling us, Fitz, old boy?" Laughter.

"Franklin?" Cindy said his name again.

"Cindy . . ." He groaned, rolled over to one side, and sat up, feeling dazed.

"You're all right?"

He rolled his head around, then shook out each arm and leg, just to be sure. "I think so. Did anyone else —"

"No," Cindy told him. "Apparently you were the chosen."

He blinked. It was an odd choice of words. "And you were —"

"On the other side of the wall. I'm afraid —"

"Thank goodness," he interrupted, accepting her hand as he got to his feet. His administrative assistant, Alice, who worked in the cubicle next to his, helped steady him on the other side. "I never would have forgiven myself if you'd been hurt, Cindy. I've been saying for years these old partitions are a danger to life and limb."

"No one can deny it now," Alice said. "Do you think we might get a remodel out of this, Franklin?"

"About time if we did!" someone else said.

Franklin brushed his sleeves and straightened his tie, once again rolling his head on his neck just to be certain he could. The crowd around him, seeing he wasn't mortally wounded, dispersed. All except Cindy and Alice.

"Anything I can get for you?" That was Alice.

"Maybe some water and a couple of aspirin? As a precaution. And I'll have to fill out an accident report, I suppose. Otherwise, I think I just need to sit down . . ."

"In your office?" That was Cindy. Sounding as anxious as she'd looked a few minutes ago.

"Well, yes. That would be the logical place."

She sighed. "Let me clear a path then."

"Clear a path?" He shook his head in confusion.

Cindy didn't answer, just turned and walked toward the opening that was the doorway to his cubicle, her shoulders slumped. Franklin followed her with a puzzled frown.

The portable wall that partitioned his office from the hallway — as well as Alice's next door — was still somewhat askew. He really was going to have to raise a stink with Filene about remodeling. Every other floor was bright and modern, including the offices upstairs. But then, marketing and merchandising were the *glamorous* divisions. Who cared about finance and accounting? "Bean counters." "Drones." "Oblivious to their environment." At least,

120

that was Filene's opinion.

But when the work environment compromised the workers' safety — well, something had to be done, Franklin told himself. If someone got hurt, Strawbridge & Fitz could be in for a nasty lawsuit. *That* argument was something his stepmother would respond to. And if she —

Franklin stopped short at the entrance to his office, thoughts of Filene, lawsuits, and remodeling suddenly forgotten. He looked around in wonder.

On the wall between his and Alice's cubicles hung three unique and beautiful evening gowns, one in shades of blue and green, one in shades of peach and cream, the last in various shades of purple. They weren't patchwork, exactly, though either the skirt or the bodice — and in the case of the purple dress, both — were created from strips of fabric sewn together. The styles were all different but tended toward the fanciful with their fitted waists and bouffant skirts and elegant finishing touches. They looked like dresses a fairy-tale princess might wear.

In the center of the room was Cindy, on her knees, sorting out other gowns from the midst of a shimmering mountain of fabric.

She looked up at him with such a forlorn expression he felt a physical pang. *As if your happiness depended on her smile,* he heard his father's words in his mind. Oh, what he would give to be able to coax her lovely smile back to her face! He wanted to gather her in his arms and tell her whatever was wrong, things were going to work out — Franklin himself was going to make sure of it.

"Cindy?" he asked gently.

"I had it all planned," she said sadly, gazing up at him from the floor, her eyes luminous. "I didn't know the foot on the partition swiveled. I was going to knock your socks off, Franklin."

He grinned. "And you swept me off my feet instead!" he teased. "I'd say that's a step up, wouldn't you?"

Encouraged by her surprised little hiccup, he leaned over, grabbed the fabric of his trousers, and lifted the legs a couple of inches. "And look at that, would you! My socks may not be gone, but they *are* falling down around my ankles."

This time she smiled. A small, sad, crescent-moon sort of a smile, not at all the smile he remembered lighting up the Kitsch 'n' Caboodle Café, but a smile nonetheless. He felt heartened.

"Your own designs?" he asked, kneeling to pick up one of the dresses from the jumble. "Aunt Min told me you were talented," he added at her nod, "but I had no idea. These are so — *original*." He rubbed a finger lightly across the velvet in his hands.

Cindy stood, a dress draped over her arms. "Glad Raggs," she said. "Do you think if we're careful, and leave the foot be, the gowns could go back on the wall? They're part of my presentation."

Presentation? he wondered.

They rehung the dresses. When Alice came in with the aspirin, she oohed and ahhed and asked interested questions, which seemed to go a long way toward raising Cindy's spirits.

Franklin was surprised and pleased to hear the part Aunt Min had played in inspiring Cindy's line of evening wear. He wouldn't put it past his aunt to have bought yards more fabric than she needed just so Cindy would have more scraps to play with.

"The idea for the two-piece gowns is one I got from Miniver too," she told Alice, pointing to an example. "I don't know if you've ever met her —"

"You mean you design Miniver

Macready's concert gowns?" Alice interrupted, squealing. "I've seen her in concert twice, and she looked as magnificent as she sounded. She's stunning, isn't she, with that mane of silver hair?"

"She is," Cindy agreed. "But her figure is — well, *challenging*. As far as a really good fit goes, I mean."

Franklin thought the description was tactful.

"Also, in concert, she needs good range of motion for her arms," Cindy went on. "Two pieces seem to work better for that. Which got me to thinking: If two pieces work better for playing piano, why not for dancing?"

"Dancing?"

"Isn't that what most evening gowns end up *doing* at some point in their lives?"

"Now that you mention it," Alice said thoughtfully, "yes, I'd say they do."

"And how many gowns have you worn that worked *well* for dancing?" Cindy asked. "They look beautiful, yes. But they pull. They strain. They pinch. So *my* thought was, why not a beautiful gown with comfort and motion built in?"

"What a good idea!" said Alice with enthusiasm.

"And *then* I got to thinking how many

people out there — how many women — are different sizes, top and bottom, like Mini Mac —"

"No one I *know* is a perfect size ten," Alice agreed. "Or a perfect twelve, or fourteen, or *anything*, for that matter . . ."

"You can buy career and casual separates," Cindy said. "So why not evening-wear separates? That way, a woman can buy a ready-to-wear gown as close to made-to-measure as ready-to-wear can be. Not just a skirt and top, either, but a real *gown*."

"Smart," Alice said admiringly.

Franklin, who in his time had analyzed a women's apparel sales report or two, had to agree. *Very* smart.

He was even more impressed by the time Cindy finished her sales presentation an hour later. For a woman unschooled in either marketing or design, she seemed incredibly savvy — not to mention talented. The dresses, the sketches, the well-thought-out business plan. It was clear to see that Glad Raggs was more than a creative exercise to Cindy. More than a business, even. It was her passion.

She had more invested in her trip to see him today than he'd ever invested in anything. Which made it all the more difficult to tell her he couldn't help her.

"I think you've got a winner, Cindy. I think you could make it go," he said when she was finished.

Something in his face or tone of voice must have told her. "But?"

He sighed. "It's true I'm the heir to my father's fortune," he said. "Or half of it anyhow. And there's nothing I'd like more than to invest in your company, Cindy, even if I *didn't* owe you my life. But at the moment my money's all tied up in the trust fund Father set up for me. My step-mother gives me a trickle every month for an allowance, but the floodgates don't open till I hit thirty. In the meantime, I'm just a manager in the accounting department at Strawbridge & Fitz. Three people report to me. I know I have the name, but so far, that's *all* I have. I'm small potatoes, Cindy."

She tried to hide her disappointment — and didn't do much of a job of it. She was as transparent as glass when it came to her feelings, Franklin thought. He doubted there was a deceptive bone in her body.

"I'm sorry," he said.

She sighed. "I was just so *sure* you were the answer."

He leaned back in his chair, staring

thoughtfully at the half-dozen gowns lined up shoulder to shoulder around the walls. "If there was some way you could start smaller . . ."

"Evening gowns just aren't small," she said. "One dress alone could cost hundreds of dollars in fabric alone. And the labor!" She rolled her eyes. "There's no way I can make them in the numbers I need without an assembly line somewhere. If I designed active wear, say, or T-shirts —"

"Like that one?" Franklin pointed to one of her two-piece evening dresses. The full skirt fell from a wide satin waistband in vertical strips of ruby-colored fabric — three different kinds — and the cropped top was a simple cap-sleeved tee with a wide neck, made out of some kind of stretchy crushed velvet in the same rich scarlet as the skirt.

"Exactly," Cindy said. "The top to that dress has four seams, a hem, and satin lingerie bias around the neck. That part of it I can whip up in an hour — two at the outside. The skirt, on the other hand —"

"Couldn't you sell that top as a high-fashion holiday T-shirt?" Franklin interrupted. "Wouldn't it look all right with a pair of designer jeans?"

Cindy stared at the velvet top, her brow

wrinkled. "The style *is* something like the T-shirts I made for Robin and Rosie's birthday . . ."

Franklin knocked on the wall between his and Alice's cubicles, then stood up and peered over it. His administrative assistant looked up from her desk with a quizzical expression. Put on for his benefit, Franklin was sure. Alice wouldn't have missed a word of his meeting with Cindy.

"Got a minute?" he asked.

"*I'd* wear it," Alice said a few minutes later, after making Franklin explain his idea again as if she hadn't heard it. "With a pair of black jeans. Or a short skirt and tights. You know, for those times you want to dress up and dress down at the same time."

Franklin didn't, but he took her word for it.

"How many of those could you make in the next three or four months?" he asked Cindy.

"Realistically? Without quitting my job and the rest of my life? Maybe ninety or a hundred. Maybe not that many — I still have work to do on the designs for Mini Mac's new gowns."

"But if your mom helped?" he prodded.

"She's the one *making* Mini Mac's gowns, Franklin."

"So if you got an order for, say, two hundred T-shirts, with delivery in October — you don't think you could do it?"

"If I actually got an order from Strawbridge & Fitz?" She hesitated. She was chewing on her lower lip in a way that made it difficult for Franklin to stay focused.

"I'd find a way," she finally said.

He picked up the phone. "Good. Let me make a call here . . ."

Fifteen minutes later, Cindy was on the floor in the junior department selling the junior-wear buyer on jewel-toned crushed panne velvet T-shirts for Christmas. Almost before she knew what had happened, she was back in Franklin's office in a daze.

"Franklin. She placed an order. Seventy-five each in ruby, sapphire, and emerald. Two hundred twenty-five T-shirts!"

"Excellent! And you're charging her what I suggested?"

"Only because I'd talked myself out of the whole idea by the time I got down there. How am I going to make two hundred twenty-five T-shirts by October?!"

"You'll find a way," he reminded her.

"I thought if I asked a hundred fifty dollars apiece she'd be sure to turn me down."

"If you'd asked *less,* she'd have turned you down. How could she justify charging the customer three hundred dollars if she'd only paid you thirty?"

"Three hundred dollars?" Cindy gasped. "People are going to pay three hundred dollars for my *T-shirts?!*"

"And why shouldn't they?" She could have sworn it was pride in his voice. "They're Cindy Reilly's Glad Raggs, aren't they?"

9

Jonathan couldn't have looked more surprised when he opened the door to find Cindy on his doorstep.

Or more handsome. The midnight blue of his eyes gleamed in startling contrast to the thick black hair and copper skin his mother swore came from some unknown Indian brave hidden in the family tree. Cindy had never known another man who turned heads the way Jonathan Crum did. He liked the attention too. A little too much sometimes.

But she didn't want to think about that now. Besides, after the last misunderstanding, they'd worked things out. He'd promised to be more circumspect, and she'd promised not to come unglued if, through no fault of his own, some woman or another should throw herself at him.

It was the price one paid for having a gorgeous boyfriend. And for the fact they'd been living a hundred miles apart for seven years. Distance had been hard on the relationship. But soon, thank goodness, distance wouldn't be an issue.

She flung her arms wide and smiled with all the exuberance she was feeling. "Special delivery, Jonathan!"

"Cindy! What are you *doing* here?" He glanced over her shoulder. Cindy followed his eyes to the vintage Packard parked at the curb. "Isn't that what's-her-name's car — the piano player?"

"Miniver Macready. Don't I get a kiss?"

An odd expression, so brief she didn't know if she'd really seen it, flashed across Jonathan's face before he said lightly, "Of course you do." The kiss was brief, but the hug made up for it. He seemed to hold her extra tight and let go with reluctance.

"I've got the biggest news!" she said.

"And I want to hear all about it." Jonathan glanced again toward the curb. "It's hot out here in the sun though. Shall I invite the chauffeur in for a cold drink?"

She'd been about to send Eustace on his way to dinner with Franklin, who'd actually invited both of them to join him. "I think he probably has time," she said, looking at her watch. It *was* a warm day, and Eustace had been waiting around for her for hours. Jonathan was so thoughtful.

Her eyes widened in surprise as she crossed the threshold into the apartment a few minutes later, Eustace and Jonathan at her heels. "You've redecorated! Jonathan — you've bought new furniture!"

"Not really," he said offhandedly. "Castoffs from a friend. Please, have a seat — I have spiced sun tea made."

"You do?" She didn't remember Jonathan's ever having made sun tea.

"Well," Eustace said as Jonathan disappeared into the kitchen. He sat gingerly on the edge of his chair, nervously spinning his cap in his hands.

Cindy understood why. For one thing, the chrome-and-leather furniture had been designed more for style than comfort. And the style was — well, not exactly what she'd call homey. In fact, the apartment had more the feel of a modern art museum than a home. The look was spare — the low-slung sofa and chair, cream-colored with black throw pillows; the cream-colored area rug; the single abstract painting on the cream-colored walls. Biddy would have had those walls filled up in no time.

The painting, which looked as if the artist had squeezed tubes of red, blue, yellow, and black paint randomly across the canvas, she actually liked. It reminded her of Jonathan's usual, colorful, comfortable clutter.

He returned with a tray of tall, slim glasses filled with an amber liquid, which he set on the black lacquered cube that served as a coffee table in front of the sofa.

"New glasses," Cindy said as she accepted one. Again she was surprised. Money had been tight for Jonathan since he'd been in school. New glasses seemed a luxury he would have foregone.

Was the expensive furniture *really* someone's castoffs?

Cindy felt immediately guilty for the thought. If Jonathan said they were castoffs, they were castoffs. He had no reason to lie. He *didn't* lie.

But *whose* castoffs?

"I found them on sale," he interrupted her thoughts. "Now then" — he raised his glass — "tell me your news."

Somehow, she'd lost the edge to her excitement. She felt — *unsettled*. As if the changes in Jonathan's apartment were significant in some way she didn't yet know.

"I've made my first big sale," she said, her tone almost matter-of-fact. "Just this afternoon."

He looked blank. "Your first big sale."

She drew a deep breath. "I've sold two hundred twenty-five velvet T-shirts to

Strawbridge & Fitz. For one hundred fifty dollars apiece."

He no longer looked blank. He looked stunned. "Wow. How are you going to do it?"

It was the first question she'd asked herself, of course. The minute she and the junior-wear buyer had sealed the deal with a handshake. But she didn't like hearing it from Jonathan.

Jonathan was supposed to be her champion, her partner, her comrade in arms. He was supposed to say, "Wow! That's wonderful! I always knew you could do it, Cindy. How can I help you?"

"I'll figure it out," she said, her voice tight.

Jonathan looked at her across his iced-tea glass for a moment, not saying anything. When he spoke, his voice was gentle. "I'm sure you will, Cindy. You can do anything you set your mind to. I've never doubted that."

Cindy felt her irritation melt away. When he spoke to her in that tone of voice, she'd forgive him just about anything.

"What shall we do to celebrate then?" she asked brightly. "Do you want to go out or stay in?"

When he didn't immediately answer, she

added, "Eustace is having dinner with a friend. I just need to let him know how late I'll be and where he should pick me up."

Jonathan leaned forward to set his glass on the tray, almost as if he was avoiding her. Avoiding her eyes. "I'm sorry, Cindy. I wish you'd told me you were coming. I already have plans for the evening."

"Oh, Jonathan." She wondered if she sounded as disappointed as she felt. "I haven't seen you in weeks! Can't you get out of it?"

"I'm afraid not." He glanced at Eustace, who was still fidgeting with his cap.

He didn't feel free to talk with Eustace there, that much was clear. And neither did she, at this point. Not with the questions she wanted to ask: *What's wrong, Jonathan? Is it something I've said? Something I've done? Whatever it is, let's talk about it . . .*

"Will you call me tonight?" she asked.

He hesitated. "I may be out late."

"Oh. Where did you say you were going?"

"I didn't." He looked at her now, but without offering any more information. She waited, her heartbeat quickening. What was it? She and Jonathan didn't have secrets.

Finally, reluctantly, he told her. "I'm

meeting a man I'm interested in working for. It's a sort of . . . an informal interview."

Cindy's breath caught in her throat. "An informal interview? With an attorney, you mean?" When he nodded, she leaned forward as he had done earlier, avoiding his eyes in the same way he had avoided hers, and set her iced-tea glass next to his on the tray. "Why would you do that, Jonathan? When you're coming home to Pilchuck at the end of the summer?"

Instead of answering, Jonathan rose abruptly. "Mr. Phillips, would you like some more tea?"

"Thank you, but no." Eustace, too, jumped from his chair. "Ol' Eustace b'lieves what he'll do, for the moment, is mosey on out to the car and catch him some winks. You'll excuse him?"

Cindy threw him a grateful look. "I won't be long, Eustace," she said.

"*Quaa-ack!*" Jonathan honked after showing the chauffeur out. He grinned at Cindy.

She frowned, more in confusion than anything, but Jonathan apparently took her expression as criticism. "Oh, lighten up," he said. "Even *you* have to admit the man's an odd duck."

Even her? What was *that* supposed to mean?

"Maybe so," she said, her voice tight, "but he's a *dear* odd duck. Now, what is it you need to tell me?"

Jonathan looked studiously at his watch. "I don't have much time."

"I'm not leaving until you tell me."

He sighed. "All right then. The thing is, this last semester I've been — well, re-evaluating. I don't know if small-town law is really what I want to do, Cindy. Don't you think I owe it to myself to check out some other options? Weigh some other opportunities?"

"Not what you want to do? But Jonathan, we've been planning this forever! It's what we've dreamed about! The whole town's waiting for you to come back home and hang your shingle!"

Jonathan ran both hands through his glossy black hair and leaned his head back on the sofa, squeezing his eyes shut. As if he didn't want to see her. Didn't want to deal with her. Finally, with a deep sigh, he lifted his head and met her eyes. "That's just it, Cindy. Can't you see? That the whole town would be waiting for such an incredibly anticlimactic event! There's nothing going on in

Pilchuck. I'd be bored out of my skin."

"It doesn't sound to me as if you're weighing anything," she said. Her throat was so tight she was surprised her words came out without squeaking. "It sounds to me as if you've already made up your mind. For both of us. Don't you think *I* should be in on this decision? You haven't said a word to me about any of this!"

He didn't deny it. "You're right; we need to talk. I'll make sure I'm home by eleven and call you tonight. You'll be home by then?"

At her nod he added, "But I've got to get going now, Cindy. I can't be late."

And that was that. A brief kiss good-bye, but no hug, no "I love you." Cindy walked out to the Packard like an automaton and slid wordlessly into the front passenger seat. Eustace sat up, pushing his cap back into place.

"Would you want to be goin' home?" he asked quietly.

She would be — but Eustace had been so pleased when Franklin invited him out to have dinner while she and Jonathan were celebrating.

Ha! Some celebration.

On the other hand . . . hadn't she been presumptuous to show up at Jonathan's apartment without any warning? To think that he wouldn't have other plans — or, if he did, that he could break them on a whim? That wasn't Jonathan. Jonathan was conscientious, steady, reliable. People could *count* on him.

You're taking this all too personally, Cindy, she told herself. Jonathan was at the end of his schooling. He was going through one of those confusing "life passages" she'd heard about on that radio show, the one with the call-in psychologist. And he hadn't talked to her about his confusion precisely be-cause he knew she'd react the way she was reacting.

Poor guy. She hadn't been very under-standing.

Well, tonight they'd talk about it — and she'd be so understanding he would think she'd had a personality transplant since this afternoon. They'd work things out. She was sure of it.

"Go home?" she said to Eustace. "Are you kidding me? I'm not leaving this town till I've done some serious celebrating."

Franklin was delighted to have Cindy join him and Eustace for dinner, especially because it meant she wasn't with her so-called boyfriend. If said boyfriend couldn't rearrange one evening of his life to help Cindy celebrate her red-letter day — well, he didn't deserve her, that was all. She was better off with Franklin and Eustace.

Except that she wasn't entirely happy about not being with the boyfriend. Oh, she sounded philosophical enough about it, but she was disappointed. Franklin could tell.

She needed distraction. And he knew just the place.

Fortunato's Ristorante was a unique combination of several things Franklin liked, not the least of which was the Fortunato family matriarch, Nonna Pippa.

He frequented Fortunato's, close to downtown near the city's historic Pioneer Square, for unhurried lunches in the lull between the noon rush and the early dinner crowd. The first time he'd gone there, on the recommendation of an acquaintance who was dating Leander Fortunato's daughter at the time, he'd been greeted by an old woman almost as wide as she was tall, her gray hair coiled in braids on top of her head, wearing a shapeless apron over her shapeless dress and sweeping the sidewalk outside the restaurant as if her life depended on it.

"Nonna Pippa," she had introduced herself, stopping her sweeping long enough to shake his hand. "Welcome to Fortunato's Ristorante. We got lotsa things you like inside."

Nonna Pippa, Franklin soon discovered, had a special place in her heart for young men who ate alone. When she came inside that first day and discovered him sitting by himself with a large bowl of minestrone and a minibaguette of extra sour sourdough, she'd pulled up a chair to his table, helped herself to a chunk of his bread, and proceeded to tell him the Fortunato family history, beginning in Genoa with her late husband's father's birth.

From then on she'd called him "Signore Franklin" and introduced him around the restaurant as a "fine boy" — which was a little embarrassing, but not half as mortifying as Aunt Min's "Isn't he precious?"

He'd been there quite a few times for dinner, too, usually as a special treat for Cookie, who enjoyed Nonna Pippa almost as much as he did. On Friday and Saturday nights, the gourmet northern Italian cuisine was served with music — a six-piece swing revival band called Brown Derby Joe. Franklin thought it an odd sort of music to go with Italian food until he learned how much Nonna Pippa loved swing dancing.

In fact, Nonna Pippa's joyful approach to dancing had given Franklin an appreciation for the pastime his many years of lessons never had. But then, his dancing lessons had been Filene's idea, not his. Until Nonna Pippa, he'd avoided dance floors like the proverbial plague. Now he always took time to take a turn around the floor with the Fortunato family matriarch, and sometimes with Cookie. Tonight, he was hoping to coax Cindy onto the floor. What could be more celebratory than dancing?

The downside to the place was that lately — unfortunately — Fortunato's Ristorante had been "discovered" by a certain trendy social set. Currently, it was *the* place to see and be seen around Seattle. Which was good for Lorenzo and Leander's business, Franklin supposed, and not a total surprise, considering the quality of food, the elegant old-world atmosphere, and the popularity of Brown Derby Joe.

Ordinarily, seeing and being seen was of little interest to Franklin. Tonight, however . . .

To tell the truth, tonight he wouldn't mind at all being seen at Fortunato's, especially with a beautiful woman like Cindy Reilly on his arm. A woman who somehow managed to be the prototype for the All-American-Girl-Next-Door-Hometown-Sweetheart and at the same time an Uncategorical, One-of-a-Kind, In-a-Class-by-Herself Original. An incredibly special woman who didn't appear to even know how special she was.

Cindy was more elegant in her comfortable, colorful clothes and her simple, subtle, hardly there makeup than Filene and her ilk were when they dressed to the nines and made themselves up for a charity ball. With her golden hair cascading down her back, with her cinnamon eyes sparkling and her generous smile lighting every dark corner of the restaurant, he was certain she'd outshine every woman there.

Cindy herself wasn't so confident. Walking into Fortunato's Ristorante felt to her like walking into someone else's life — someone cultured, sophisticated, and rich. It was not the sort of place one would find in Pilchuck, nor even in Bellingrath. It was clearly a Big City Restaurant — and Cindy had never in her life felt more like a Small-Town Girl.

She actually gasped when Franklin held

the ornately detailed bronze-and-copper door for her and she caught her first glimpse of the interior. A sweep of curved marble stairs descended from street level to a waiting area right out of the Renaissance, except that the men and women milling about — attractive without exception — were dressed in modern clothes.

The foyer had a *fountain*, for heaven's sake! With a marble Cupid on a pedestal, his arm drawn and his arrow pointed at the heart of an oblivious and very expensive-looking woman seated on one of the velvet-cushioned benches.

The woman looked up as the door opened, her eyes slipping past Cindy as if hardly registering her existence, but resting on Franklin with a flicker of recognition. She inclined her head toward him — it was almost more a dismissal than a greeting, Cindy thought — and returned her attention to the leather binder in her lap.

She was the most exotic creature Cindy had ever seen in real life — almost as striking, in fact, as the high-fashion models who graced the pages of *W* or French *Vogue*. Her straight, shoulder-length hair was black — as black as Jonathan's — and cut above her perfectly arched eyebrows in fashionably wispy bangs. Her skin, in contrast, was the palest ivory, stretched over incredible bones and uninterrupted by even the faintest blush. Her perfectly formed Cupid's-bow lips and her long fingernails were painted brilliant red. The same shade as the short, beaded dress — an Antonio Fusco, if Cindy wasn't mistaken — that revealed every womanly curve beneath it.

The effect was so dramatic it nearly took Cindy's breath away. She'd held her own with the Strawbridge & Fitz receptionist in her pearls and understated suit earlier in the day. But now, next to this woman, she felt like a frumpy housewife. No — make that a gangly scarecrow.

Almost without thinking, she took Franklin's arm — as if the action could steady her nerves. Straightening her shoulders, she breathed deeply and stepped down.

And it was a good thing she'd taken Franklin's arm too: She misjudged the distance and stumbled over nothing. If he hadn't grabbed her, she likely would have tumbled to the bottom of the steps and crumpled in a heap beneath Cupid's vacant stare — and directly at the feet of Miss Perfection.

10

"Are you all right?" Franklin asked anxiously.

"I'm all right." Except for her pride, which was suffering more by the second. Her cheeks were flaming.

To make matters worse, Franklin stopped at the bottom of the stairs, right in front of the gorgeous woman in the short red dress. "Hello, Aubrey."

She arched an eyebrow flirtatiously without giving Cindy or Eustace so much as a glance. "Franklin Fitz. We meet again so soon." Her voice was low and sultry, and there was a certain wry twist to her red lips when she spoke, as if she were secretly amused.

Which she probably was, Cindy thought, her cheeks flaming again. Amused that someone like Franklin Cameron Fitz III, heir to the Strawbridge & Fitz department-store fortune, was with a country bumpkin like Cindy Reilly.

The woman raised her hand as if expecting Franklin to kiss it — which he didn't, thank goodness. Cindy would have been sick right then and there. She certainly hoped this wasn't the girl Franklin had told Eustace he "had in mind." Frumpy housewife, gangly scarecrow, country bumpkin, or not, *she'd* be a better match for him than — what was her name? Aubrey? What kind of a name was *that,* anyhow?

Franklin placed his hand firmly over Cindy's where it clung to his arm, as if to calm her. It did give her confidence, somehow, his hand on hers. "Cindy, Eustace — I'd like you to meet Aubrey du Puy. A friend of my stepmother's," he said. Aubrey flicked a glance at Franklin's companions, nodded shortly, and pointedly returned her attention to the binder on her lap.

Franklin's hand tightened on Cindy's as they turned away. She glanced at him, startled, and saw that he was scowling fiercely.

"Franklin?"

His brow cleared as their eyes met and held. He loosened his grip on her hand. "Cindy Reilly," he murmured, "you are worth a thousand *thousand* Aubrey du Puys. Don't ever let anyone make you think otherwise."

Before she could do anything but drop her jaw and snap it shut again, he was shepherding her and Eustace toward the hostess stand. Was he a mind reader?

"Good evening, Signora Felicia!" he called.

"Signore Franklin!" The thin, dark woman who stood behind the podium had a pinched, fretful sort of face, but it softened and lit up when she saw him.

"You got the message I need a table for three instead of two?"

"I did. You make me scramble again after we have the table all set for you," she scolded.

"Ah, Felicia, I would so enjoy seeing you scramble!"

"Harrumph." She rolled her eyes, but she clearly enjoyed his teasing. "He mocks me," she said to Cindy and Eustace. "And still I put up with him. Why is this?"

Franklin was grinning as if that dark scowl had never crossed his face. "Because I'm just so darn likable, maybe?"

"Ha!"

He held up a hand. "Felicia, before we come to blows, I'd like you to meet two special friends, Cindy Reilly and Eustace Phillips. We are here tonight to celebrate."

"To celebrate what?"

"Life. Success." He suddenly thought of Aunt Min's question: *Are you happy?*

Well, tonight he was. "And happiness!" he added.

"To celebrate is good, Signorina and Signore," Felicia said with a little bow to Franklin's guests. "You honor us to celebrate under our roof." Lifting her penciled eyebrows at Franklin, she added: "So! You finally bring a girlfriend to Fortunato's! And a pretty one too. Nonna Pippa will worry she won't be dancing tonight."

"Oh, I'm not —" Cindy started to say.

"Nonna Pippa knows I always save a dance for her," Franklin said before she could get her words out.

The dinner was as delightful as it was delicious — not in small part due to the company of this very Nonna Pippa. Almost the moment their warm basket of bread arrived — *Bruschetta al Pomodoro,* which turned out to be the fanciest and most mouth-watering garlic bread Cindy had ever eaten — the Fortunato family matriarch pulled up a chair and joined them.

She was a squat, round woman with a lifetime of joys and sorrows engraved on her old face, and she talked a mile a minute, her hands moving almost as fast as her tongue. It took Cindy a moment to realize she wasn't speaking a foreign language, but a wonderful, rollicking, heavily accented version of English, punctuated here and there with Italian words and phrases.

The old woman had so much to say — making recommendations, asking questions without waiting for answers, and regaling them with family news that Cindy could only half keep up with — it took Franklin several minutes to get a word in edgewise just to introduce her audience.

At which point Nonna Pippa took one of Cindy's hands between her own and said, "So! My Franklin finally got a girlfriend! A fine boy, is Franklin," she added, leaning toward Cindy with an air of confidentiality. "I tell him over and again he needs a good woman. For the dancing. For *amore*. For making the babies."

Cindy blushed. "Oh, but I'm not —"

"For some things, Signora Cookie and Nonna Pippa do fine," she interrupted. "For others . . ." She lifted her eyebrows and shook her head. "Now — how do you find the *bruschetta?* Leander, he uses only the most firm of the plum tomatoes and the most fresh of the basil leaves . . ."

She stayed through the *zuppa* and *insalata* courses, excused herself for the *Taglioni con Pesto al Caprino* — thin noodles with goat cheese pesto — and returned toward the end of the main course. *Gamberi al Forno con gli Aspáragi,* Cindy had chosen: baked shrimp with asparagus.

Cindy enjoyed the way the Italian names rolled over her tongue almost as much as she enjoyed the exquisite flavors of Leander Fortunato's culinary creations. Better yet, she enjoyed sitting back, having someone wait on her hand and foot — instead of the other way round.

After trying several times early in the evening to inform Nonna Pippa she *wasn't* Franklin's girlfriend, Cindy had given up. Nonna Pippa had made up her mind. What did it matter anyhow? Cindy would never see the old woman again. She'd leave it to Franklin to explain to Nonna Pippa. Some other time.

In the meantime, the Fortunato family matriarch added as much color and authenticity to their Italian feast as the garlic and pesto and extra virgin olive oil, the sweeping mural of vineyard-covered hills wrapping the walls of the dining room, and the marble fountain in the entryway. Eustace was clearly charmed with their hostess, though he never got in more than a word or two at a time when she was seated with them.

More than anything else, Nonna Pippa

— and Franklin, too, to give him his due — helped Cindy relax, forget her insecurities, and do what she'd come to do: celebrate. Celebrate her first big sale. Celebrate the fact that she, Cindy Reilly, was finally on her way to the big time. Celebrate that fairy tales come true . . .

It was Franklin who explained to their hostess exactly why they were there. He sounded as proud of Cindy's accomplishment as if it had been his own.

For a brief moment, Cindy thought of Jonathan's less-than-enthusiastic response to her news. *He had other things on his mind,* she told herself. *Besides, I hadn't even told him I was making a pitch to Franklin today. If I know Jonathan, he's probably kicking himself but good right now. And wishing he was with me instead of some dull old attorney.*

"Look out, world!" she cried, banishing Jonathan from her mind and raising her glass.

"Viva Glad Raggs!" Franklin toasted.

"So what are you waiting for, Signore Franklin?" said Nonna Pippa, clapping her hands. "The *sorbetto,* he can wait. The *celebrazione,* she cannot. Also, the dancing is good for the . . . how do you call it?" She patted her stomach.

"Digestion," Franklin offered.

She nodded vigorously. "Yes. And for the soul."

Franklin pushed back his chair. "Of course it is. May I have this dance, Nonna Pippa?"

She waved her hand dismissively. "Dance with your *innamorata!*" Glancing at Eustace with a coquettish smile, she added, "I got another partner in mind. Signore?"

Eustace hurriedly rose from his chair and helped Nonna Pippa from hers.

"Ol' Eustace is honored," he said.

"Innamorata?" Cindy asked Franklin as they disappeared from view.

Franklin hesitated, then said, "I'm not sure. Girlfriend, sweetheart, something like that."

What was it about being around Franklin that made her blush so furiously? "You'll have to set her straight, Franklin. I couldn't get her to listen to me."

"I'm not sure I can either," he said. "Once Nonna Pippa gets something into her head, she doesn't like to let go." Again he hesitated. When he did speak, his words seemed to fall all over themselves. "In the meantime, would you . . . I'd be . . . shall we . . . dance?"

She stared up at him, all her insecurities

suddenly flooding back from wherever they'd retreated the last couple of hours.

He wanted her to *dance?*

She hadn't danced since the annual Pilchuck High School Spring Fling her senior year. Even then, she hadn't exactly been what anyone would call an accomplished dancer. It hadn't mattered much then — dancing in high school had been more about fun and exuberance than about rhythm and form. And she and Jonathan had been at pretty much the same level of competence — or *incompetence*, the truth be told. She was quite sure what they'd done on the dance floor in the Pilchuck High School gymnasium wouldn't pass for dancing at the elegant Fortunato's Ristorante.

"I — really don't know how," she said.

"What?! You design dresses for dancing and don't know how? It's time you learned, Cindy. Dance with me," he urged. "I'd love to teach you."

She turned her head to look over her shoulder toward the dance floor. "But there's hardly anyone out there," she wailed. "People will see us!"

"Look how much fun Eustace and Nonna Pippa are having," he coaxed.

It was true. At least, they *looked* as if they

were having fun. But even at *their* ages, they were more agile and graceful than she could ever hope to be.

A flash of red caught her eye as another couple moved onto the dance floor. Her heart sank. *Aubrey.* She'd managed to put the unpleasant woman out of her mind. No way was she getting out there, putting herself up for comparison with a woman like that. She couldn't hold a candle to Aubrey du Puy. Just look at how gorgeous she was. Just look at how beautifully she danced. Graceful, light on her feet, perfectly in sync with her handsome, debonair —

Jonathan!

Before she even knew she was out of her seat, Cindy was pushing her way through the tables toward the dance floor. If she'd been a dragon, she would have been spitting fire.

She must want to dance after all, Franklin thought, hurrying after her. And she must want to do it *now* — she was zigzagging through the tables like a gold-medal skier on a slalom run. He didn't catch up with her till they reached the coveted see-and-be-seen tables at the edge of the dance floor, where she stopped so abruptly he nearly ran over her.

Not until then did he see Aubrey du Puy,

in her formfitting scarlet dress, dancing co-
zily with a tall, good-looking man about
Franklin's age. They were so smooth together, they looked as if they'd been
dancing together all their lives.

Great. Just what Cindy needed when
Aubrey had already shaken her confidence
once tonight. "Don't forget — you're
worth ten times an Aubrey du Puy," he
murmured in her ear.

She didn't look at him. "Last time it was
a thousand *thousand* times," she spat.

"Cindy?" He was shocked at her tone of
voice — but not as shocked as he was the
next moment when she marched across the
hardwood dance floor, grabbed Aubrey
du Puy's dance partner with both arms,
and literally dragged him away from her.

"Cindy!" Franklin called, his heart
beating in triple time as he ran after her.

"You lying, two-timing, cold-hearted
cheat!" Cindy shouted, flinging the man's
arm away from her as if it were garbage.

Franklin stopped dead in his tracks.
Surely not! Surely the man with Aubrey
du Puy wasn't Cindy's *boyfriend!*

He felt suddenly sick to his stomach. As
much as he wanted Cindy not to have a
boyfriend, he would never have wished on
anyone — let alone *her* — losing a boy-

friend the way Cindy was losing hers.

To say she wasn't taking the situation well was to put it mildly. She was practically jumping up and down in front of the guy, punching the air with her fists to emphasize her shouts: "So *this* is the *business* appointment you couldn't get *out* of to help your *fiancée* celebrate the most important event of her *life?*"

The boyfriend — or was it fiancé? Or *ex*-fiancé, at this point? Whoever he was, he looked stricken. Possibly even fearful.

Aubrey, on the other hand, didn't look the least bit afraid. She stepped between Cindy and the man — the Creep, as Franklin was beginning to think of him — with her arms crossed and her face set in the kind of cold expression Franklin had only seen, before tonight, on his stepmother's face. "You're making a scene," she snapped. "And you aren't his fiancée."

By then Franklin was at Cindy's side. He reached an arm around her shoulders, but she flung it away. "Darn *tootin'* I'm making a scene, you little snip!" she yelled. "And what would *you* know about our engagement anyhow?"

"I know everything about you, Cindy Reilly," the other woman said, her voice as cold as her expression. "Or should I say

Little Miss Pollyanna?"

Cindy gasped. If Franklin hadn't grabbed her and pulled her away, he was sure she would have let Aubrey have it. He knew already she was a take-charge kind of person, but never in a million years would he have guessed she was such a spitfire!

To make matters worse, at that very moment Nonna Pippa swooned in Eustace's arms, right there in the middle of the dance floor. Seeing as how she weighed probably twice as much as he did, they both went crashing to the floor. *That* brought Cindy back to her senses in short order.

"Eustace! Nonna Pippa! What have I done?" she moaned, and dropped to her knees beside them.

Nonna Pippa, being indisposed, didn't answer. Eustace groaned.

Signora Felicia, the bartender, and a pair of waiters materialized on the scene simultaneously. "Is there a doctor in the house?" the bartender bellowed. Within seconds a doctor was there, kneeling beside the fallen pair. Fortunato's attracted doctors and lawyers in droves.

Franklin pulled Cindy up from the floor and put his arm around her. She was shaking like the proverbial leaf. The circumstances weren't anything like what he'd imagined, but the way he felt with his arms around her was everything he'd dreamed. Didn't the Creep feel it too? What was wrong with him, to leave a real woman like Cindy Reilly for a Barbie doll like Aubrey du Puy? Speaking of whom . . .

He looked around, but Aubrey and the Creep had quietly disappeared. The see-and-be-seen crowd was on its feet at the edge of the dance floor, craning its collective neck to see what in the world was going to happen next. This was *not* the kind of thing that happened at places frequented by the trendy social set. The air was abuzz with excitement.

The Fortunato brothers, Leander and Lorenzo, raced from the back of the house just as the doctor was extricating Eustace's left foot from under Nonna Pippa. "Mama!" Lorenzo cried. "Mama! Can you hear me?"

With the help of the doctor, Eustace sat up, wincing in a way that made Franklin's heart skip a beat. Nonna Pippa's eyes fluttered open. "She's alive!" Leander breathed.

"Lie still," the doctor ordered the old woman. "I need to check for broken bones."

Nonna Pippa didn't appear to have broken any bones — probably thanks to Eustace, who'd taken the brunt of the fall. While Lorenzo and Leander fussed over her like a pair of hens over the last remaining chick, the doctor examined Aunt Min's chauffeur.

"Could be just a sprain," the doctor said when he pressed against the top of the old man's left foot and Eustace yelped in pain. "On the other hand, could be a break in the metatarsal. You'll need an x-ray, old boy. And I hope you drive an automatic. You aren't going to be too interested in working a clutch, the way that's feeling."

The '49 Packard, of course, was *not* an automatic. "Do you know how to drive a stick shift, Cindy?" Franklin whispered.

Cindy worried her lower lip for a moment before answering. "It can't be *that* hard, can it?"

Franklin almost grinned. That sounded like Cindy — willing to try. If it had to be done, she'd do it. "Never mind," he said. "Help me get him up and into a chair."

Eustace winced as they made the short trip to a nearby table. "Don't worry, old friend," Franklin told him. "We'll get that foot taken care of, and then I'll get you and Cindy home."

"That ol' foot *can't* be broke," Eustace said stubbornly, as if saying it could make it so. "Ol' Eustace won't stand for it."

Nonna Pippa, when she revived enough to know what was going on, was distressed at Eustace's injury. "I am so sorry, signore," she told him, setting a huge bowl of blackberry *sorbetto* in front of him as if blackberry *sorbetto* could make everything better.

He shook his head. "Ain't nobody's fault, Miss Pippa. That was some dancin', though, wasn't it? Even ol' Eustace has got to say — that was some dancin'." He shook his head again.

"It *is* somebody's fault," Cindy said. "You *know* it is, Eustace. I lost my head, and I frightened Nonna Pippa so bad she fainted, and now here you are with a broken foot, and —"

"Ain't broke," Eustace insisted.

"— I feel *awful*."

Nonna Pippa eyed her with a dark scowl. "For having a second *innamorato* to the side of Franklin — *this* is what should make you feel awful," she said severely.

At that point, Franklin thought he'd better set the record straight. "You've got it wrong, Nonna Pippa. Cindy is only my friend, not my sweetheart. The man on the dance floor — *he's* the boyfriend."

"*Si?*" Nonna Pippa sounded profoundly perplexed. "So why does he dance with the Scarlet Woman?"

"That's what *I'd* like to know," Cindy said mournfully.

Without even thinking, Franklin reached over and gave her hand a squeeze.

11

They took Eustace to the hospital, Franklin driving the Packard and leaving his Jeep in the hands of Leander Fortunato, who promised to take good care of it till Franklin could come back to pick it up.

It was after midnight by the time they loaded Eustace back into the limousine outside the emergency room. On a warm Friday night in the city, a fractured metatarsal — which Eustace could no longer deny in the face of his x-ray — was hardly considered an emergency. He'd had to wait his turn.

"If you don't mind," Franklin said to Eustace as they wheeled him out and set him up in the roomy backseat with his plaster-encased foot propped up, "I'd like to drop by my place to pick up a change of clothes and my toothbrush. It's not too far out of the way."

Eustace's painkillers had kicked in; he had no objections to anything. Cindy didn't seem to care either way. Cindy, in fact, had been so subdued since they'd left the restaurant, Franklin was more worried about her than he was about Eustace. Fractured metatarsals healed quickly; fractured hearts took longer.

He tried to fill the car with cheerful conversation as they drove, pointing out interesting sites along the route to Washington Park — as many as they could see in the dark anyhow. Once they started winding up the hill toward the Fitz family estate, Cindy livened up a bit. Franklin was so used to the neighborhood he hardly paid attention anymore, but for a first-time visitor, the residences along the way must be eye-catching. Any one of the beautifully landscaped homes could have graced the cover of *Architectural Digest.*

"Wow," Cindy breathed as they passed the home of the president of Duwamish University, its carefully placed floodlights casting dramatic shadows against the red brick walls and gleaming Georgian porticoes. "Double wow!" she exclaimed as they pulled into a curving driveway at the top of the hill. The house where Franklin had grown up loomed ahead.

It *was* impressive, he thought as he slowed the old limousine — even from this angle, which oddly enough was the back of the house, even though it faced the street. The sixteen-thousand-square-foot mansion sat on its wooded lot with its imposing entrance facing a spectacular view over Lake Washington and the lights of Bellevue shining across the dark expanse of water.

Of course, the view from his cozy apartment above the carriage house — now the garage — was just as spectacular. Filene might like living in a museum, but he preferred something a bit more homey.

The concrete drive curved past the streetside French doors and the massive mullioned window above them. On the other side of the window a huge crystal chandelier lit the grand staircase, which led down to the ballroom and up to the third-floor bedrooms. The second floor, at ground level here at the back of the house, accommodated four thousand square feet of living areas.

As they followed the drive around the east wing to the front of the four-story limestone edifice and the twin towers came into view, Franklin heard Cindy gasp.

"Franklin! You didn't tell me you lived in a castle!"

"Hard to believe my great-grandfather arrived in America at age sixteen with five dollars in his pocket, isn't it?" he said.

"Really?"

Good, Franklin thought. Something to take her mind off the Creep.

"He worked his way across the country from New York to Seattle just in time for the Alaska Gold Rush," he said, idling the Packard in front of the house so Cindy could take it in. "He was one of the lucky ones. Made what in those days was considered a fortune — enough to invest in lumber, pulp and paper, real estate. But his father had been a tailor and his mother a shopkeeper, and clothes and retail were in his bones."

"A tailor!" Cindy said, sounding interested in spite of herself.

Franklin drove on past the house to the triple garage farther up the drive and parked the car in front of one of the doors. "Cameron Fitz and his friend Charles Strawbridge opened their first store in 1901, right in the middle of downtown. Seattle had a reputation as a wild and woolly town back then, so of course all the 'new money' wanted to prove they weren't anything of the kind. In those days, Strawbridge & Fitz was considered the ticket to East Coast sophistication. I'll have to give you a tour of the house sometime, Cindy. When we're not so rushed."

Which at the moment they were. Cindy

had already told him she had a five-thirty breakfast shift, which meant she wasn't going to get a lick of sleep tonight except what she could snatch in the car on the way home.

"I'll be just a minute," he said as he closed the door of the Packard.

But when he descended the stairs from his apartment a few minutes later, duffel bag in tow, Cindy was gone from the limousine. He peered into the backseat, where Eustace was punctuating the quiet night with soft, irregular snores. He straightened and called softly, "Cindy?"

Then he saw her silhouetted against the sky, at the edge of the drive where the yard dropped off into the canyon, gazing out over the lights of the city. She looked lonely and lost, and he had a sudden impulse to walk up behind her and put his arms around her, to hold her, to protect her from the world — or at least from the Aubrey du Puys and the Jonathan Crums of the world.

Jonathan Crum. The creep! How could she let a guy like that suck up all her wonderful energy?

A yellow arc of light swung around the corner of the house, catching Cindy by surprise. She whipped around, one hand to her chest as if to keep her heart from jumping out of it.

The black Jaguar screeched to a halt. His stepmother's car. Franklin's heart sank. A run-in with Filene was the last thing he wanted at the moment. To be honest, it was the last thing he wanted *ever,* at *any* moment.

He was at her car door by the time she had it unlocked. "Filene," he said as politely as he could gather the strength for. "I'm so glad you arrived in time to meet Cindy."

Filene emerged from the low-slung car like a black cat, slinky and sinuous. She raised her chin and her eyebrows. "A bit late to be entertaining a lady friend in your apartment, don't you think?" she murmured.

Franklin flushed. "She hasn't been in my apartment, Filene," he said in a low voice.

Cindy came around the back of the Jaguar. He had no choice but to introduce them. His stepmother looked Cindy over in the dim light of the lamps planted on either side of the front walkway. Franklin felt anger flare at the insolence in her slow study.

"Cindy who?" she asked, unsmiling. Ignoring Cindy's outstretched hand.

"Reilly," Cindy answered, her voice unsure. She dropped her hand.

Franklin set his mouth in a grim line and moved closer to Cindy, placing an arm around her shoulder and giving her a quick squeeze — as if by touching her even briefly he could protect her from Filene's venom.

"Cindy is an apparel designer," he said evenly. "Strawbridge & Fitz will be carrying her line this Christmas."

Filene raised a perfectly arched eyebrow toward Cindy. "Indeed! I don't recall the name, my dear. What line would that be?"

"I call my line of evening gowns Glad Raggs, Mrs. Fitz," Cindy replied. Franklin ached at the eagerness in her voice. Filene was going to eat her alive. "But it's a velvet T-shirt I've sold to Strawbridge & Fitz. Actually, it's the top to —"

"We just stopped by on our way out of town," Franklin interrupted, grabbing Cindy's hand and squeezing a warning. Filene was already looking down her nose at Cindy. She was quite capable of calling the whole deal off if she didn't think the idea of Glad Raggs — or Cindy herself — fit the image of Strawbridge & Fitz.

"Out of town?" His stepmother's eyes narrowed.

"To Aunt Min's. I'll be gone for the weekend."

"Your aunt allows you to bring along . . . *company?*" She made it sound like a bad word.

"Oh, Mrs. Fitz!" Cindy sounded horrified. "I'm not *staying* with Franklin! I live in Pilchuck, and Mini Mac's chauffeur brought me to Seattle this morning for my appointment with —"

"The junior-wear buyer," Franklin supplied. Filene would not be happy to know that Franklin had stuck his nose outside of accounting.

"— but Eustace broke his foot and the Packard's a stick, which I don't know how to drive, though I did tell Franklin I thought I could figure it out —"

"Which I'm sure you can," said Franklin, "but now isn't the time."

"— and he's offered to drive us both home. Mrs. Fitz —"

"Please. Filene." She looked pained.

"Filene, then, you really do have the nicest son in all —"

"Stepson," said Franklin and Filene in unison.

"Stepson," Cindy echoed, her flow of words faltering.

Franklin took her elbow and firmly

turned her toward Aunt Min's limousine. "I'll take the train back Sunday night," he said over his shoulder.

"She doesn't like me," Cindy whispered as he helped her into the car.

"Don't take it personally," he murmured back. "She doesn't like me either."

"I'll bet she'd like Aubrey du Puy."

Franklin sighed. "As a matter of fact, she does."

Cindy didn't have another word to say about Filene — or about Aubrey du Puy — but she had hundreds of words to say about Jonathan Crum. *Thousands,* maybe. Franklin heard more in the next two hours about the Crumb — a name he'd decided fit even better than the Creep — than he really cared to know.

She didn't sleep a wink the whole way back either. She cried, though, off and on. It nearly broke his heart.

By the time he showed her to her door in Pilchuck in the wee hours of the morning, he was a mess. Part of him wanted simply to declare himself to Cindy: "I've lost my heart. You're the woman for me. Please forget about Jonathan Crum, who is so aptly named it's not even funny, and give me a chance."

172

Another part of him knew that a woman like Cindy Reilly wouldn't forget a man she'd loved for almost a decade in a minute — or a day or a week or a month or possibly even a year — and that if he pursued her now he was likely to lose her forever. He was likely to end up her "rebound fling" or the apparently necessary "transition person" he'd overheard Alice and her friends talk about around the water cooler at work.

He might have met Cindy only a week ago, but already he knew the idea of being a temporary replacement in her life until she patched up things with Jonathan had no appeal at all. Neither, for that matter, did being a temporary replacement in her life until she met "The One," as his admin assistant termed it — the person on the other side of the requisite transitional relationship. He didn't want to be temporary. In fact, as ridiculous as it seemed, he had his mind set on being The One.

But Cindy wouldn't be ready to hear that. Not yet.

"Call me whenever you need to," he said instead. "You have my work number and my home number and my pager number. I'll be at Aunt Min's on the weekends unless I let you know. I'm available anytime, Cindy."

"All right," she sniffled. "Thanks, Franklin."

"I'll call tomorrow to see how you're doing," he said. "And give you an update on Eustace."

"All right," she sniffled again as she turned the key in the front-door lock.

"Umm . . . Cindy . . ." Franklin took a deep breath. "Could you use a hug from a friend?"

"Could I!" Cindy turned around and practically flung herself into his arms. Franklin nearly lost his balance — plus his resolve to stay silent on the subject of his feelings.

Suddenly she was crying into his shoulder. "Where did he learn to *dance* like that?" she sobbed. "Jonathan can't dance, Franklin. Any more than I can. And —" She choked on her tears. "Pollyanna," she said helplessly. *"Pollyanna!"*

"Get outta here!" Biddy stared wide-eyed at Cindy from behind her cat's-eye glasses. "You're makin' this up!"

Cindy, elbow deep in the day's supply of creamy coleslaw, shook her head. "I'm not," she said sadly. "I don't have that kind of imagination."

"You're tellin' me in the space of twelve

hours yesterday" — Biddy held up a hand and started counting off on her fingers — "you knocked over a wall in Franklin Fitz's office —"

"I'm afraid I did."

"Got turned down for the money to expand Glad Raggs —"

"Only because Franklin didn't have it. *Doesn't* have it. His stepmother controls the purse strings till he's thirty, you see . . ."

"Took an order for over thirty-thousand dollars' worth of T-shirts you have no idea how you're goin' to fill —"

"Actually, I *do* have a couple of ideas . . ."

"Had dinner in a restaurant with a *fountain* in the *foyer,* for pity's sake —"

"It was amazing. Biddy, that dinner would have cost Franklin three hundred dollars if the Fortunato brothers hadn't insisted on paying for it!"

That stopped Biddy's recital for a moment. Three hundred dollars was more than a hundred Breakfast Specials.

"We'll come back to that," she said. "Meanwhile, you caught Jonathan not only in a bald-faced lie but out on the town with a glamorous woman —"

"I haven't heard his side of the story yet," said Cindy. "Maybe there's a perfectly innocent explanation."

"Maybe the moon's made of green cheese." Biddy switched hands and folded down another finger. "Be that as it may, you then upset an old woman so badly she fainted —"

"She thought I was cheating on Franklin."

"Cheatin' on Franklin!" Biddy shook her head and then ticked off the final item on her list: "And to top things off, the old woman ended up breakin' Eustace's foot. Did I leave anything out?"

"You got it all," said Cindy, her shoulders slumping in dejection over the tub of coleslaw. She worked Buster's special dressing through the shredded cabbage in silence for a moment. "I was *awful,* Biddy," she finally said. "Ugly, nasty, rude . . . I'd be surprised if Jonathan even wants to *talk* to me."

"It does seem to me you had good reason for bein' upset," Biddy philosophized.

"But I didn't give him a chance to explain!"

"So maybe you did jump to conclusions. Who wouldn't in your shoes? It isn't as if he hasn't strayed before, Cindy."

"You're right. And he's always come back —"

176

"That's not the point. What I'm sayin' is, you're not the one who should be feelin' guilty here."

Cindy didn't respond.

"Did you get any sleep last night?"

"No. We didn't get home till three this morning. Mr. Sandman didn't wait up for me."

"I shouldn't have scheduled you for this mornin'," Biddy fretted. "Vestal could have worked a breakfast for once."

Cindy shook her head. "The Saturday morning regulars wouldn't have it, Biddy. They're going to want a full report. I couldn't disappoint them, not after all their advice. And the genuine faux snakeskin portfolio they all chipped in to buy me."

She pulled her arms out of the coleslaw. Biddy turned on the water at the sink so she could rinse the dressing off. "I'll give Louise a call and see if she can't come in early," Biddy said. "Sometimes Louise doesn't mind workin' a split."

Over the next four hours, Cindy served fifty-seven customers, told the T-shirt-sale story thirteen times, and drank eight cups of industrial strength Pretty Darn Good coffee, which kept her going until ten, when Louise — praise be to the Almighty

— did come in to relieve her. Then she went home and slept ten hours straight.

Her mother was getting herself a bedtime snack when Cindy woke up and stumbled yawning into the kitchen, looking for something to eat. Cait Reilly was an older version of Cindy, with a slightly less generous mouth and her blond hair cut short and swept away from her face. So far she'd heard only the bare-bones version of Cindy's Seattle experience, in a phone call from the hospital last night. Cindy filled her in on the rest of the story over a bowl of chicken-noodle soup and buttered toast — all except for the Catching-Jonathan-Red-Handed incident. She shouldn't even have said anything to Biddy, she thought, until she'd talked to Jonathan and heard his side of things.

"You'll need to find a good wholesale source of that crushed velvet," Cait said. "I still have contacts through the Fabric Faire. When do you get paid for the order?"

"Not till delivery," Cindy said. "I figure materials are going to run me close to four thousand dollars. I'll have to spread it out over all my credit cards."

"You don't think Pete Pickle will give you a loan now that you've made a guaranteed sale? The interest rate would be better."

Cindy brightened. "Oh! Maybe he will."

"Doesn't hurt to ask anyhow. Have you worked out a production schedule?"

"Not exactly. But I know I have to put together seventy-five shirts a month for the next three months to get them delivered on time." Cindy worried her lower lip. "I hope I didn't bite off more than I can chew."

"We'll figure it out, sweetheart." Cait laid her hand on her daughter's. "Do you know how proud I am of you? And how proud your dad would be?"

Cindy felt tears pricking at her eyeballs as a sudden wave of longing for her father swept over her. She knew she believed in herself because Joe-Joe had believed in her. He'd nurtured her dreams, helped her put feet to them, and celebrated her triumphs, however small. *Like Franklin did yesterday,* came the surprising realization.

"I know," she said, and left it at that.

Her mother yawned. "I'm ready for bed," she said. "Oh, by the way, you had several phone calls earlier."

"Jonathan?" Cindy asked eagerly.

"Jonathan once, Mini Mac's nephew twice. Franklin said to have you call as soon as you woke up."

"What about Jonathan?"

"He'll call back tonight at eleven." Cait paused. "Is everything all right with you and Jonathan?"

Cindy's heart skipped a beat. "What do you mean, all right? Why do you ask?"

"Just a mother's intuition . . ."

"I don't want to talk about it right now," Cindy said, and her mother — bless her soul — let it go.

12

Franklin's conversation with Cindy Saturday night wasn't everything he'd hoped it would be. She was expecting a call from Jonathan, she said, and couldn't talk long.

"But I wanted to say how much I appreciate everything you did for me yesterday, Franklin. The introduction to the buyer. The dinner. The ride home."

"My pleasure."

"And to apologize, which I don't think I ever did in all the confusion. I know I must have embarrassed you."

"Oh no! You didn't embarrass me."

"I didn't?"

"You *worried* me a little. But mostly you astonished me. I'm still in awe."

"In awe!"

"Of your spontaneity. Of the way you stood up for yourself."

"You have a nice way of looking at things." He could hear the smile in her voice. She sobered as she added, "I've been thinking more along the lines of 'lacking self-control' and 'making a fool of myself.' If I didn't embarrass *you*, I *did* embarrass me."

"It's all in your perspective," Franklin said. "Which reminds me, Cindy — about Pollyanna. Pollyanna gets a lot of flak, but she was happy, wasn't she? And she made the people around her happy. What's so bad about looking on the bright side of things?"

"Hmm . . ." Cindy thought about it for a moment. Then: "You're right," she said, cheerful once again. "I'm positive Jonathan has a perfectly reasonable explanation for being with Aubrey du Puy last night."

Franklin's heart sank. He'd meant to encourage her, not give her reason to go easy on the Crumb.

"I have to go, Franklin," she said. "Thanks again."

"Please — watch out for yourself," he said. "And call me whenever you need me."

"You're so sweet."

"Promise?"

"All right. 'Bye now!"

And she was gone.

Pollyanna. Cindy had to admit Aubrey's derisive tag still stung. Who but Jonathan could have given her such an idea? He'd always teased her about the way she looked

at the world through rose-colored glasses
— but only teased. It was one of the things
he liked about her, he said — that she
found the good in every circumstance. In
every person. Had he changed his mind?

The phone rang. Cindy's heart fluttered
with anxiety as she picked up the receiver
in the middle of the ring. "Hello? Jonathan?"

"Hello, Cindy. Are you all right?"

She relaxed a smidgen. Maybe this
wasn't going to be so bad. This was the
Jonathan she knew, asking right up front
how she was doing. Concerned. Solicitous.

"Oh, Jonathan. I'm not even close to all
right. I am *so* embarrassed!"

He made a sound that was almost a
chuckle, and Cindy relaxed a smidgen
more. "I have to say it was a bit of a
shock," he said. "In all the years I've
known you, I don't think I've ever seen you
so mad."

"I don't think I've ever *been* so mad."

"I deserved it, Cindy. If I'd been more
honest with you up front, it never would
have happened."

Her throat tightened with renewed anxiety. More honest about what?

"I'm just happy Aubrey's father had already left," Jonathan added. "Or I really

183

would have had some explaining to do."

"Aubrey's father?" Cindy asked blankly.

"Dominick du Puy, who happens to be a senior partner in the most prestigious law firm in Seattle. Aubrey was gracious enough to set up the dinner appointment at Fortunato's so I could meet him."

"But who's *Aubrey?*" Cindy wailed.

"A law-school colleague. We did our practicum together last quarter, Cindy. I'm sure I mentioned her," he said smoothly.

Had he? Maybe. Once at the beginning of the term. But still —

The light came on in her head. "Her father's the attorney you want to work for."

"Bingo. It would be a major coup to land a position in his firm."

So the whole thing was about a job! It was the reasonable explanation Cindy had been waiting for, but somehow it didn't make her feel much better.

"But Jonathan, why didn't you tell me sooner you were rethinking your plans to practice law in Pilchuck?"

"I should have, Cindy. But I knew you'd be upset."

"At first, maybe. I admit, I've always seen us living out our days in Pilchuck. Pilchuck is the only home I've ever known." She wound the telephone cord around her arm. "But you know I'm flexible. I can adjust, if you decide Seattle is where you want to practice law. Maybe I could get a job at Fortunato's —"

"What?! Cindy, Fortunato's is *the* place to see and be seen in Seattle. And I don't mean wearing a waiter's uniform!"

Hurt welled up inside her. "You know I don't always mean to be a waitress, Jonathan," she said, trying to keep the tremor from her voice. "Did you hear what I told you yesterday? About my sale to Strawbridge & Fitz?"

"Of course I did," he soothed. "I'm thrilled for you, Cindy."

"Then what is it?"

He sighed audibly. "I worry about you in the city, that's all. I just don't think you'd like it. You have to admit . . ." But he didn't say what she had to admit, asking instead, "Do you really see yourself fitting in with the crowd at Fortunato's?"

"I had dinner with the family matriarch last night," she answered, trying to keep her tone light. "She seemed to like me fine."

"That fat old woman in the baggy dress and apron who hangs around the dining room? She's as odd a duck as that chauffeur who brought you around yesterday.

185

Hardly the standard to hold yourself to."

"What are you saying, Jonathan?" she asked slowly. "That I'm so hopelessly small-town I couldn't learn to be a big-city lawyer's wife?" She remembered suddenly how she'd felt next to the sophisticated, glamorous Aubrey du Puy.

"Don't put words in my mouth, Cindy. You know I think the world of you. I just don't think you understand the demands, that's all."

"And I suppose your little friend Aubrey does?" Cindy couldn't keep the sarcastic tone out of her voice. It was either that or cry — and she was not about to cry.

"There's no reason to get snippy," he said tightly. "Jealousy doesn't become you, my dear."

"Are you telling me I don't have a reason to be jealous?"

The seconds ticked off. Cindy knew what was coming. She'd heard it before: *Just an innocent flirtation that got a little out of hand. You know that you're the one I love . . .*

The confession didn't come. "I'm not sure you have a right to ask that question," he said instead. Then, out of the blue, as if it related: "Aubrey says it was Franklin Fitz the Third you were with last night."

Cindy's heart tripped over itself. "It wasn't a date," she protested. "I had business with Franklin yesterday, and . . ." Her voice trailed off.

"Exactly," he said triumphantly. "And do you know what? I'm not the least bit jealous, because *I trust you*. And I think it's great you've made a connection with Franklin Fitz. There's a whole world out there we never knew existed in Pilchuck, Cindy. Maybe Fitz can show you the ropes. Take you to the next level, like Aubrey's done for me."

Cindy felt sick to her stomach. *The next level.* Hadn't she known from the moment she laid eyes on Aubrey du Puy she was totally outclassed?

She didn't even have to ask where Jonathan had learned to dance.

"So you're going to keep seeing Aubrey?"

"Spending time with people who can help advance your career just makes good business sense, Cindy," he said reasonably. "I'd never ask you to stop seeing Franklin Fitz."

But there was "seeing" and there was *seeing*, Cindy thought. Wasn't there?

"What about *us*, Jonathan? What about you and me?"

187

"You know I'll always care about you. The way I know you'll always care about me."

Cindy could hear the *but* coming from a mile away. No — a *hundred* miles. *He's breaking up with me,* she thought numbly. *This can't be happening!*

"But . . ." said Jonathan.

She held her breath.

"I think we both need to think about whether caring for each other is enough," he said. So gently! With such compassion! "Are we really compatible? Do we have the same goals? Do we want the same things out of life?"

Cindy was silent. She'd never doubted the answers to those questions before.

"Maybe we need to take a break from each other for a few weeks, Cindy."

"We haven't seen each other since Easter! We've *had* a break, Jonathan."

"But you have some new things to think about now. If I do decide I need to pursue my career in the city, well, is that really what you want?"

"I want to be with you," she said stubbornly. "Whatever it takes."

"You're not being rational. This is a serious issue, Cindy! What if you moved here for me, and you hated it, and you started

188

to resent me? Do you know how often that happens?"

She was beginning to feel dizzy trying to keep up with him. "I couldn't resent you."

He sighed again. "Look — I've been planning to come up and take you out for your birthday. Why don't we both take a little time between now and then to think about what we really want — I mean alone, no contact, no phone calls — and then we'll talk again. See how we're feeling."

She didn't like the idea one little bit, but after another five minutes of talking with Jonathan, she was so confused she would have agreed to anything. Well, anything within reason. And he *did* sound so reasonable . . .

"We'll talk again on my birthday then," she finally agreed.

"On your birthday," he promised. "It's only a few weeks. This will be good for both of us, Cindy."

She didn't see how, but he must be right. He always was.

After the conversation ended, she sat in the overstuffed chair by the phone with her knees drawn up to her chin and her arms wrapped around her legs, thinking furiously. Jonathan was right, she told herself — she *was* small-town. She *didn't* know how to act in the social situations she'd find herself in as Jonathan's wife. She was a rube.

But she wasn't so stupid she couldn't figure it out. Didn't the self-improvement section at Looking-Glass Books down the street take up almost as many shelves as the cookbook section? Didn't every women's magazine the Apple Basket Market carried feature monthly beauty makeovers?

She could learn to dance. She could learn to carry on intelligent conversations. She could learn whatever it was she needed to learn to be a big-city lawyer's wife. She could change. After all, Jonathan had. He'd had a chance to, living seven years in Seattle.

It hadn't been her choice to stay behind in Pilchuck, had it? She'd had a scholarship to the Beaux Arts School of Design. She'd been ready to move to the city then.

Her twenty-fifth birthday was just over three weeks away. If it was big-city glamour and sophistication Jonathan needed from her — well, big-city glamour and sophistication was what he was going to get. By her birthday she'd be a new woman.

And as far as Aubrey du Puy went — well, she just wasn't going to worry about her. This wasn't about Aubrey. Not really. It was about that glamorous, sophisticated, big-city aura Aubrey carried around with her. It was about that "whole new world" she'd opened up for Jonathan.

But Cindy and Jonathan had something Aubrey and Jonathan could never have: a history. With time to think, Jonathan surely wouldn't want to give that up.

Everything was going to work out — she just knew it was. After all, weren't she and Jonathan meant for each other?

Wasn't he her fairy-tale prince?

Aunt Min was between weeks on her cabbage soup diet. Franklin got up early on Sunday and made oatmeal for them both, sprinkling his with brown sugar and burying a slab of I Can't Believe It's Not Butter in the center. A healthy handful of fresh blueberries and skimmed milk topped both bowls.

"Are you sure you wouldn't like to take the summer off from your job and be my cook and chauffeur?" Aunt Min asked as she scraped the bottom of her dish. "Till Eustace is back on the job?" She didn't sound like she was kidding either.

The idea had appeal, though he didn't know about the cooking. More often than not he ate meals out. Or with Cookie, who — despite being ousted from Filene's kitchen shortly after Fitzy's death three years ago — still loved to cook, especially for hungry, appreciative fans like her "little Biscuit." Fortunately, Franklin's father had provided her with a small annuity and lifetime use of the groundskeeper's cottage she and Clement had shared for so many years, or Filene would have ousted her from the estate entirely. Filene had her own ideas about how things ought to be run.

Spending a couple of months tooling around Tillicum County in the '49 Packard though — that part was tempting. Especially when Cindy Reilly lived only a dozen miles away. The fact that it wasn't a good idea to *date* her right now didn't mean he couldn't spend time getting to know her as a *friend*. Letting her get to know him . . .

He sighed. "I wish I could, Aunt Min. I'd be happy to help you out on weekends — would that help?"

"It would. Starting this morning, if you'd be so kind. I'd like to go to church in Pilchuck this morning."

"You would? I thought you had your own church here in town."

"No service this morning. Most everyone's at the all-church retreat at Jubilation Campground on Mount Balder."

"Sure you don't want me to drive you up to the campground?" He glanced at his watch. "We might be a little late, but we should make it in time for most of the morning activities. It can't be more than a couple of hours away."

"No thank you." She dabbed at the corners of her mouth with her napkin. "I have my heart set on hearing Pastor Bob at the Pilchuck Church of Saints and Sinners this morning."

"Really? He's that good?"

"You'll have to see for yourself," she said. "I can be ready in half an hour."

Franklin knew the minute he walked into the little church why Aunt Min had her heart set on the Pilchuck Church of Saints and Sinners. Cait Reilly was standing in the foyer greeting worshipers and handing out church bulletins; he assumed that meant Cindy was somewhere right around the corner.

Not that he minded. He was just surprised. Aunt Min had never shown an interest in matchmaking before. She was making it easy for him too. Coming alone

— if he'd even known the Pilchuck Church of Saints and Sinners was Cindy's church and thought of coming in the first place — might have insinuated something he wasn't yet ready to insinuate. Especially to Cindy, who had probably spent the night crying her eyes out after her phone conversation with the Crumb last night. He'd stayed up late, hoping she'd call, but she hadn't.

"Miniver and Franklin! It's lovely to have you with us this morning," Cait said, smiling her welcome. "How's Eustace?"

"Cranky," Aunt Min said, accepting a bulletin. "Which for Eustace is extraordinary behavior. We tried to get him to come along this morning, but he says he's miffed at the good Lord at the moment and needs to wrestle it out on his own. Doesn't think he deserves a broken foot. I told him the rain falls on the just and the unjust — it's not a matter of deserving."

"And excellent counsel that was, Miss Miniver."

Franklin turned to see who belonged to the deep, resonant voice. It was a round-faced, balding man in a suit and tie.

"Pastor Bob." Aunt Min extended her hand, and he gave it a hearty shake. "I don't believe you've met my precious nephew."

Franklin felt his face grow warm. He was going to have to talk to her about that "precious" business. It was mortifying!

Pastor Bob let go of Aunt Min's hand and reached for Franklin's. "So this is the man our Cindy saved from choking to death! Franklin Fitz, isn't it? Pastor Montgomery Bob. My, but you do look healthier than you did in that newspaper photo. Happy to see it, son."

"Newspaper?" Aunt Min asked.

"The chicken-bone-choking was the lead story in last week's *Post*," Cait said. "I have extra copies at home, Mini Mac. And extra chicken for the grill too. Why don't the two of you join us for Sunday dinner after church?"

"We'd love to. Wouldn't we, Franklin?"

"We would," he said, even though he was feeling somewhat annoyed with Aunt Min. She seemed set on taking charge of his life without asking.

"Cindy's sitting up front if you'd like to join her," said Cait.

Franklin recognized several faces from the Kitsch 'n' Caboodle Café as he followed Aunt Min up the center aisle like a dinghy tied behind a yacht. There was the owner of Strip Joint Furniture Refinishing and Drive-Through Espresso — Some-

body Muncey, if he remembered right —
and Suzie Something-or-Another, with a
pretty redhead and an impish kid, and old
Mrs. Pfefferkuchen. Several people waved.

They were a friendly bunch, he thought
as he nodded and smiled his way to the
front of the church. Already he felt at
home. The large church he'd attended all
his life in Seattle was so formal and imper-
sonal he sometimes felt more like a visitor
than a member. The Pilchuck Church of
Saints and Sinners, on the other hand, *invited* one to get involved.

As usual, Cindy's welcoming smile hit
him like a train light in a dark tunnel. She
certainly didn't look as if she'd been
crying. "Mini Mac! Franklin! What fun!"

"More fun ahead," Aunt Min said as she
seated herself in the center of the pew.
"Your mother's invited us for dinner."

Franklin debated. Next to Aunt Min, or
next to Cindy? His aunt hadn't left room
enough for him to sit between them. When
she placed her large handbag on the pew
next to her, the decision was made. Aunt
Min and her handbag together took up a
formidable amount of space.

He sat down next to Cindy. She held a
shiny flute across her lap, one hand clasped
around the mouthpiece.

"You look —" he almost said "beautiful," which she was, in a yellow sundress splashed with giant aqua, white, and violet flowers. Her golden hair was pulled back in a thick, loose braid tied with a purple ribbon.

"Happy," he said instead. His brows drew together slightly. Did her smile mean the conversation with the Crumb had gone well after all? Did Jonathan have her so wrapped around his little finger after all these years he could do anything and she'd forgive him? He didn't appreciate what he had in Cindy, *that* was clear —

"You don't," she said.

"What?"

"Look happy. What's wrong?"

"Oh!" He shook his head. "Nothing. Really. Playing your flute for church this morning?"

Cindy nodded. "During the offertory."

"I play sousaphone," he volunteered.

"You do! We're always looking for instrumentalists, Franklin. Maybe you'd like to play some Sunday."

"A sousaphone isn't exactly a solo instrument," he said.

A lean, athletic, sandy-haired man got up from the facing bench and approached the podium.

Cindy whispered, "Maybe we could do a duet sometime."

By that time the man at the podium was greeting the congregation and announcing the opening hymn. Franklin didn't have a chance to say it might be hard to find music for a sousaphone-flute duet. "Maybe," he whispered back instead and opened the hymnbook.

13

The sermon was about Esther, who happened to be one of Cindy's favorite Old Testament characters. It was something of a Cinderella story, when it came right down to it: the lowly Jewish maiden, an orphan and a descendant of slaves, chosen by King Xerxes out of all the girls in Persia to be queen of the land. Of course it went far beyond Cinderella, what with Esther risking her very life to bring the evil Haman to justice and to save her people from destruction. Esther was no namby-pamby princess, that was for sure.

"One of the qualities that brought Esther to power in the palace," said Pastor Bob, "was her *teachability*. The king's eunuch, Hegai, gets short shrift in the story of Esther —"

Cindy, in fact, didn't even *remember* a character named Hegai in the story of Esther.

"— but for twelve months, Hegai was Esther's personal mentor, not to mention her diet and beauty consultant. In charge of her makeover, if you will."

Cindy perked up. Her makeover!

"There was something about Esther that Hegai liked," Pastor Bob continued. "Perhaps her humility. Her willingness to learn. He gave her special attention, and she blossomed under it.

"When it was finally time to go before the king, Esther consulted Hegai one last time. How should she act? What should she say? What should she take with her? We don't know what Hegai told her — only that Esther listened, and learned, and 'won the favor of everyone who saw her,' as the writer tells us — including the king, who 'was attracted to Esther more than to any of the other women,' and she 'won his favor and approval.'

"Esther was wise to seek the counsel of others who knew the things that she did not. May we follow her lead and be always teachable."

There was more, but Cindy didn't hear it. Her mind was tripping all over itself. Why, Esther's situation might as well have been her own! A simple girl who hadn't had the privileges some others might have had, put in a position where she had to somehow capture the king's attention and then his heart. In competition with the most beautiful girls in the land, no less . . .

Her fingers tapped absently at the keys

of the flute in her lap, making quiet little popping sounds that echoed her growing excitement. Wasn't this just what she'd decided last night — that she could learn what she needed to learn to get Jonathan back? That she could figure out "glamorous" as well as anyone? That she could play the same part Aubrey du Puy had learned to play?

Jonathan Crum might not be a king, but he was king of her heart. And Cindy might not have all the advantages of Aubrey, but she was teachable. Surely Pastor Bob's sermon was confirmation that her self-improvement plan was the will of the Almighty.

Why, without even thinking about it she could come up with a grocery list of possible mentors. She had True Marie, down at the Belle o' the Ball Beauty Salon, and the twins, who'd taken a charm course last year. Not that much of their learning had stuck, but they still had their notebooks.

She had the twins' friend Narcissa, who was only eighteen, but already an independent beauty consultant for Carrie Mae Cosmetics. If she got brave enough, she had Nadine, who sold curve-enhancing foundation garments along with the not-your-basic-black dresses that were the mainstay of her Bellingrath store. She had Ina Rafferty at the Pilchuck Public Library, who would be happy to steer her to reading materials that would make her conversation sparkle . . .

She sneaked a glance at Franklin, who was scribbling sermon notes on the back of his bulletin, and thought of Jonathan's words: *Maybe Franklin Fitz can take you to the next level.*

Did she have Franklin in her corner for this project, she wondered? Because Jonathan was right. Who could possibly be better to "take her to the next level" than Franklin Cameron Fitz III?

She'd already called in her favor for saving his life. The sale to Strawbridge & Fitz would never have happened without him. But hadn't he told her just last night to call him *whenever* she needed him? Hadn't he made her *promise?*

Dinner with the Reillys was a delightful affair. What was it about eating food outside that made it taste so good, Franklin wondered. The grilled chicken and corn on the cob, the baked potatoes loaded with everything, the sweet, crisp watermelon — it was every bit as delicious, if in a different way, than their gourmet Italian dinner at

Fortunato's Friday night.

And the company! Cait Reilly was charming, the twins were entertaining times two, and Cindy was —

Well, Cindy was utterly beguiling, is what she was. Without even trying to be. If he didn't have the story of his own parents' romance to go on, he would never believe he could feel this way about someone in such a short time. He wasn't ready to call it *love,* but he was definitely deep into *like.*

If only he knew what was going on with Cindy and the Crumb since that phone call last night!

"Franklin, you'd best have another piece of this chicken," Aunt Min said, placing a sizzling drumstick on his plate without even asking. "Franklin gets faint when he's low on protein," she explained to the Reilly women. As if he couldn't talk for himself — or even feed himself.

But before he could protest, she was on to something else: "Cindy, I did enjoy your flute solo this morning. A *rousing* rendition of 'Onward Christian Soldiers.' "

Franklin sighed. He might as well forgive her and move on, himself. There was no controlling Aunt Min.

"It was, Cindy," he agreed. Actually, *startling* was the word he would have used.

Cindy had played "Onward Christian Soldiers" as *fortissimo* as a flute could get, with triple-tongues and trills and glissandi galore.

"Thank you and thank you," Cindy said, sounding pleased. "I hope it wasn't too much for Mrs. Schlichenmeier's heart. She was nodding off in her pew, and I knew she'd be embarrassed if the offering plate came around and Mr. Hammond had to nudge her awake. That's why I held on to that high F trill so long."

"Did it wake her up?" Franklin asked curiously.

"Oh yes! She nearly lost the feathers on her hat, the way her chin bobbed up!"

"Cindy says you play tuba," Mrs. Reilly said to Franklin around a bite of watermelon. "Does that mean you played it in high school and probably still could in a pinch, or you really play it?"

"It's a sousaphone," he corrected her. "And yes, I really play it. In fact, last week I joined the Leschi Senior Center John Philip Sousa Memorial Concert Band."

"A concert band to play marches? John Philip would roll over in his grave!" Cindy said.

"It's either John Philip rolling *over* or the band members rolling *into* their graves,"

Franklin said. "I'm the only one under sixty-five. Avery Farnsworth, our drummer, is eighty."

"No way!" the twins said in unison.

"Way. We wouldn't get very far on a parade route."

"How'd *you* get in there?" Robin asked. Or was it Rosie?

So he told them all about Cookie and how she'd twisted his arm to join the band for the summer season. Cindy said it sounded like great fun and she wished she had a place besides church to play her flute. Aunt Min suggested she start up a Pilchuck High School alumni band and Cindy said maybe, after the T-shirts were done.

Normally Franklin would have liked the way the conversation meandered, like a Sunday drive in the country, with no particular destination in mind. But time was running out, and he desperately wanted to talk to Cindy alone. It was driving him crazy, not knowing what had transpired between her and the Crumb.

"Franklin, Precious — do you think you and Cindy could find a pharmacy for me while Cait and I clean up dinner?" Aunt Min said just at the moment he thought he was going to fidget right off the bench where he sat.

"We'll go!" the twins said in unison.

"Thank you, girls, but it's — well, *personal*," she said. "I'd rather have my nephew go, if you don't mind."

He wondered briefly what in the world Aunt Min could need from the pharmacy on such short notice. And what could be so personal she'd rather have *him* get it than a pair of seventeen-year-old girls.

She dug a pen out of her handbag and scribbled something on her napkin, then folded it and handed it to Franklin along with a twenty-dollar bill. Curious, he peeked at the note. *Think of something!* it read.

He ducked his head to hide his grin. Trust Aunt Min! "Cindy?" he said, sliding out from the picnic table.

"Sure." Cindy followed him. "Let's walk — it isn't far. After all that good food, I'll fall asleep unless I get some exercise."

They were barely out the front gate before he asked her, trying for a casual tone, "So how'd it go with Jonathan last night, Cindy?"

"We sort of broke up."

"Sort of?" What in the world did *that* mean? And why was she being so calm about it?

Maybe she'd finally realized the Crumb

was a crumb. Maybe she'd been doing her grieving for years and was already over him. Maybe she was ready for someone who could treat her the way she deserved to be treated. Someone like Franklin Cameron Fitz III. His heart jumped.

"We're taking a break from each other for a few weeks. The truth is, Jonathan doesn't think I have what it takes to be a big-city lawyer's wife. But he's wrong, Franklin." There was a determined tilt to Cindy's chin.

"He's wrong?"

"He doesn't *know* how wrong he is. I'm not stupid."

"Of course you're not."

"You did tell me to let you know if there was something you could do for me?"

"*Anything,* Cindy."

She sighed loudly, as if a huge burden had rolled off her back. "I knew I could count on you, Franklin. I want you to be my Hegai."

He looked at her blankly. "I beg your pardon?"

"My mentor. Like Hegai was to Esther. Jonathan's — well, *wandering.* I want you to help me get him back."

"You agreed to do *what?!*"

Franklin sighed. "What else could I do, Aunt Min?" He met her eyes briefly in the rearview mirror. "She looked at me with those big brown eyes, and I just melted."

"Considering the way you feel about her, do you really think this course of action is wise?"

Wise? he thought. Since when did *wise* enter into it? When it came to matters of the heart — well, a man had to do what a man had to do.

"I keep thinking about the postman," he said slowly.

"The postman?"

"You know, the story about the guy who goes off to war and writes his girlfriend letters every day, and then one day he hears from her and she's engaged to the postman."

"Aha." Miniver was silent for a moment. "I suppose you thought of 'Enry 'Iggins and Eliza Doolittle too."

"I hadn't, but now that you mention it —"

"She's been in love with Jonathan Crum for a long time, Franklin."

"I don't get it, Aunt Min. What does she *see* in him?"

"All of what's good and true and none of what's rotten. It's how she sees everyone."

Franklin knew that wasn't entirely true. Cindy had told her a lot about Jonathan on their long ride home Friday night. Enough to know she did see Jonathan's weaknesses.

"Do you think there's such a thing as being too forgiving?" he asked.

"Seventy times seven," his aunt reminded him.

"But if a person hurts you over and over?"

"The good Lord expects us to hold each other accountable," she said briskly. "Forgiving is not the same as giving license — as some people seem to take it. Jonathan included."

Franklin decided he'd think on that one for a while. "Anyhow, I promised to teach Cindy how to dance by her twenty-fifth birthday. Jonathan is supposed to come take her out, and she seems to think he won't let her down. She wants to surprise him."

"And her birthday is . . . ?"

Once again he sighed. "Three weeks from Tuesday."

"He's an awfully nice young man," Cindy's mother said thoughtfully as they watched Mini Mac and Franklin drive away.

"He is," Cindy agreed.

"We like him," Rosie and Robin said together.

"You do?" Cindy asked, surprised. "What happened to 'Too old, too square, too status quo'?"

"He's too-too-too for *us*, Big Sister," Robin said. "But not for *you*."

Cindy snorted. "Uh-huh. As if I'm looking."

"We like him better than Jonathan," Rosie said.

Cindy jerked her head around, startled. "What do you mean?"

"He's not so stuck on himself," Robin said.

"You think Jonathan's stuck on himself?" Cindy was astonished. She'd never heard the twins say anything negative about Jonathan.

"Like gum on a shoe," said Rosie.

"How come he never comes to see you anymore, Cindy?" Robin asked.

"You know very well why," Cindy said crossly. When they raised their eyebrows in what Cindy took as identical looks of skepticism, she couldn't help but defend him. "You know he had hard classes last term. And papers and a practicum and midterms and finals."

"Weren't finals over, like, three weeks ago?" asked Rosie innocently.

"Girls," Cait tried to intervene.

"He's studying for the bar exam, in case you'd forgotten!"

"Girls!" Cait reprimanded.

Cindy fell silent. She didn't want to argue with her sisters. They were only saying what they saw. Things she herself had been making excuses for.

"Jonathan and I . . . we sort of broke up last night," she said, avoiding their eyes.

Robin and Rosie gasped.

"Just for a while," she added hastily. "It's like a — well, like a trial separation."

"Oh, honey!" her mother said.

"We're really sorry," Rosie said.

"We didn't mean to be rude," said Robin. Then she brightened. "But with Jonathan out of the way —"

"Maybe you and Franklin —" Rosie added.

"Girls!" Cait rebuked them again.

"Jonathan isn't 'out of the way,' " said Cindy with as much dignity as she could muster. "He's just . . . temporarily sidetracked."

"Sidetracked?" Robin's eyes grew wide.

"You mean, like, by another *woman?*" cried Rosie.

"Oh, honey!" her mother said again.

Cindy raised her hands. "No, no — it's all right. It isn't about the woman, I'm sure of it."

"*What* isn't about the woman?"

"The problem. Between me and Jonathan. Although she is gorgeous and sophisticated and rich and —"

"Cindy, dear," her mother interrupted, "if there's another woman — and *especially* if she's gorgeous and sophisticated and rich — she's a problem."

Cindy shook her head. "I think it's more what Aubrey represents," she said.

"Aubrey? Her name is Aubrey?" asked Rosie.

"Cool name," said Robin.

Cait frowned at her younger daughters and shook her head. "What do you mean, 'what Aubrey represents'?" she asked Cindy.

"It's this whole other *world* out there that Jonathan's discovered," Cindy said, her voice going dreamy. "An exciting, glamorous, fast-paced, big-city world I got just the barest glimpse of Friday night . . ."

"Exciting and fast-paced we can see," Robin said.

"But *glamorous?*" Rosie finished the thought. "You ended up in the emergency room!"

"So the problem between you and Jonathan is . . ." her mother prompted, ignoring the twins.

"The problem is, Jonathan's having second thoughts about practicing law in Pilchuck. He *likes* that exciting, glamorous, fast-paced, big-city world. And he isn't sure I'm going to fit in."

"*You* think you will?"

Her mother's doubtful expression doubled Cindy's determination. She thrust out her chin. "Maybe I wouldn't, right now at this very moment. But that doesn't mean I *can't* fit in. I'm not so stupid I can't improve myself, am I?" she demanded.

"Of course you're not! But honey — do you really *want* to fit into this 'whole other world' of Jonathan's?"

"I do, I can, and I will!" How could her mother even ask such a thing? "I'll be so self-improved by the time I'm done," she added, "that Jonathan Crum will come crawling back to me!"

"You go, girl!" squealed the twins in unison.

"We'll help," said Rosie, flopping an arm across Robin's shoulder.

"Good," said Cindy. "First things first. You've still got those instruction manuals from Miss Demeanor's School of the Social Graces?"

The words were barely out of her mouth before they were off and running.

Cait threw her hands in the air. "Cindy Reilly, you've got a stubborn streak in you from here to the moon and back. Just like your father before you, God rest his soul. Heaven help Jonathan Crum. Heaven help us all!"

14

"Biddy," Cindy announced when she walked into the Kitsch 'n' Caboodle Café for her breakfast shift the next morning, "we've been doing it all wrong."

Biddy blinked. "Doin' what all wrong?"

"The whole thing. Standing. Sitting. Walking."

"Wha— ?"

Cindy held up the pink plastic binders Rosie and Robin had found under their beds after hours of searching. "According to Miss Demeanor — who as you know is an expert on the Social Graces — even the basics don't come naturally. Retraining — that's the key."

"Retrainin'? As in learnin' how to walk all over again?" Biddy looked doubtful behind her rhinestone-studded glasses. "Get outta here!"

"I've got to do it," Cindy said. "There's no way around it."

Biddy wiped her hands on a bar towel. "I suppose this has somethin' to do with Jonathan Crum."

"It does." She updated Biddy on the Jonathan situation as they filled the salt-and-pepper shakers at the break table in the back of the diner. Biddy tried to offer consolation, but Cindy cut her off.

"It's not such a bad thing, Biddy — what's happened between me and Jonathan. Oh sure, it threw me for a loop at first. But you know what?"

"No, what?"

"Hearing Jonathan talk about Aubrey du Puy and life in the city and big-city lawyering — well, it was just the thing I needed to shake me out of my doldrums. Just the thing to pull me out of the horrible rut I'd dug myself into."

"Hadn't noticed the doldrums," Biddy said mildly. "Haven't heard you complain about bein' in a rut either."

"That's just the thing — I've been in such a rut I didn't even know what a rut I was in! Of course Jonathan's outgrown me! But now that I'm *aware*, I've got a place to start. And that book" — she nodded toward the pink notebook on the break table — "is it."

Biddy's gaze shifted from Cindy to the notebook and back again. "And where, exactly, do I come in?"

"I need someone to read the instructions to me till I get the basic motions down. It's awfully hard to do both at once, the reading and the maneuvering. The twins tried to help, but you know the twins. All they were good for was giggling." She started placing salt-and-pepper shakers on a tray to distribute to the tables. "Miss Demeanor was wasted on Robin and Rosie, Biddy."

"I'm all for self-improvement," Biddy said, placing her hands on her hips and giving Cindy a critical eye. "But to tell the God-honest truth, it seems to me you walk just fine the way you're doin' now. I sure haven't heard the customers complain."

"They wouldn't notice, Biddy. As dear as they are, the Kitsch 'n' Caboodle crowd isn't exactly what you'd call discriminating."

"Well, now, a couple of 'em got a prejudice or two —"

"Never mind that," Cindy interrupted. "The point is, Jonathan's associates *would* notice. And more important, *I* would. I want to be my best for Jonathan."

"And what about Jonathan bein' his best for you?"

"He loves me, Biddy," she insisted. "He's just confused about it at the moment. When I'm as self-improved as I intend to get — he'll see."

217

"If he doesn't see already, he's blind and a fool, is my opinion," Biddy grumbled. "But if Jonathan is who your heart is set on —"

"In all these years, has it ever been set on anyone else?"

"No, more's the pity."

Cindy wrinkled her brow. First the twins and now Biddy. What was all this anti-Jonathan sentiment all of a sudden?

Biddy sighed and added, "All right then. Where do we start?"

"I knew you wouldn't let me down!" Cindy gave Biddy a spontaneous hug that Biddy immediately wriggled out of. Biddy wasn't the touchy type.

Mondays were slow. After they opened and the regular breakfast crowd thinned out, Cindy hauled out one of Miss Demeanor's manuals and flipped it open. "It's all about projecting grace and confidence, Miss Demeanor says. The twins did at least get that far last night." She touched her fingertips to her temples, trying to remember, then recited in singsong: "Know what you're doing and do what you know, and you'll fit in wherever you go."

"Hmm. 'The Basic Walk,'" Biddy read over her shoulder. "All right — you ready for this?"

Cindy handed the manual to Biddy. "I'm ready."

"Beginning position," Biddy read. "Shoulders back, chin up, tummy in, tush tucked."

"Shoulders back. Chin up. Tummy in. Tush tucked," Cindy repeated as she followed each directive. She took a deep breath, which the "beginning position" seemed to encourage. She felt good.

"Left foot at eleven o'clock, right foot at one," read Biddy.

"Left foot at eleven. Right foot at one."

"Lifting the heel of the left foot off the floor, keeping the angle at eleven o'clock" — Biddy stopped to make sure Cindy understood — "step forward and slightly in front of the right leg, touching the ball of the left foot to the floor."

Cindy stepped out, arms rotating as she tried to keep her balance.

"As you lower the left heel to the floor, lift the right heel, step forward and slightly in front of the left leg — keeping the one o'clock position — and touch the ball of the right foot to the floor."

But too much time had gone by. Cindy lost her balance and fell in a heap on the black-and-white checkered tiles. Her feet not only were at the wrong o'clocks; they were waving in the air. A good thing she wore pedal pushers to work, and not a skirt.

"Grace and confidence," she mumbled as she picked herself up.

"Repeat as often as necessary to get to where you're going," Biddy concluded. "Think ballerina. Do not think lumberjack." She peered at Cindy over the top of her cat's-eye glasses. "Shall we try again?"

"We shall," said Cindy, acutely aware of the stares she was getting from Jonas Muncey and Alf Mayer, who sat at the counter nursing their morning coffee. Even the velvet Elvis on the wall appeared to be watching her with his hooded eyes. She'd never noticed before how smarmy his smile was.

Later that afternoon, after the lunch rush, Biddy had Cindy practice walking around the restaurant with the binder balanced on her head, "which, in *my* opinion, is a better use for the durned thing," she said.

"We're workin' up to a tray of glasses," Biddy explained to Harley Burns, who was gaping at Cindy with unconcealed wonder. "First empty, then full." Cindy hoped she was kidding.

Shoulders back, chin up, tummy in, tush

tucked. Shoulders back, chin up, tummy in, tush tucked. Shoulders back . . . It was Cindy's new mantra, repeated silently a hundred times a day as she practiced walking, standing, kneeling, rising — fortunately, the activities of her trade.

"Grace and confidence," Biddy reminded her hourly.

"Know what you're doing and do what you know, and you'll fit in wherever you go," Jonas Muncey chanted every time he dropped by for a cup of coffee, his blue eyes twinkling merrily.

"Think ballerina. Do *not* think lumberjack," old Alf Mayer teased her from his seat at the counter, once in the morning and once in the afternoon.

Cindy didn't care. She had three weeks to accomplish her makeover from country bumpkin to city sophisticate. With two hundred twenty-five velvet T-shirts awaiting her attention, too, she had to make every minute count.

Franklin had great fun playing his sousaphone with the Leschi Senior Center John Philip Sousa Memorial Concert Band on the Fourth of July, but he did wish Cindy had been there. Avery Farnsworth's percussion solo was well worth the price of admission — more, actually, as the price of admission was free.

He supposed he should have warned Filene he was bringing the entire retinue back to the house to watch the fireworks. Then again, she hadn't bothered to tell *him* she'd invited a number of well-heeled friends and business associates to do the same. There was a bit of confusion when Filene's guests started arriving in their fancy cars and found the driveway blocked by a convoy of senior citizens in portable aluminum rocking chairs.

Otherwise, none of Franklin's guests set so much as a foot inside the mansion. And since Filene had *her* guests set up on the second-floor terrace off the master bedroom suite with champagne and caviar on water crackers, the two groups didn't even have to breathe the same air.

Still, it wasn't that she minded Franklin having guests, he realized. Filene's problem was that they weren't the right *kind* of guests — in the same way Cindy Reilly wasn't the right kind of woman for Franklin. His stepmother had let him know *that* in no uncertain terms.

"Your point is moot, Filene. Cindy's not interested. She's" — he'd paused, finding it painful to say the words — "in love with someone else."

"I don't like the way you were looking at her."

I don't like the way you look at me sometimes, he'd thought of saying. *Like right now.* But, as usual, he hadn't said anything.

"It was a bang-up Fourth of July, Cindy," he told her after church on Sunday, the following day. He'd made the drive up from Seattle early enough to take Aunt Min to church in Bellingrath, but she'd already found a substitute chauffeur, a retired school-bus driver who was "tickled pink" at the opportunity.

"You go on up to Pilchuck, Hegai," Aunt Min had told him. "Esther awaits." Which had filled him with anticipation, until he'd remembered Xerxes.

"The concert got rave reviews from the audience — even the ones who turned off their hearing aids," Franklin told Cindy. "And the estate is the perfect spot to watch the fireworks at Bellevue, straight across Lake Washington."

"But that's so far away!"

"There is that," he acknowledged.

"I like being right spang in the middle of things," she told him. "Lying on my back on a blanket in Homesteader Park with fireworks exploding right over my head."

"That does sound exciting, all right." Funny how he already knew that about her — that she liked to be right spang in the middle of everything. Cindy wasn't one to stand by and watch from a distance.

Which reminded him: "I brought a boom box and some CDs. What's the plan for the dancing lessons?"

"Oh, Franklin! I've barely learned how to walk this week. Do you really think you can teach me how to dance?"

"Barely learned to walk?" He looked at her blankly.

"Watch." She took a deep breath and walked away from him down the pavement, awkwardly, her back stiff and her arms held out from her body at an angle as if ready to catch herself if she fell. Which seemed likely, the way she was wobbling.

She did a funny sort of pivot and started back toward him — as if walking an invisible tightrope, he thought, puzzled. One foot directly in front of the other, feeling for the rope, and the fear of falling written all over her face. But when she stopped in front of him, her intent expression dissolved into her trademark sunny smile. "There! What do you think?"

"I — ah —" He stopped, not sure how to put it delicately. Not certain, actually, that he should "put it" at all. "What, exactly, was wrong with the way you were walking last week?" he tried.

"I don't know, really." Cindy sighed. "But this is the way Miss Demeanor says it ought to be done."

"Miss . . . Demeanor?"

"You know, of Miss Demeanor's School of the Social Graces."

"Ah. Miss Demeanor." He scratched his head, trying to think of what else to say. He'd never heard of Miss Demeanor, but obviously Cindy took great stock in what she said. "Did I hear recently that Miss Demeanor has — fallen out of favor, shall we say?"

"Really?"

"I'm not sure . . . but Cindy, I have to tell you, the first time I saw you at the Kitsch 'n' Caboodle Café — well, let's just say I noticed the way you walked." He felt his face grow warm. "That is, I —"

What was he getting himself into? "I found it very appealing," he finished quickly, before he could lose his nerve.

"Really?" she asked again. "You're not just saying that?"

"I'm not just saying that. You looked so

— *natural.* Relaxed. Like someone who knew exactly what she was doing."

"Grace and confidence," Cindy said. She sounded surprised.

"Exactly."

"Know what you're doing and do what you know, and you'll fit in wherever you go."

Franklin looked at her quizzically.

"One of Miss Demeanor's principles," she explained.

"Oh! Well, grace and confidence certainly haven't gone out of style. Maybe it's Miss Demeanor's *methods* that have fallen out of favor."

"I *have* been walking a long time on my own," Cindy mused.

"Any of your customers at the Kitsch 'n' Caboodle ever complain about the way you get around?" he asked.

"That's what Biddy said! No, I can't say as they have. Though Harley Burns says I don't really walk. I sail, he says."

"Perfect," said Franklin.

"Harley has a boat out at Heron Bay," she added. "He says he marvels at how I sail around the restaurant loaded down with plates and never run aground."

Franklin smiled. She was going to be a wonderful dancer.

"You really like the old way better?" Cindy asked.

"I really do."

Her sigh sounded profoundly relieved. "So be it then. What do you think of Miss Demeanor's Basic Position, though, Franklin? It feels good to me." She demonstrated as she recited: "Shoulders back, chin up, tummy in —"

She stopped abruptly.

Franklin took a deep breath. His face felt as warm as hers looked. "The Basic Position is excellent," he said.

She took him home for dinner, which she insisted was the least she could do in return for his mentoring. Again, it was a delightful affair. Dinner with his father and Filene had always been frightfully formal and virtually silent. He very much liked the way the Reillys served up conversation and laughter along with their meals.

The four Reilly women were a family in a way the Fitzes had never been. The closest he'd come to a family meal when he was growing up was dinner with Cookie and Clement in their little cottage, once in a blue moon when his father and stepmother were both away. Even dinner at Fortunato's Ristorante with Cookie and Nonna Pippa had more of a family feel to it than dinner in the Fitz mansion's mahogany-paneled dining room. As a child, Franklin had lived in fear of scratching the Chippendale dining set or knocking over the Chinese coromandel screens. Filene would have been furious.

"Has Cindy told you about her progress on the T-shirt project?" Cait asked him as she served him thick slices of pot roast and mounds of mashed potatoes with dark gravy.

"Not yet."

"I've been up to a lot more than studying Miss Demeanor, I can tell you," Cindy said cheerfully.

She had. Contacting manufacturers, ordering fabric samples, sizing T-shirt patterns, reapplying for loans. This on top of working thirty-five hours at the Kitsch 'n' Caboodle Café. "Mr. Pickle seems more positive this time around," she said. "Since I have an actual order. It may take a few weeks to get the money though. I'll have to use my credit cards till then."

"Tell him about the Great Books," one of the twins said eagerly.

"Tell him about the Stuff Every Cultured American Really Should Know," said the other, just as eager.

"Just another piece of my self-improvement program," Cindy explained modestly. "Ina Rafferty — she's Pilchuck's head librarian — helped me come up with a list of books I should know about."

The Great Books list was daunting. "I haven't read a third of these!" Franklin told her as he looked it over after dinner. "You're planning on getting through all these books before your birthday?!"

"Oh no! Just Jane Austen before my birthday. Ina said Jane Austen would be 'apropos' under the circumstances. '*Apropos:* both relevant and opportune.' I looked it up. Isn't that a good word, Franklin?"

"I've always liked it," he said, feeling dizzy.

"It's not as overwhelming as it looks," she said, reaching for the Great Books list. "See all these with stars? They've been made into movies. *All* the Jane Austens, for instance — lucky for me! And the ones with checks Ina says she can order through interlibrary loan as books on tape. Those I'll be able to listen to while I'm sewing."

"Pilchuck's head librarian suggested you see the *movies* instead of read the books?!"

"Only because, as Ina says, 'time is of the essence,' " Cindy said. She sighed. "I don't know how she knew about me and

Jonathan, but I can't say I'm surprised she did. Everyone in Pilchuck knows. Everyone in Pilchuck always knows everything." She sighed again.

"It's the way of the world in small towns," Cait said philosophically. "No sense getting all worked up about it, Cindy. Besides, you know the whole town's rooting for you."

"True. Just like the whole town was rooting for me when I asked you to invest in Glad Raggs, Franklin."

"They were?"

"The regulars at Kitsch 'n' Caboodle even pitched in to buy me that genuine faux snakeskin portfolio I had with me."

Franklin tried to imagine what it must be like to have not only a family rooting for your success, but an entire town. It made no sense in his experience, that was for sure. "What about this 'Stuff Every Cultured American Really Should Know?' " he asked.

"Ina insisted I had to have this one in my personal collection," she said, hauling out a book nearly as thick as the Seattle phone book. *The Dictionary of Cultural Literacy*, its cover read. "I figure if I read ten pages every day, five after morning devotions and five before bedtime prayers, in a couple of months I'll know enough not to sound stupid in front of Jonathan's friends. Ina says probably even Jonathan doesn't know all the stuff in here."

"You're reading a dictionary cover to cover?!"

"It's really interesting, Franklin! The first chapter was easy — it's about the Bible, and if there's one thing I know after twenty-four years at the Pilchuck Church of Saints and Sinners, it's the Bible. Now I'm on Chapter Two, 'Mythology and Folklore.' And I was always pretty good at that kind of stuff in school too. You know, all about the gods and goddesses. Here —" She thrust the book toward him. "Ask me anything up to page forty-five."

What could he do but humor her? He opened the book near the front and ran his finger down the page. "Okay. Brünnhilde."

Cindy pressed her fingertips to her temple. "Okay. Don't tell me . . . Brünnhilde . . . I've got it! She was a servant of some god — Norwegian, I think. And she was in love with a guy named Siegfried. But he lied to her and she had him killed."

One of the twins walked into the room from the kitchen just then, a wet dish towel over her shoulder. "Wow! Jonathan better

231

be glad you're not Brünnhilde," she said.

"*I'm* glad I'm not Brünnhilde," Cindy said. "After she had Siegfried killed, she killed herself."

The second twin — Franklin had given up trying to figure out which was which — followed her sister into the dining room. "I hope he was worth it," she said.

"*No* man is worth that," Cindy said. "Not even Jonathan."

For some reason, Franklin took hope from the statement.

15

Cindy was nearly in tears after her first half-hour of dancing lessons. There was no way she was ever going to figure this out before her birthday! She had today and two more weekends, and that was it. Franklin looked — and sounded — just as frustrated as she felt.

"Relax!" he told her. "You're trying too hard. You've got to *feel* it, Cindy. Remember, this is supposed to be *fun*, not work."

But the more he told her to relax, the more tense she got. And the more tense she got, the more she bumped into him, stepped on his toes, twirled left when she should have twirled right, let go when she should have held on.

Poor Franklin!

She flopped down on the living-room rug, which was rolled up at one side of the room to expose the hardwood floor beneath it. Perfect for dancing, Franklin had said. But that was before he'd put Duke Ellington on the CD player, led her to the middle of the floor, and tried to lead her through "I'm Just a Lucky So-And-So."

Franklin hit the Pause button on the boom box once again and paced up and down in front of her, chin in hand.

"I'm sorry, Franklin," she said. "I'm just hopeless."

"Of course you're not!" he said. "I've seen the way you maneuver the tables at the restaurant, Cindy. Talk about grace and confidence! You've got what it takes. We just have to figure out how to transfer it to the dance floor."

We. That was awfully nice of him, she thought — not leaving her failure entirely on *her* shoulders.

He snapped his fingers. "I've got it! Do you have a tray somewhere, like the ones you use at work? Something you could balance on the fingers of one hand?"

"I don't think so . . ." She frowned, thinking. "The pizza pan maybe. It's the right size, and it's a good heavy one."

"Would glasses slide around on it?"

"I could drape it with a tea towel."

"Great! Do it. Three or four glasses, filled with water. I'll get the room ready."

She was too intrigued to argue. She didn't have the faintest idea what a tray of glasses could have to do with dancing, but Franklin must have something up his sleeve.

He did. But rearranging the furniture?

"I don't think Mom's going to like the new floor plan," she teased, stopping in the doorway with the loaded pizza pan balanced in one hand. "Especially if she gets up in the middle of the night for a midnight snack and doesn't turn the light on."

"Very funny," Franklin said.

The room looked more like an obstacle course than either a dance floor or a living room. Franklin had moved the chairs in from the dining room and set them about at random.

"What do you want me to do with the tray?"

"Deliver it to me," he said. "But I want you to circle every chair at least once on the way."

So it *was* an obstacle course! *Very* strange, Cindy thought, but she did as she was told. At this point she was willing to try anything.

"Fine," he said when she reached him. "Let's do it again. But this time, it's the middle of the lunch rush."

This, Cindy thought, she could do. This she had experience with. She raced around the room, cutting corners, swerving around chairs, confidently balancing the pizza pan with its load of glass tumblers —

now pushing it out in front of her, now swinging it to the side, now pulling it in toward her body . . .

She stopped in front of Franklin for a second time.

"How much water did you spill?" he asked.

"How much water did I spill? I don't spill water, Franklin. I'm a professional!"

"Good. Let's do it again, this time to music." He pushed the Pause button on the boom box to restart the tunes. Duke Ellington's big-band sound poured from the speakers. "Take the A Train," Franklin said.

"Chug-a-chug-a," said Cindy as she set out on her roundabout route through the chairs. It was kind of fun weaving in and out of the living room obstacle course in time with the music. Duke Ellington's band was definitely more energizing than the Muzak Biddy favored for the Kitsch 'n' Caboodle.

She took a spontaneous turn in the middle of the floor to flash a smile back at Franklin, pulling her tray of glasses in close to her waist to keep it balanced. He grinned back, encouraging.

She sailed around the living room with her pizza pan through "Satin Doll,"

"Perdido," and "Love You Madly." Hamming it up and having the time of her life, but telling herself Franklin was crazy. So she was finally having fun. So he'd gotten her to relax. She still wasn't dancing.

Or was she?

The thought stopped her in her tracks — so abruptly she almost lost control of the tray. She actually spilled a drop or two of water.

"Franklin!" She called across the room. "Have I been *dancing?* With a *pizza pan* for my partner?"

"You might say that," Franklin said smugly. "Now think about what you were doing for a minute, Cindy. As you were moving around the chairs, where was your balance centered?"

Cindy puckered her brow. "At my waist, I guess. No — a little higher." She pressed her hand above her navel, below the vee of her rib cage, and rotated her hips, testing. "What do you call this? Your solar plexus?"

"Your . . . solar . . . plexus." Franklin's voice sounded strangled, as if he were having trouble breathing. And not a chicken bone in sight. Cindy hurried across the room and handed him a glass from the pizza pan, eyeing him with concern. He took a deep breath and then a long drink.

"You're all right?" she asked anxiously.

He nodded, coughing lightly. "Thanks. Yes. So you found your center of balance." He took another swig of water and set the glass on the end table where Cindy had placed the tray. "And how did you keep the water from spilling?" he asked.

She thought for a moment. "Well — I didn't really think about it. I just moved the tray wherever it had to go to keep it balanced. The way I do at work when I'm coming around the corner of the counter or trying to keep out of Biddy's way."

He held out his hands to her, palms up, fingers cupped. "Hook your fingers over mine — lightly — good! Now — do you think you can imagine me as you and you as the pizza pan?"

"The pizza pan?"

Another half-hour, and she finally started to get it. In the same way she moved her tray of glasses around to keep it balanced while she worked, Franklin was moving her around the living room dance floor: now pushing her out in front of him, now swinging her to the side, now pulling her in toward his body, now spinning her under his arm.

"If you let go of my hands," he warned, "I'll lose you. It's my hands that tell you where I'm going and where I need you to go — to keep the water from spilling, so to speak." He pulled her in and grinned down into her upturned face. "Your tray wouldn't go jumping out of your hands on its own, now would it?"

At the slight pressure against her fingers, Cindy moved away from him again, holding tightly so as *not* to jump out of his hands. He pulled her in closer again and swung her around. She laughed, exhilarated. "I'm dancing, Franklin! I'm really dancing!"

The moment she said it, of course, she lost her balance and stomped on his toe.

He winced. But only for an instant. Then he smiled and said, "Of course you are."

Franklin didn't know if Cindy invited him to stay and watch Jane Austen after their dancing lesson out of politeness or if she really wanted him there. Either way, he wasn't about to say no — even if *Sense and Sensibility* wouldn't have been his first choice for film entertainment.

He was disappointed when the evening turned into a family affair — but then again, a family affair was probably safer than watching a romantic movie alone with Cindy. Especially after having her in his arms all afternoon.

The Reilly women provided popcorn, iced tea, and a running commentary on the story, which Franklin found annoying at times and fascinating at others. This household was so unlike the one he'd grown up in. Cindy and her sisters had obviously been encouraged from an early age to have opinions and to express them. He wished he could have known Joe-Joe Reilly. He wished he could have known his *own* father in the way this family seemed to know one another.

"They're getting kicked out of their *house?*" Robin squealed after the opening scene. Franklin knew it was Robin because, while he and Cindy had been engrossed in dancing lessons, the twins had gotten into an argument with the neighbors' Siamese cat, and Robin had a wicked scratch across one cheek. At present, she was clearly outraged that Mr. Dashwood's will provided handsomely for his son and barely at all for his second wife and his daughters. "That's criminal!"

"It *wasn't* criminal then," Cindy said reasonably.

"Well, it should have been," Rosie declared. And later, after a revealing conversation between two characters, "You mean women couldn't even have *jobs* back then?"

"You're never going to find *me* waiting around for a husband to take care of me," Robin said.

"It's the way things were done back then," said Cindy.

Franklin, to his surprise, found himself drawn into the story — and especially into the love triangle between Colonel Brandon, Marianne, and Willoughby.

Couldn't she see? Couldn't she *tell* that the Colonel was the better man for her? Didn't she know that depth and character were more important than charm and a pretty face?

Cait and the twins voiced the same opinion, but Cindy got sucked in by Willoughby. "He's so *perfect* for her," she insisted. But Franklin noticed she got quieter and quieter as the story played itself out and Willoughby showed himself for a cad and a scoundrel. In the end it was the Colonel who won Marianne's love — but not before Willoughby broke her heart.

Please, God, Franklin prayed silently, gazing at Cindy. *Don't let Jonathan break her heart.*

Even if it means you can't have her?

He wasn't willing to carry that internal conversation any further.

"That's so sad," Cindy said, her cinnamon eyes moist with unshed tears.

Franklin forced his attention back to the screen, though what he wanted to do was reach his arm around her and pull her close.

On the screen, Willoughby sat on his horse on a hill overlooking the wedding festivities of Marianne and the Colonel. After a moment he bowed his head, turned his horse, and galloped away.

"*So* sad," Cindy repeated meaningfully.

"Only for Willoughby," Rosie said, matter-of-factly.

"And he brought it on himself," said Robin.

By Tuesday afternoon, Cindy had found suppliers for the crushed panne velvet and the satin lingerie bias binding she needed for her T-shirt project. She maxed out three credit cards to pay for the supplies and to have them delivered express. She couldn't afford to waste any time.

By Wednesday evening she'd finished the chapter on "Mythology and Folklore" in her cultural resource book and worked through the next two chapters, "Proverbs" and "Idioms." She especially liked learning the foreign words and phrases: *savoir-faire*, for instance, which was exactly what she was aiming for in her self-improvement program — along with *sangfroid* and a certain *je ne sais quoi.*

C'est la vie, coup de grâce, fait accompli — she loved the way the words rolled off her tongue. "Just this morning, Biddy, I've learned how to say good-bye in five languages," she told her boss one day, nearly bursting with the thrill of discovery.

Just for fun, she tried out her new knowledge on the regulars, trying to match languages with heritages where she could — though in Pilchuck that made for an overabundance of *auf Wiedersehens.* After a while she *adios*ed, *aloha*ed, *arriverderci*ed, and *au revoir*ed without discrimination.

Thursday afternoon the fabric arrived: bolt after bolt after bolt of gorgeous, jewel-toned velvet. The delivery driver was nice enough to stack them in the corners of the sewing room, which had once been the garage. Joe-Joe Reilly had done the original remodel, and after his death, when Cindy started working with her mother, the women had rearranged the workspace to accommodate them both.

It was a small space for two women and all the equipment their trade required: two commercial-quality sewing machines, a serger, an ironing board, a steam iron and other specialty pressing tools, a pair of dressmaker's forms, a drafting table, and a huge cutting table. Rows of built-in shelves for fabric storage lined one wall, floor to ceiling. The others were covered either in corkboard, so sketches, directions, and small pattern pieces could be pinned directly to the wall, or in pegboard, to keep notions and tools — bobbins, buttons, zippers, pins and needles and threads, scissors, tape measures, markers — within easy reach.

At present, however, the space looked more like a fabric warehouse than a sewing room. After the delivery van pulled away, Cindy experienced a moment of such heart-palpitating panic she almost ran after it, arms waving, to beg the driver to reload the bolts of cloth and "return to sender" right then and there. She probably would have done it if the phone hadn't rung just then.

It was Franklin, wanting to know if she'd like to practice her fine dining techniques the following evening. There was that golf resort north of Pilchuck, he said. Lummi-

Ah-Moo, with its four-star restaurant . . .

She protested the expense, but only mildly. Just hearing Franklin's calm, steady voice slowed down her heartbeat to near normal; going to dinner at the Inn at Lummi-Ah-Moo might be just the thing she needed.

"You've fed me twice already," Franklin reasoned. "And I'm expecting two more Sunday dinners before your birthday."

"Well, of course! But that's to pay you for my mentoring."

"My mentoring's to pay you for saving my life."

She was certainly getting the mileage out of that chicken bone, Cindy thought. And she hadn't even made a conscious wish on it.

"All right then." She perked up. "And I can tell you what I've been learning! I started the chapter on 'World Literature, Philosophy, and Religion' this morning."

"I know. I bought a book just like yours this week and did some extra reading to catch up with you."

"You did?"

"I thought that way — if we're both on the same page, so to speak — we could practice making scintillating conversation."

"Scintillating?" Cindy asked, trying out

the unfamiliar word on her tongue.

"Brilliant. Sparkling. Not that you don't sparkle already," he added hastily. "You sparkle like nobody I've ever known."

He really was the sweetest man! "The more polished I am, the more I'll sparkle, Franklin. I think it's a wonderful idea. But I really hate to impose."

"No imposition," he said. "You're right — all this cultural stuff is really interesting."

"But don't you know it already? You went to college, didn't you?"

"I did, and I don't. There's so much to learn and so little time and so many other demands when you're in college. A lot gets left out — or doesn't sink in. Believe me, Cindy, I'm enjoying myself."

So it was settled. He'd drive up from Seattle after work and pick her up at eight. For dinner at the Inn at Lummi-Ah-Moo! What in the world was she going to wear?

She brushed the question aside. At this point it was more appropriate to ask how in the world she was going to turn the mountain of fabric in the sewing room into two hundred twenty-five T-shirts by October.

16

It was funny how much like a real date Cindy's practice dinner with Franklin at the Inn at Lummi-Ah-Moo turned out to be. Funny odd, not funny ha-ha. Maybe it was because it had been so long since she'd been out on anything like a real date.

She felt awkward at first, the way she'd felt at Fortunato's Ristorante when she first walked in, but only for a minute or two. This time there was no Aubrey du Puy to make her feel deficient — and no dance floor threatening. After her single lesson, she wasn't ready to go public yet.

This time, too, she knew Franklin better. And Franklin had a way about him that made her feel pretty and interesting and *valued,* somehow. The touch of his hand at her elbow, the appreciation in his glance, the way he listened with his head cocked like a parakeet's when she talked, the pause before he answered, as if to consider what she'd said. He was every bit the gentleman that Jane Austen's Colonel Brandon was: attentive, responsive, complimentary.

"You're the prettiest woman here, Cindy

Reilly," he murmured, leaning confidentially across the table as she opened her menu.

She actually blushed. "You don't have to say that, Franklin."

"And I wouldn't if it wasn't true. But may I give you a bit of advice, sweet Esther?"

"Advise away, dear Hegai. You *are* my mentor."

"In the social circles you're aiming for, the gracious way to answer a compliment is to smile and say thank you. You'd do well to practice," he teased, "because you're sure to get compliments galore."

"That's sweet of you to say, but —"

At his look she stopped herself, smiled, fluttered her eyelashes, and said, "Why, thank you, Franklin."

He laughed. "A nice touch, the eyelashes. Just be careful who you flutter them at, Cindy. You may have more than puppy dogs following you home."

Later, home again and preparing for bed, she reviewed the evening in her mind. She did think Franklin had gone overboard with his "prettiest woman in the restaurant" spiel. She certainly hadn't spent any extra time primping. When her shift at Kitsch 'n' Caboodle was over, she'd gone straight home to the sewing room and worked until half an hour before Franklin's arrival, then taken a two-and-a-half-minute shower, slipped into a colorful Hawaiian print sundress, and plaited her still damp hair into a single braid.

As far as makeup went — well, when your workday started at five-thirty in the morning, you learned to dispense with everything but the necessities. A little moisturizer, a flick of mascara, a layer of lip gloss — that was all she usually managed. An extra forty winks was so much more important than forty minutes' worth of beauty regimen.

Of course, that was going to have to change. *Make appointment with Narcissa for beauty makeover,* Cindy had already written on the message board next to the phone. Quick and natural wasn't going to do for the wife of an important big-city attorney like Jonathan Crum was going to be. If Aubrey du Puy was any indication, Jonathan would want his wife to have a more polished, sophisticated, finished look. And since Aubrey du Puy had managed to turn Jonathan's head, even temporarily, she obviously *was* an indication.

Jonathan! Cindy realized suddenly she'd barely thought of him all evening. Here she'd been with another man — thoroughly *enjoyed* herself with another man, for heaven's sake — without giving Jonathan a moment's thought! She felt a pang of guilt, even though her datelike time with Franklin had definitely *not* been a date.

Had it?

Of course it hadn't! It had been a *lesson*. A way to learn what all those forks and spoons were for, and how to pronounce *châteaubriand with béarnaise sauce,* and how to cut brandy-glazed baby carrots without having them fly across the room. It had been a way for her to practice scintillating dinner conversation.

And it had been so much fun! What a world of ideas there was out there to talk about! From fatalism to free will to fundamentalism, from Kafka to Kant to Kierkegaard, they covered the gamut of their morning reading on world literature, philosophy, and religion. "It's so interesting how it all overlaps," Cindy marveled. "And how often Christianity crops up. I mean, I know how much my faith means to *me,* but I guess I never thought about how much it means in history."

Franklin had warned her up front that, generally, religion and politics were considered inappropriate topics for polite conversation at dinner. But in light of their recent readings they had agreed to put the restriction aside.

"It's just us," Cindy said.

"Yes, it is," Franklin agreed. "We can go wherever we want to in this conversation."

And so they had.

Why she hadn't even *thought* of Jonathan during their discourse, she couldn't begin to fathom.

"I hope you know what you're doing," Aunt Min told Franklin late Sunday night when he got in from Pilchuck. He'd been with Cindy Friday evening, Saturday evening, and all day Sunday.

"I've never cared much about fitting into Filene's social scene, it's true," he said, deliberately misunderstanding, "but I certainly know *how* to. Cindy's learning a lot from me. You should see how she's dancing, after only two weekends."

"And you're feeling fine about this? Preparing Cindy for another man?"

Franklin was silent. He'd managed not to think about the Crumb all weekend. Cindy hadn't brought him up once, and to tell the truth . . .

"I think she's getting over him, Aunt Min."

"And you base this belief on . . . ?"

"I just have a *feeling*."

Miniver sighed and shook her head. "My dear Franklin!"

She might as well have said "My poor, foolish Franklin!" The adjectives were there in her tone of voice.

He *was* foolish, of course, he admonished himself on the trip back home to Seattle. Cindy may not have talked about Jonathan, but neither had she done anything to make Franklin think she felt more for Franklin than friendship. Sure, she'd had a good time over dinner at the Inn at Lummi-Ah-Moo Friday night. And dancing around the Reilly living room Saturday night. And sharing a pew and a hymnbook with him Sunday morning. And sharing a picnic lunch and more dancing Sunday afternoon, under the trees at Homesteader Park, to the sounds of Glenn Miller's band . . .

But Cindy Reilly was a happy person. She would have enjoyed herself with anyone; that's how she was. A Pollyanna through and through.

And he loved her for it. He really did. He couldn't deny it anymore.

He had two messages on his answering machine when he got home — both, oddly enough, from elsewhere on the estate. One was from Cookie, to say she missed him being there for dinner and a game of Scrabble on the weekends, but she hoped things were going well for him and his "girl." The other was from his stepmother, her voice imperious: "Call as *soon* as you get in."

It was late, but the lights were on in the master-bedroom suite. Filene would have heard him drive in. There was no way to get out of it.

He wished he had it in him to stand up to her, but somehow it never seemed worth the anticipated fight. She made his life miserable enough as it was — no sense in giving her further reason.

"Filene. It's Franklin."

"So you've found your way home again." Acid-tongued.

"Yes." She made him feel like an idiot-child. Or the prodigal son. Or a *tomcat*, for Pete's sake.

Her voice sweetened. "How's your aunt?"

He was surprised. Filene never asked about Aunt Min. In fact, he'd never understood Filene's lack of interest in Miniver Macready. As a world-famous concert pianist, hers was a worthy name to drop —

and dropping names was one of Filene's favorite pastimes. Now that he knew more about the family history, he wondered if the fact of Aunt Min's fame meant less than the fact of her relationship to Molly Macready.

"Fine," he said. He'd learned to answer her questions and comments as succinctly as possible, to make her unbearable interviews as short as possible.

"What did you do all weekend?"

He felt his hackles rise. He was twenty-six years old. He was his father's legal heir. He had just as much right to be on — or off — the estate as she did. He didn't have to answer to his stepmother.

But he didn't want to antagonize her either. "This and that," he answered, trying to keep his tone neutral.

"You're seeing that *woman*, aren't you?" The acid tongue again.

"Woman?" He pretended innocence.

"You know exactly who I mean. Your little Pilchuck . . . *patootie*."

Anger boiled up inside him, but he held his tongue. "Was there anything else you wanted, Filene?" he asked evenly.

"Yes, as a matter of fact, there is. The coordinator for the Greater Seattle Combined Arts Council Most Eligible Bachelor

Auction called and wanted to know what your date package was. Since you weren't here and the programs had to be printed, I decided for you."

"The who-what-*which?*" Franklin said, a feeling of dread settling over him like a pall. "What are you talking about?"

"Don't tell me you've forgotten, Franklin. You volunteered for the bachelor auction months ago."

"Volunteered! For a bachelor auction!"

"You offered to do whatever you could to help out with fund-raising for the Arts Council, Franklin. Don't try to deny it — I was there when you said the very words to Justine Pomeroy."

Franklin did remember talking to Mrs. Pomeroy, one of Filenc's tennis partners, in the driveway one afternoon after work, probably six months ago now. She was a talker, and what he remembered most was what a difficult time he'd had getting away from her.

"I thought I was volunteering my financial expertise," he protested.

"You told her whatever you could do, Franklin. After all, you *are* one of Seattle's most eligible bachelors. And it's simply too late to back out at this point. The auction's next weekend. If you've made other plans, you'll have to cancel them."

Franklin's heart sank. Next weekend was Cindy's last chance for dancing lessons. She still wasn't as confident as he'd like, and he'd planned on a full weekend of practice. "When on the weekend?"

"Rehearsal Friday night, auction Saturday. Seven o'clock both evenings. Don't plan on getting away until after midnight on Friday, Justine says."

Friday and Saturday both! And Cindy worked Saturday morning. She was going to be so disappointed.

He was disappointed. And not a little flustered about the whole idea. "What, exactly, does a bachelor auction entail, Filene?" he asked cautiously.

"Just what it sounds like. Women bid on a date with the bachelor of their choice. The right *kind* of women, Franklin. Suitable women for Seattle's most eligible bachelors."

Aubrey du Puy flashed into his mind. A whole *roomful* of Aubrey du Puys. He shuddered.

"You don't have to do anything but walk the runway and look pretty," his stepmother added.

Walk the runway and look pretty! This was sounding worse and worse. "And what did

256

you tell Mrs. Pomeroy was the 'date package' that comes along with me?" he asked, dreading the answer.

"That was easy. The Gallowglass Gala."

Of course. Filene's annual end-of-the-summer charity ball — her chance to show off the Fitz family estate in all its glory. Still, the elegant black-tie event raised lots of money every year for lots of worthy charities. Everyone who was anyone in Seattle came to the Gallowglass Gala. Franklin had made an appearance every year since he was six and stayed for the party every year since he was sixteen. It was one of his duties as the Fitz family heir.

Last year — to Filene's chagrin — he'd brought Nonna Pippa as his date. He'd have invited Cookie, too, except that she'd already signed up for a trip to Blake Island for a salmon dinner in a Native American cedar long house. The Leschi Senior Center crowd did get around.

Besides, Cookie said, she'd been to every Gallowglass Gala until she retired — though always through the service entrance. "I wouldn't enjoy myself," she'd told Franklin. "I'd want to be back in the kitchen making sure everything was running smooth. You have your fun with Pippa."

Which he had. More fun than he'd ever had at the Gallowglass. For one thing, it was Nonna Pippa who'd taught him that social dancing was an expression of celebration — not a form of torture. For another, bringing someone as "unsuitable" as Nonna Pippa to the Gallowglass Gala was one of the few acts of rebellion against Filene he'd dared since his father's death. He had to admit there'd been pleasure in displeasing her.

No doubt being "volunteered" for the Greater Seattle Combined Arts Council Most Eligible Bachelor Auction this year was his punishment for embarrassing Filene last year. Or maybe her method of controlling him. Or both. He wouldn't put it past his stepmother to pay off some so-called suitable woman to bid for him at the bachelor auction just to make sure he didn't pull another stunt at the Gallowglass Gala as he'd done the year before. "Suitable" meaning, of course, some clone of herself, like Aubrey du Puy.

More likely, though, Filene just wanted to embarrass him. What could be more mortifying than being auctioned off like a prize bull?

As Franklin saw it, the auction had two possible outcomes. He'd either end up going to the Gallowglass Gala with the kind of woman who had to resort to buying her dates, or he'd suffer the humiliation of having no one bid for him at all. He didn't know which was worse.

He shuddered. There had to be a way —

Something suddenly clicked in his brain. There *was* a way.

"Franklin!" Cindy wailed over the phone when he called from his office the following day. "You can't not come this weekend! I need you!"

Franklin's heart leapt at her words. But when he reminded himself the reason she needed him was to get her boyfriend back, it immediately lay down again.

"I know," he said. "I need you, too, Cindy. You'll never believe what my stepmother's roped me into."

He was right. She didn't, at first. She'd never heard of such a thing. "You mean like a *cattle* auction?"

"Exactly. You can see why I need you to come down here next weekend, can't you?"

It took some talking to convince her.

She hated to take the time away from her T-shirt project . . .

"You've got to take a break sometime," he said.

If he was on the platform, she'd be all alone in the crowd . . .

"I've already talked to Cookie. She'd be happy to go with you for moral support."

She couldn't leave her mother and the twins without the car on a Saturday night.

"I'll pick you up. And take you home."

Wouldn't that make an awfully late night for him?

"You could stay overnight with Cookie. Go to church with us in the morning. And I'll give you a final dancing lesson in the ballroom. You'll love it, Cindy."

The ballroom! The mansion had a ballroom? That perked up her interest.

But she didn't know if she was self-improved enough yet to pass muster in "high society."

"Of course you are," he said with more confidence than he felt. He had an idea the atmosphere at the bachelor auction was going to be more like a shark feeding than a garden party. Would Filene and Aubrey and their ilk eat sweet, innocent Cindy alive?

"Why don't you just give the money to Cookie and have her bid for you?" Cindy asked.

"If you could see it as an opportunity," he said, ignoring her question because he didn't have a good answer — not one he was willing to share, at least. "A learning experience. Another chance to put yourself in your chosen social setting and get more comfortable being there." He closed his eyes, hating to say it: "Do it for Jonathan, Cindy."

She was silent for so long he thought he'd lost the phone connection. "Are you there?" he asked.

"I'm here. All right," she agreed, her voice resigned.

She didn't want to do it, Franklin could tell, but she'd decided to do it for Jonathan.

He was pleased, of course. After all, she was doing what he wanted.

But his heart ached too. She wasn't doing it for him.

Face it, man, he told himself, staring bleakly at the phone after he'd said good-bye. *You're nothing more to Cindy Reilly than a means to an end.*

17

"It was awfully nice of you to drive all the way to Pilchuck for me," Cindy said to Franklin as he loaded her overnight bag into the back of the Jeep. "Mom really needed the car this weekend."

"It was the least I could do when you're saving my neck," he said. "You don't know how much I appreciate your coming to the rescue, Cindy. Especially with your time crunch. How are the T-shirts going, by the way?"

She worried aloud for the next twenty miles about production problems — how the serger had gone on the blink and cost a fortune to fix, how the satin bias tape had finally arrived, but in the wrong colors, how cutting out the pattern pieces was taking more time than she'd anticipated.

"At the rate I'm going, I *might* have all the pieces cut out by the time the order's due. Unfortunately, none of them will be sewn together, let alone edged and hemmed," she said, only half-kidding.

"You're making me feel guilty about

tearing you away from your work," he told her.

"Forget it — like you said, I needed a break. In the whole scheme of things, what's a day and a half? Besides, I have the entire Kitsch 'n' Caboodle crew noodling on the 'challenges' of my project, as Buster calls them. Maybe they'll have it all figured out for me by the time I get back. In fact," she added, "Lon Shoemaker — his company makes furniture, actually, not shoes — thinks maybe I could speed things up by cutting out the pieces with a jigsaw instead of scissors."

"Really?"

"That's how clothing manufacturers do it, he says — six-inch stacks at a time. It's not exactly the same kind of jigsaw Lon uses in his woodshop, but he thinks maybe he can modify one of his."

Franklin shook his head. "I'm amazed, Cindy. At how everybody in that restaurant is pulling for you."

She nodded absently, her mind still on the so-called challenges of her project. She sighed. "It's funny, you know? Not funny *ha-ha*. Funny *ironic*."

"What is?"

"Getting my line into a store like Strawbridge & Fitz is a dream come true

— but it feels more like a nightmare!"

Franklin took his eyes off the road for a moment to look at her. "Aunt Min has a theory about that. Dreams are easy, she says. But when they come true, they metamorphose into real life. And real life's hard."

"Metamorphose . . ." Cindy mused. "Oh, I remember. Transform. Like the guy who woke up and discovered he'd turned into a giant bug. Now *that* was a nightmare!"

"Franz Kafka. You're a good student, Cindy."

"I work hard."

"And dream big."

"I guess you could say that." She cocked her head curiously. "What about you, Franklin? What are your dreams?"

"I've never really . . ." He hesitated. "That is, officially, I haven't had dreams of my own. I'm a Fitz. I have responsibilities to my family line. The business. Especially since my father died . . ." His voice trailed off.

"And unofficially?"

"If my future wasn't already cut out for me?" he mused. "I used to dream about opening a business of my own. Starting from scratch like my great-grandfather did with Strawbridge & Fitz. Building a company from the ground up. I'd want to stay in retail," he said, warming to his subject. "I like the business. But I'd want to do specialty stores — boutiques. Smaller, more personal . . ."

Cindy stared at him as he continued talking. There was a light in his eyes, an excitement in his voice, an *energy* about him she hadn't seen before in their short acquaintance. Franklin had been holding back on her. *Franklin's been holding back on himself,* some inner voice told her.

"That sounds wonderful, Franklin!" she said aloud. "Really, it sounds like something you should try. Did you ever get a chance to talk to your dad about it?"

The light went out of him.

"Once," he said, his voice oddly flat. "He was terribly upset. I was his only child, he said. His heir. He was counting on me. Strawbridge & Fitz was my destiny."

"So he wouldn't even think about letting you start your own business."

"He didn't have time to think. He died that night. A massive heart attack. He was only forty-five."

Cindy was thunderstruck. "Oh, Franklin, I'm so sorry! But surely you don't blame —"

"Of course not," he said too quickly. "It was just one of those things. One of those very sad things."

She reached across the seat and lightly touched his arm. "I know. Like my father's accident." Joe-Joe Reilly had fallen from a scaffolding at the Heron Bay oil refinery where he'd worked. He'd always been safety-conscious and there had been no safety violations. It had just been one of those things.

They were silent for a long time. When Franklin spoke again, it was about the view outside the window, and then about the Sousa Concert Band, and then about Cindy's dancing lessons. He seemed to have shed his burden of gloom like a dog shaking rain off its coat.

He really is the nicest man, Cindy thought. So personable. So easy to be around. Not one to keep her thoughts to herself, at some point in the conversation she said impulsively, "I sure do like you, Franklin."

She was surprised how instantly crimson he turned. And how speechless he seemed.

"The gracious way to answer a compliment . . ." she prompted.

He looked properly chagrined. *"Gracias, merci,* and *danke schön,"* he said, and flashed her a smile.

266

"Let's see. That would be Spanish, French, and — don't tell me — German?"

"Spanish, French, and German," he agreed.

He was *much* better looking than she'd thought the first time she met him, Cindy thought, staring at his profile as he drove. Not in the same way as Jonathan, of course, but —

Her eyes narrowed. Her mouth thinned. She didn't want to think about Jonathan. The truth be told, she was feeling a bit cross with her boyfriend. Or should she call him her *ex*-boyfriend? It didn't seem clear anymore.

"So who are the other bachelors in this auction?" she asked Franklin, deliberately banishing Jonathan from her mind.

The pristine groundskeeper's cottage on the Fitz estate, complete with an English country garden out front and wild roses climbing the porch, looked almost as cheerful and as charming as its tenant. Cookie Simms had the front door open before Franklin even stopped the Jeep.

Cindy liked her at first sight. The kind, congenial lines imprinted on her face could only have come from a long-held habit of joy. The pair of sturdy, dwarflike dogs that came rollicking out to the car to greet them on their short little legs — ears on the alert — had foxlike faces with smiles as sweet as Cookie's. One was golden yellow and white, the other black, brown, and white, and neither had a tail; when Franklin bent to pet them, they wagged their entire hind ends.

"Pembroke Welsh corgis," Franklin informed her as he opened her door. "The same kind who attend the Queen of England, Cookie likes to point out. Come on, let me introduce you."

The eyes behind Cookie's fashionable gold-toned glasses were the color of faded denim, but there was nothing else faded about her. She wore turquoise pants and a bright yellow T-shirt with a forest of umbrellas printed on the front under the logo, "Seattle Rain Festival, Jan. 1–Dec. 31." Cindy didn't know what color her hair had been during Franklin's boyhood — or even yesterday — but at present it was the copper of a newly minted penny.

Her personality matched her appearance — she practically bubbled over with energy and optimism. "I've heard so much about you, Miss Cindy! Saving Biscuit's life the way you did. Mercy!"

"Biscuit?" Cindy stole a glance at

Franklin and found him once again red-faced. He caught her eye and frowned, his meaning clear: *Don't you dare tease me about this. Now or ever.*

"He loved my buttermilk biscuits when he was a boy," Cookie explained, oblivious to the exchange between Franklin and Cindy. "And I loved him the way he loved my biscuits. Franklin's been *my* Biscuit ever since."

She prompted them into the cottage, Cindy first and then Franklin, carrying Cindy's overnight bag. The house smelled wonderfully of onions, herbs, and spices.

"I see Zollie and Zelda have already taken a liking to you," Cookie said to Cindy as she followed her guests inside. "They don't take to just anyone. Won't give the time of day to Biscuit's stepmother, Filene, for instance. No sir. They've never liked Filene. Not one little bit."

Cookie directed them to the cheerful living room, which was decorated in pink-and-white striped wallpaper with a rose-trellis border. She lowered herself to the sofa, upholstered in colorful rose-patterned chintz, and invited Cindy to follow suit. Franklin seated himself in the overstuffed chair set at an angle to the sofa.

Zollie and Zelda sank to the floor at Cookie's feet. "Best companions an old woman could have," she said affectionately, reaching down to scratch the head of first one and then the other. "Except for Biscuit, of course, who lets me win at Scrabble. But Biscuit's not always around, what with his job and his new girl."

Cindy's heart fluttered oddly. "I thought you told me you didn't have a girlfriend," she said to Franklin.

His face, once again, turned violently crimson. "I don't." He looked down at his lap, and then back at Cindy. "She means you, Cindy." He sighed. "I've tried to tell her we're just friends, but —"

"Friends are a fine thing," Cookie interrupted. "We'd be lost without 'em. But friends aren't going to keep you warm at night, Biscuit. No sir."

Cindy felt her own face flush as Franklin abruptly and mercifully changed the subject. "That wouldn't be your famous chicken pot pie I'm smelling in the kitchen, Cookie . . . ?"

It was. And it was delectable, Cindy discovered not long after they'd sat down at the kitchen table for dinner. "Mmmmm! My boss — I work in a restaurant, Cookie — my boss would kill for the recipe."

"I hope not," Cookie said cheerfully. "I've got too much living yet to do."

"Including that cookbook you've been talking about for years?" Franklin tweaked her.

"What a good idea!" Cindy said.

Cookie waved a hand dismissively. "I'm not the one's been talking about it for years," she said. "It's Biscuit been doing the talking. And my, he does go on!"

Cindy didn't know about "Biscuit," but Franklin clearly was the apple of Cookie's eye. After he left for his pre-auction duties, while Cindy helped her clean up the dinner dishes, Cookie sang his praises: He was loving and loyal, thoughtful and generous, intelligent and earnest — but humble and blessed with a wonderful sense of humor. And could he play the sousaphone!

Zollie and Zelda lay on the kitchen floor with their chins on their paws, gazing up with their big brown eyes, as interested in the sound of Cookie's voice as Cindy was in her words about Franklin. She'd seen some of these qualities in Franklin herself, of course, but there was something about hearing it from someone else. Someone who'd known him nearly all his life.

Franklin had made arrangements for a

town car to pick them up at the estate and deliver them to the Four Seasons Olympic Hotel downtown, where the Greater Seattle Combined Arts Council Most Eligible Bachelor Auction would be held. Luxurious, but not as fun as riding in Mini Mac's Packard, Cindy decided.

On the way, Cookie filled her in on Franklin's history: his mother hit by a car when he was only four, just after Cookie and her husband, Clement, had come to work for the Fitzes; Filene Downing "moving in like a vulture after a kill" when Franklin Cameron Fitz Jr. was at his most vulnerable; Franklin growing up in a house more like a museum than a home, with a workaholic father and a stepmother who found him "more a bother than the real treasure he was," Cookie said.

"It sounds as if you, at least, let him know he was a treasure," Cindy told her. "He was lucky to have you and your husband in his life. He knows it too — he's always talking about you, Cookie."

"He's been here for me in a special way since Clement died," she said. "And he's always talking about you, too, Miss Cindy. How pretty you are, and smart and plucky."

"He is?"

"All of which I can testify to, now I've met you," she said, reaching a hand across the seat to touch Cindy's arm. "I'm glad he's met you, Miss Cindy. And don't you worry; I don't believe a word of it when he says you and he are 'just friends.' I know that boy better than he knows himself."

"Oh, Cookie! I do hope you're wrong!" Cindy said, distressed. She remembered all at once how flustered Franklin had been when she'd told him how much she liked him. Could it be —

Of course it couldn't. "I'm *sure* you're wrong," she added before Cookie could form a reply. It was ridiculous even to think of. Franklin was, after all, doing everything he could to help her get Jonathan back. Why would he be doing that if he himself were interested in Cindy?

Besides, he knew how she felt about Jonathan —

"I don't think so, Miss Cindy," Cookie said.

Cindy stared at Cookie across the car.

How *did* she feel about Jonathan?

Franklin tugged at his tuxedo pants where they pulled uncomfortably across his thighs, wishing he'd tried them on before this afternoon. The last time he'd worn his tuxedo was last summer's Gallowglass Gala, before he'd made the stationary bikes and the leg weight machines at the gym part of his fitness routine. He'd bulked up more than he realized.

The family doctor had warned Franklin after his father's third and fatal heart attack that he couldn't afford to sit at his desk all day without some form of regular exercise. So he'd approached the fitness task with the same diligence he approached his work. By now his thrice-weekly workouts at the Washington Athletic Club felt as necessary to his mental health as to his physical well-being.

And to think he could have been dressed in a pair of shorts and a Washington Athletic Club T-shirt instead of his ill-fitting penguin suit! Bachelor Number Twelve, a local TV news personality Franklin had run into a time or two at the club, was wearing exactly that. Each bachelor was dressed to express the nature of the "date package" that went along with him, and Bachelor Number Twelve's happened to be an afternoon and evening at the exclusive athletic club: exercise in the gym, kick-back time in the spa, dinner in the Library Grill, dancing in the piano bar off the lobby.

If only Filene had given him fair warning and let him choose his own "date package"! Of course, if Filene had given him fair warning he wouldn't even be here. Which was undoubtedly why she hadn't bothered.

He took comfort in the fact that not too many of Seattle's other Most Eligible Bachelors looked as if they really wanted to be there — even the ones dressed for skiing, sailing, hiking, or some other form of dressed-down activity. A few of the more outgoing, public personality types — including Channel Five's Bachelor Number Twelve, who was scheduled to walk the runway in front of Franklin — were playing it up for the news hounds hanging around backstage. Not Franklin. Not on your life! None of the photographers even looked at him, and that suited him just fine.

The noise in the ballroom had been steadily accelerating. Justine Pomeroy had told the gathered bachelors last night at their rehearsal that three or four hundred women were expected for the auction. The *spectacle*, is how Franklin thought of it. Three or four hundred! Most of the ones with the money to bid, thank goodness, would be bidding for those same outgoing, public personality types who were currently hamming it up for the cameras. The five hundred dollars he'd given Cindy would be more than enough to buy a date with a low-profile player like himself. "It's more than I can afford," he'd told her, "so whatever you can do to keep the bidding low . . ."

He'd been embarrassed to hear that the Kitsch 'n' Caboodle regulars had been giving Cindy tips about the auction all week long. Were there any secrets in Pilchuck?

But their advice seemed sound. Cindy was going to start the bidding low, then drop out till she heard the auctioneer's "Going once" — at which point she'd jump back in with a large enough increase in the bid to discourage any rivals.

"How will you know the increase is enough to do the trick?"

"I'll double whatever the last increase was," she said. "Alf Mayer says that usually does it. But Franklin, I'll bet the bid goes over five hundred, and I won't have to spend any of your money at all. You're a great catch, even without that fancy ball that comes with you."

"I am?" His heart had soared. It wouldn't happen, of course — especially not following Bachelor Number Twelve, who would go for a fortune, and who made him feel practically invisible — but it felt good to hear her say he was a great catch. He'd almost asked her to expound, but that seemed a bit egotistical.

He peeked around the curtain that served as a backdrop for the runway, hoping to catch a glimpse of Cindy and Cookie before the spectacle began.

What he saw instead, front and center, was a table full of raucous women raising their wineglasses in some kind of toast. The blood drained from his face. It was Filene, with seven other giddy women whooping it up like drunks at a ball game. He recognized at least four of them as women his stepmother had thrown up to him over the last six months as "suitable matches."

Including Aubrey du Puy.

18

By the time Cindy and Cookie arrived at the hotel, the ballroom where the bachelor auction was being held was bursting at the seams — and not a man in sight except the tuxedoed waiters moving around the room with trays of drinks.

This would have been just the place to practice dancing with her pizza pan, Cindy told herself as she accepted a printed program from an usher. That Franklin! Who else would ever have thought to use a tray of glasses to teach her how to dance?

The room was set up with tables, but she saw at a glance the chairs around them were all taken. She didn't mind standing, but it wouldn't do for Cookie to be on her feet for hours. Spying a cart of folding chairs against one wall, she left Cookie in a likely spot behind the center row of tables and squeezed her way through the crowd to get to them.

My, but it was noisy! The big room sounded a bit like a barnyard, Cindy thought as she returned to Cookie with a chair beneath each arm. The braying, the gobbling, the bleating going on!

And once the auction started — well, it was a revelation, that was all. She'd never thought of high society as having such a crude, crass, indelicate side. High-society ladies, especially — if *ladies* even applied in this situation. Even as a teenager, she'd have been grounded for a month and had her mouth washed out with soap for the kind of things she was hearing. And this was the — what was that term from the chapter on idioms in her cultural literacy resource? *crème de la crème?* — the crème de la crème of society.

She was embarrassed for them. She was embarrassed for her entire gender!

But she couldn't have been one tenth as embarrassed as the poor, red-faced MEBs — Most Eligible Bachelors — skulking across the stage to a blaring rendition of "Here She Comes, Miss America." They looked more like slaves waiting for the whip than candidates for a beauty pageant. Or more to the point — considering the whistles and catcalls and swarming around the stage — like sides of beef waiting for the hook. Talk about a meat market!

Some of the MEBs had excellent credentials, too, according to the printed program. But nobody appeared to care about their credentials at the moment — at least, not the kind that could be written about. Nobody appeared even to care what their names were; the mistress of ceremonies might as well have been calling out their names to an empty room for all the attention she got. Who needed names? After all, every MEB was identified by a number pinned to his back.

"Ooh, baby, Number Seven!" someone cried. Bachelor Number Seven cringed. "Hot stuff, Number Nine!" Bachelor Number Nine looked ready to bolt and run.

Not that a certain percentage of the MEBs weren't enjoying themselves. Cindy's eyes widened, for instance, as Bachelor Number Twelve strutted and swaggered down the runway to the accompaniment of shouts and wolf whistles — as puffed up as a rooster at dawn. And she was completely bug-eyed when he reached the end of the walk, turned around, and gyrated his hips suggestively.

"Ow-OOOH," someone howled like a coyote after a kill. "Shake that booty, baby!" someone else hollered amidst the whistles and laughter that filled the room.

"There's Franklin," Cookie said, poking Cindy in the side. "Mercy! He looks like a whipped dog, slinking along up there! Too bad he had to come after that peacock."

Franklin clearly was not enjoying himself. Cindy felt instantly sorry for him, especially having to follow the "peacock." In fact, he looked as if he'd rather be flailed with a cat-o'-nine-tails than be walking down the stage in the spotlight as Bachelor Number Thirteen.

"Number Thirteen," said Cookie, clucking her tongue. "Seems to me he could've picked himself a luckier number than that! Looks about ready to bust out of his tuxedo too. Mercy! I could've let it out for him."

His trousers did seem to be straining at the seams. Cindy was surprised — Franklin was never flashy, but he always took care with his appearance. He always looked nice, in his understated, accountant sort of way.

After their group introduction the bachelors came out one by one, most of them walking the runway as fearfully as if it were a gangplank thrust out over shark-infested waters. Which in a sense, Cindy recognized, it was.

The emcee described each MEB's background and the date package that came along with him, and once he'd finished his walk back up the runway, the auctioneer took over for the bidding. A few of the bachelors postured like body builders during the auctioneer's spiel, but most of them just stood there like lumps. Miserable, terrified lumps.

Then came Bachelor Number Twelve. Some local TV celebrity, Cindy discovered from her program notes because she couldn't hear the emcee over the noise of the crowd. His date package — a workout, whirlpool, and dinner and dancing at some athletic club — didn't sound nearly as interesting as some of the others listed: a ride in a hot-air balloon with a gourmet picnic lunch aloft, for instance. Or a day trip to Victoria, British Columbia, with afternoon tea at the Empress Hotel. Or even an afternoon of sailing in Puget Sound, ending with dinner and dancing at Gig Harbor.

But Bachelor Number Twelve knew how to work a room. When he reached the end of the runway and once again "shook his booty," the crowd went wild. Where bidding for the first eleven bachelors had started under a hundred dollars and not gone over four-seventy-five, the opening bid on this guy was *four* hundred! He had women climbing up on their chairs waving fists full of money. At one table near the front, women were even hopping up on the table: "Five hundred!" "Six hundred!" "Six-fifty!"

Cindy's hand flew to her mouth as the music coming over the sound system suddenly switched to a tune she'd played for years with the high-school pep band: "The Stripper." She knew what was coming.

Bachelor Number Twelve loosened his T-shirt from his shorts, and to the accompaniment of whistles, shrieks, and catcalls, teased the audience for five minutes before ripping off the shirt and flinging it into the crowd. There must have been fifty women diving for it — scratching and clawing at each other. High-society *ladies!* Acting like — what were those creatures from *Gulliver's Travels?* Yahoos! That was it. Crude, boorish, uncivilized Yahoos!

But still, she had to admit, the electricity in the room had her own blood pumping. It was all she could do to keep from jumping up on her chair to get a better view. The whole scene was so incredibly ridiculous it was funny. Funny? It was *hilarious!*

By the time the auctioneer banged his gavel, the crowd was worked into a frenzy and Bachelor Number Twelve had garnered twelve hundred dollars for the coffers of the Greater Seattle Combined Arts Council. "Mercy!" Cookie gasped, fanning herself. Cindy was laughing so hard she had tears running down her face.

The crowd was still abuzz with commotion when Franklin stumbled out on the stage. Cindy abruptly stopped laughing. Poor Franklin! After the booty-waggler, he looked like a babe in arms. Or more to the point, like a lamb to the slaughter.

He should have refused, Franklin thought miserably. He should have donated his five hundred dollars to the Greater Seattle Combined Arts Council and been done with it. He wouldn't even be out here now if Bachelor Number Fourteen hadn't pushed him onstage.

Why, oh *why* did he have to follow Bachelor Number Twelve? For a brief moment he thought of Cindy's reaction to Aubrey du Puy and understood it from the inside out. The audience had gone wild over the TV guy. He'd brought in a fortune! Franklin knew his strengths, and showmanship wasn't one of them. Gallowglass Gala or not, he couldn't help but be anticlimactic after that kind of act — especially with Cindy starting the bid at fifty dollars, as they'd agreed. He'd be lucky to have someone outbid her at seventy-five.

He heard the mistress of ceremonies droning on. He was supposed to be doing something, but his brain had turned to mush. The spotlight felt like a giant heat lamp as he stood motionless in its glare. He could feel the sweat dripping down his face, crawling down his neck, pouring down his torso. He had put a handkerchief in his inside pocket, hadn't he? Yes — there —

He dug it out and mopped his face. It was instantly soaked. His hands shook nervously.

"Walk the runway!" someone hissed behind him.

Oh! The runway . . .

He stepped out hesitantly, crumpling the handkerchief in his hand. His legs felt stiff, wooden, and somehow disconnected from his brain. *Twenty feet,* he told himself. *Twenty feet down, turn around, twenty feet back. Five minutes, and the whole thing will be over.*

One step. Two. Three . . .

No one was even *listening,* Cindy thought indignantly as the emcee profiled Franklin and described the Gallowglass Gala. They were all still talking about Bachelor Number Twelve — who had nothing going for him, really, besides a well-known face and that booty-waggle. No one was paying the slightest attention to Franklin.

She sighed. And no wonder! He looked like a robot as he made his way down the runway — stiff-legged, stiff-backed, stiff-faced. Dull as a day in February — especially compared to the booty-waggler.

But Bachelor Number Twelve had nothing on Franklin, she thought, her indignation growing. Sure, Number Twelve knew how to entertain a crowd. But would a man so full of himself have the slightest interest in his date? Would a man like that make sure his date was enjoying herself? Would he even let a date get a word in edgewise? No, he would not. Cindy was sure of it.

A man like Franklin, on the other hand — well, as Cookie said, Franklin was thoughtful and generous. Easy to be with. Unpretentious. Smart and funny. And he might not be a Jonathan Crum — especially in that poorly fitting tuxedo — but he was certainly no slouch in the looks department.

All that, and the heir to a fortune on top of it!

Any woman would be downright *lucky* to win a date with Franklin Cameron Fitz III, she told herself. She couldn't for the life of her understand why he didn't have girls standing in *line* to go out with him!

Franklin took a deep breath as he reached the end of the runway. He flexed his shoulders to help relieve his tension, stretched his arms, flexed his fingers.

The crumpled handkerchief dropped to the floor. Drat! He automatically bent to retrieve it —

Rrr-rip!

Oh no. Please, God, not this. Not now!

But it was too late for that particular prayer. The seam at the back of his too-tight pants had given way.

Just in time for his return trip up the runway. And he couldn't count on the split tails of his tuxedo to hide it.

What to do?!

Cindy gasped. Surely Franklin wouldn't —

She clambered up on her chair to get a better view.

"What's going on?" asked Cookie.

"I think he's following Number Twelve's lead! He's taking off his jacket!"

"No!" Cookie cried. "Not Biscuit!"

"He's pulling his shirttails out of his trousers! Oh my word, Cookie!"

"Lord, help us all!" cried Cookie. "Help me up there, Cindy!"

A moment later Cookie, too, stood on her chair, leaning on Cindy for support. She gasped.

And Cindy groaned. Franklin was backing up the runway, trying unsuccessfully to twirl his tuxedo jacket on the ends of his fingers. He looked ridiculous; there was no other word for it. If he'd practiced for a million, billion *years,* he could never carry off Bachelor Number Twelve's routine.

She couldn't stand it. She couldn't stand the thought of Franklin's suffering the utter humiliation of having the opening bid drop back down to fifty dollars and increase in twenty-five dollar increments to two or three hundred at most. Not after Bachelor Number Twelve had just taken in twelve hundred.

"What am I bid?" the auctioneer cried.

She waved her arms. "Five hundred!" she bellowed.

There was a moment of shocked silence in the room — the first moment of silence in the entire event. Cindy held her breath.

"Six hundred!" someone called, and

then it was as if a dam had broken. "Seven hundred!" "Seven-fifty!"

Maybe it was leftover delirium from the Bachelor Number Twelve exhibition. Maybe it was the promised glitz of the Gallowglass Gala. Maybe it was the allure of the Fitz family fortune.

Whatever it was, Cindy decided, it couldn't have been Franklin, who was standing center stage as if his feet were nailed to the floor, his shirttails hanging out, his face scarlet and his expression miserable.

Poor Franklin.

Yet, somehow, he'd never looked so appealing.

Maybe she was wrong — maybe it *was* Franklin the bidders were responding to. It was so hard to find a man willing to be vulnerable.

For a moment Cindy regretted her opening bid. With it, she'd effectively ruled herself out as Franklin's date for the Gallowglass Gala. They could have had fun — they were getting to be such good friends. And what an opportunity it would be to see what a fancy-dress ball was all about. The Gallowglass Gala, after all, was the kind of ball she designed her evening gowns for. She really should have the experience.

But maybe Franklin could get her tickets. Why, she could take Jonathan! What a way to show him how much she could help him advance his career!

"Twelve hundred!"

Cindy didn't have to crane her neck to see the woman who'd just matched the high bid of the auction so far. She was part of that noisy table of women at center front, right at the end of the runway, and at present, the spotlight was trained on her. She was up on the table, wearing a red, Flamenco-inspired gown, posing like a Spanish dancer, one elegant arm stretched toward the ceiling. She turned to let the masses envy her beauty, her money, her invincibility. She was —

Aubrey du Puy!

Suddenly Cindy saw red — and it wasn't just Aubrey's dress. She'd already horned in on Jonathan. Now she was going to horn in on Franklin, too?

"Fifteen hundred!"

A collective gasp went up from the crowd.

Aubrey du Puy's arm fell to her side as her mouth fell open.

"Cindy!" Cookie whispered fiercely in the breathless, waiting silence. "I thought you only had five hundred dollars!"

It was Cindy's first clue that *she* was the one who'd just bid fifteen hundred dollars for a date with Franklin Cameron Fitz III.

"I have fifteen hundred dollars!" cried the auctioneer.

Aubrey, still facing the crowd, flipped her perfect hair away from her perfect face, lifted her perfect chin, and swept her perfect eyes arrogantly over the crowd. "Not even for the Gallowglass," she said, her voice carrying throughout the room. "*No man is worth fifteen hundred dollars.*"

"Going once, going twice, SOLD!" the auctioneer cried, his voice almost lost in the raucous hilarity Aubrey's comment seemed to have inspired.

Cindy didn't think it the least bit funny. Franklin was worth every bit of fifteen hundred dollars.

Even if it *was* his own money.

Franklin didn't think it was the least bit funny either. He had never been so humiliated in all his life — even *without* the split in his pants, which, with any luck, *maybe* no one had noticed. He supposed he should be grateful to Aubrey for drawing attention away from him with her little table-top drama. Someone had actually swung the spotlight away from him and onto

Aubrey long enough for him to escape behind the curtain as the auctioneer crashed his gavel to the podium.

But somehow Franklin couldn't bring himself to gratitude. Aubrey couldn't have made it more clear the Gallowglass Gala was the only reason she'd made her bid for him. He might as well have been a ham hock, with a ticket to the ball attached.

Well, Filene had made sure he wouldn't embarrass her by showing up at the Gallowglass with the likes of Nonna Pippa again. But at least he'd avoided a date with Aubrey — by the skin of his teeth.

There was no guarantee the woman who was paying fifteen hundred dollars for him was any better than Aubrey, of course. He sighed. Whoever would have guessed someone would start the bidding at five hundred? Cindy hadn't even had a chance. And Cindy was the only woman he wanted to be with — at the Gallowglass or anywhere.

But at least she was here, right now, at the auction. If nothing else, he could be with her for the rest of the evening.

Maybe they'd just blow this joint. Maybe he'd take Cindy and Cookie somewhere and squander that five hundred dollars Cindy still had in her handbag on some fun.

"He's going to kill me," Cindy groaned. "I can't believe I spent a thousand dollars more than he gave me!"

Cookie had saved the day by putting the full amount of Cindy's winning bid on her own credit card, pocketing the five hundred in cash Franklin had given Cindy. "Biscuit's good for the rest of it," she said. "And of course he's not going to kill you. Far from it, is my speculation."

Franklin, looking more himself already, found them a few minutes later. He'd changed from his tuxedo back into the casual slacks and shirt he'd been wearing earlier.

"What were you thinking, Biscuit?" Cookie scolded him. "Taking off your jacket and pulling out your shirttails? Thank the Lord you didn't go on the way that peacock did. Mercy!"

"Bachelor Number Twelve," Cindy clarified.

Franklin's face lit crimson. He didn't say a word until he'd hustled Cookie and Cindy out of the ballroom and sat them down in a private corner of the lobby, where he told them the story.

Cindy probably shouldn't have laughed, but she couldn't help herself. She and

Cookie, in fact, both laughed until the tears streamed down their faces. "If you could have *seen* you, Franklin!" Cindy said when she finally calmed down.

"I'm quite happy I couldn't, thank you."

He was in remarkably good spirits himself, Cindy thought. Considering. She hated to ruin the mood by confessing to her crazy, impulsive, expensive action, but she figured the sooner she got it over with, the better all around.

Franklin stared at her when she'd finished her confession. "You mean — *you're* the one who bid the fifteen hundred?"

She looked at her lap, took a deep breath, and met his eyes again. "Strictly speaking — it was *your* fifteen hundred," she said.

"Cindy!" He leapt from his chair and swept her up in his arms. Then, to her astonishment, he lifted her clean off the floor and swung her around, laughing and carrying on as if he'd just won the Publishers Clearing House ten-million-dollar prize. And when he set her down again . . .

He kissed her full on the mouth.

It was a good thing he still had hold of her after that kiss, too, Cindy told herself later. Otherwise, she'd have been flat on the floor from the shock of it.

"Then you're not mad at me?" she asked him once she'd gathered her wits about her.

"Mad at you? After you've saved my life once again?"

She looked at him blankly.

"Some things are worse than death, Cindy. Spending an entire evening with a woman as shallow, conceited, and downright mean as Aubrey du Puy is one of them. As I said — you've saved my life again."

Shallow, conceited, and downright mean. From what Cindy had seen of the other woman, she couldn't disagree. Aubrey was beautiful and smart and sophisticated, but Franklin saw right through her. Franklin knew there were more important things.

So —

Why didn't Jonathan?

19

Cindy wasn't thinking about Jonathan when she woke the next morning. She was thinking about Franklin.

Franklin and that utterly astonishing kiss. So unexpected. So sweet. And so *confusing.*

Of course he hadn't meant anything by it. It was just a spontaneous, joyful, probably even *accidental* kiss . . .

But then she heard Cookie's words in her mind: *Don't you worry; I don't believe a word of it when he says you and he are "just friends."*

It really was too confusing. She was simply going to put it out of her mind.

Cindy and Cookie joined Franklin in his apartment over the carriage house for a simple and delicious breakfast — bacon, eggs, and hash browns to go along with Cookie's contribution: her famous home-made melt-in-your-mouth buttermilk biscuits, soaked with butter and drizzled with honey. The biscuits she'd named "Biscuit" after.

Cindy liked Franklin's home. It was

small, but the open floor plan and plentiful light from the windows overlooking the lake, the city skyline, and the Cascade Mountains beyond gave it an open feeling. With its white-painted walls, hardwood floors, and mission-style furniture, it was tidy, comfortable, and unpretentious — like Franklin, she thought.

She offered to help him with the breakfast dishes, but he insisted she and Cookie have another cup of tea while he cleaned up. It was quite delightful, actually, watching him at work in the kitchen while she sipped at her tea. Jonathan didn't cook or do dishes, either one.

Franklin looked over and caught her staring. "What?" he said.

She shook her head. "Nothing. I'm glad to be here, is all. I've been so crazy-busy the last three weeks I've hardly had time to breathe. This is a perfect break."

"Good."

He did have a nice smile, she thought. Open and genuine. And nice lips too. Which reminded her once again of the way he'd kissed her.

"You two keep makin' puppy eyes at each other and we're goin' to be late for church," Cookie said, her voice smug.

Cindy flushed and dropped her eyes to

her teacup. At least Cookie hadn't noticed she was staring at Franklin's lips and not his eyes.

The Church of the Blessed Redeemer, which Franklin said he'd attended since childhood with Cookie and Clement, was a very different sort of church from the Pilchuck Church of Saints and Sinners, which tended toward the casual and unstructured. The dark stone walls and woodwork, the high, vaulted ceilings, and the beautiful stained-glass windows seemed to whisper, "Be still."

Trust me, she seemed to hear God say. *I am here for you.*

Yes, Lord, she answered the stillness, feeling it seep into her soul. *I know you are . . .*

She was glad she hadn't come alone. The service was foreign to her, and she'd have been lost without Franklin sitting by her side to guide her through it. Everybody else seemed to know when to get up and when to sit down and when to say *amen* without being told.

"God Exalts the Humble," was the sermon title listed in the bulletin. But before the sermon, the theme revealed itself in a series of Scriptures read aloud: an Old

Testament lesson, a reading from the Psalms, a reading from the Epistles, and a Gospel lesson. Cindy liked the approach. It felt as if God were speaking directly to her, no middle-man needed.

First came the story of Samuel's anointing a young shepherd boy as the next king of Israel. Then they all read together that most familiar of all psalms: "The Lord is my shepherd; I shall not want. . . ." Next came Paul's charge to the Philippians: "Let this mind be in you, which was also in Christ Jesus. . . ." And finally they stood to hear the familiar story of Jesus' washing the feet of his disciples.

It was the words from Philippians that lingered in Cindy's mind as she stood. The Son of God, she thought — struck as always by the wonder of it — making himself of no reputation! Taking the form of a servant, humbling himself, becoming obedient even to death: "Wherefore God also hath highly exalted him, and given him a name which is above every name. . . ."

After the readings the reverend, a white-haired gentleman in clerical robes her own Pastor Bob wouldn't have worn on a bet — if he were a betting man, which of course he wasn't — delivered a thought-provoking homily on obedience, service, and grace.

"Your message was made for the waitresses of the world," Cindy told him as she shook his hand on the way out the door. "Like me."

"Or for those of us who might learn a thing or two from the waitresses of the world," he returned, his blue eyes twinkling.

"Either way — thanks for the encouragement."

"And thank you for *yours.*"

They stopped by the market on the way back to the Fitz estate and picked up ingredients for a shrimp-and-avocado salad. "My turn," Cindy insisted when they got back to Cookie's with the goods. "Why don't you two get out the Scrabble board while I fix lunch?"

The truth was, she wanted some time alone to think over the morning sermon. Now it was that Old Testament story that kept playing in her mind — God sending Samuel to the house of Jesse with instructions to anoint the new king. "I'll tell you which one when you get there," he'd told the old priest.

Samuel must have been pretty sure he wouldn't have to look any farther than Jesse's eldest son, Eliab. He was tall and good looking. Probably bright and ambitious and self-assured too. The very image of a prince!

But Samuel was wrong. Cindy imagined the scene:

"Forget about it," God says to Samuel. "Eliab's not the one."

"But God — he's perfect!"

"Handsome is as handsome does, Sammy. You've got to understand — I don't see the same things people see. People look on the outside, but I look on the heart."

So the old priest says to Jesse, "I'd like to meet your other sons."

And Jesse introduces seven sons to Samuel, and God keeps saying, "No. He's not the one."

"There's no one else?" the priest asks Jesse.

"Just David, my youngest. He's out tending the sheep."

So David is sent for. And finally God says, "Yes! He's the one."

God had known what he was doing too. He always did.

What are you trying to tell me, Lord? Cindy asked silently as she stared out the kitchen window, half an avocado in one hand and a paring knife in the other.

The words came to mind once again:

301

You've got to understand — I don't see the same things people see. People look on the outside, but I look on the heart.

Cindy closed her eyes for a brief moment. *Teach me to see what you see, Lord,* she prayed.

Oh, but I am, God seemed to assure her in the secret places of her soul. *I am.*

"As I said, I thought we'd have our final dancing lesson in the ballroom," Franklin told Cindy after lunch. "After a tour of the mansion, if you're interested."

"Interested? You'd better believe it!" she said. And then: "So there's really a ballroom in the house!"

He loved her sense of wonderment and the way her cinnamon-colored eyes widened when she was in discovery mode. "Where else would the Gallowglass Gala be held?" he teased.

He didn't understand at first why Cindy's interest in the house and its furnishings didn't bother him the way Aubrey's had, but he figured it out before long. The thing was, Cindy didn't care that the marble around the front entrance was Italian or that the linen on the walls in the breakfast room was Belgian or that the lace curtains in Filene's bedroom suite were

Irish. She liked the coolness of the marble and the texture of the linen and the way the light filtered through the lace.

She didn't care that the rug in the drawing room was an antique hand-knotted Aubusson or that the porcelains on the mantel were Sevres and Meissen. She cared that they were exquisitely and lovingly made.

She didn't care that the massive crystal-and-gold-leaf chandelier hanging over the grand staircase cost more than some people's houses cost. She wanted to know how the chandelier was cleaned . . . and whether Franklin had slid down the banister of the staircase as a boy.

"Not after my stepmother moved in, I didn't," he said. "And I only used the ballroom for a skating rink once."

"A ballroom! I can hardly imagine it!" Cindy marveled again, hands clasped to her chest, when he ended their tour on the lower floor. "In your *house!*"

"You can see it would make a fabulous skating rink," he said, pointing out the quarter-sawn oak floorboards curved to follow the walls of the oval room. The slope of the building site put the ballroom at ground level on this side of the mansion. Four large, curved windows overlooked the same incredible view as the windows on the main floor upstairs. "Filene was probably worried about you going through one of those windows and hurting yourself," said Cindy.

Filene would have been more angry about the broken window than worried about the kid who'd gone through it, Franklin could have said. But he kept the thought to himself. Filene would give Cindy plenty of reasons not to like her without his contributing past history. And Cindy, bless her Pollyanna heart, would undoubtedly give Filene the benefit of the doubt anyhow.

"I thought we'd start with some traditional waltzes," he said, setting his boom box against the wall and plugging it in. "And maybe a fox trot or two — just to warm us up for the swing and the cha-cha."

"You must have read your Stuff of the Day this morning," Cindy said, referring in their personal shorthand to their cultural-literacy dictionaries. She looked over his shoulder as he pulled a handful of CDs from their canvas storage bag. "So have you got anything from the Waltz King?"

"You mean Johann Strauss the Younger, of course," Franklin said. They were into the "Fine Arts" chapter by now. "And I believe I do . . ." He shuffled through the disks and held one up. "This one has both 'On the Beautiful Blue Danube' and 'Tales from the Vienna Woods.' I've got some good tunes from the King of Swing for later too."

"Benny Goodman," Cindy supplied without a moment's hesitation. She really was taking this self-improvement thing seriously, Franklin thought admiringly. And for a creep like Jonathan Crum! *Please God,* he prayed for the umpteenth time. *Don't let him break her heart . . .*

He tried not to be too familiar with her on the dance floor. He'd surprised himself with that spontaneous kiss yesterday — and scared himself a little, too, the truth be told. His feelings were coming so close to the surface, he wasn't sure he could hide them much longer. And here was Cindy, two days away from her fateful date with Jonathan. Would the Crumb finally recognize himself for a fool and come back to Cindy begging? Franklin didn't see how he could help it.

He drove her home in the late afternoon with the top down on the Jeep and the radio cranked up — oldies from the sixties and seventies this time. Sometimes they sang along, sometimes they just listened, and sometimes one or the other turned the volume down to make a comment or ask a question. They were cresting the last hill before the Pilchuck exit when Cindy reached for the volume control right in the middle of "You've Lost That Lovin' Feeling," to which, just a moment before, she'd been singing at the top of her lungs.

"Franklin," she said, her voice serious.

He gave her a quick glance and saw that her expression was as somber as her voice. A lump of anxiety formed in his throat. "What is it?" he managed around it.

"Do you like me?"

He choked. And wheezed. And started in on a coughing fit. She was so incredibly unexpected!

"Oh dear! Franklin!"

He almost missed the only Pilchuck exit from the freeway. At the last possible minute he swerved the Jeep onto the off-ramp, throwing them both against their seat belts.

She was going to be the death of him yet.

He pulled the car over to the side of the road, right in front of the *Welcome to Pilchuck* sign, and held his hand to his heart, which was pounding like a jackhammer. Whether it was from Cindy's question or from flying around the Jeep, he wasn't sure.

"City Motto: We Like It Like This," he muttered aloud, reading from the sign. Then he leaned his head back against the seat and closed his eyes.

"Franklin?" Cindy asked meekly. He was quite sure it was meekly. Which was the only reason he had the nerve to turn his head and open his eyes.

"I mean, just the way I am," she said, her expression earnest.

Had he ever seen a more beautifully sincere face in all the world? A more sincerely beautiful face?

Did he *like* her, she wanted to know! Just the way she *was!*

He took a deep breath to steady his nerves. "Of course I do, Cindy."

"I was thinking of dyeing my hair for my birthday," she said, chewing on a thumbnail.

"Dye —"

"And getting it straightened," she added.

"What color?" he managed, still trying to grapple with her first comment.

"Black."

"Black! Cindy! What in the world are you thinking?"

"Blond and curly isn't very sophisticated," she said, pulling at a long, honey-colored strand and wrapping it around her finger.

"Blond and curly is beautiful. Blond and curly is *you*."

"*I'm* not very sophisticated," she said, sighing. "I'm too tall and too thin and too tanned —"

" 'You can never be too rich or too thin,' " Franklin quoted from somewhere. Probably his administrative assistant, Alice.

"Too — *bony* then. I could never get away with a dress like Aubrey du Puy was wearing last night."

Ah. So this was about Aubrey. Raven-haired, curvaceous, scarlet-clad Aubrey. And, by extension, Jonathan Crum.

"Cindy, why in the world would you want to pattern yourself after a shallow, conceited, mean-spirited woman like Aubrey du Puy?"

"I don't want to be shallow, conceited, and mean. But I wouldn't mind *looking* like Aubrey. Having a little of her — *flair*."

He didn't know what got into him. He didn't know where he found the nerve — except that he couldn't bear to see her beating up on herself anymore. Just because the Crumb had "lost that lovin' feeling."

He reached across the cab and took

Cindy's chin in his hand, and he looked her straight in the eyes. "Cindy Reilly, you are the loveliest woman, inside and out, I have ever known. Do you hear me? If I had the *power*, I wouldn't change a hair on your head."

"You wouldn't?" Her voice was suddenly husky, her eyes wide.

"I wouldn't. And if I had the *chance*, what I *would* do is find a hundred ways to tell you every day how much I adored you."

Cindy gulped. "You would?" They stared at each other. Her eyes flickered down to his mouth. Franklin groaned.

And then he leaned across the seat and kissed her. On purpose this time.

She liked it too. He knew because she kissed him back.

Cindy didn't say a word all the way through town. But then, neither did Franklin. He looked the way she felt. Dazed.

And scared.

He didn't say a word as he brought the Jeep to a stop and parked it in front of her house, or when he helped her down from her seat, or when he reached into the back for her overnight bag.

"So . . . ," she finally said when they

reached the front porch of the little Victorian home.

"So," he agreed.

"Did you want to come in?"

"Oh, I don't think so. I'd better get home . . ."

Another awkward silence.

"I'll see you around then," Cindy said.

"Yeah. I'll call you."

He was down the walk and in the Jeep like a bullet out of a pistol.

The front door burst open.

"Cindy!" Robin cried.

"We heard the news!" Rosie crowed.

Cindy stared at them, uncomprehending. "What news?"

"He kissed you!" they chorused together.

Her mouth fell open.

"Narcissa was coming home from a beauty makeover in Bellingrath," Rosie explained.

"Suzie and Priscilla were on their way back from a day at Heron Bay with Gordie and Gregor," said Robin. "Suzie wants you to call, by the way. As *soon* as you can."

"True Marie —"

"Enough, already!" Cindy interrupted Rosie. Her face was burning.

No *wonder* Jonathan didn't want to live in Pilchuck!

20

"I can't say as I understand why you're feelin' guilty," Biddy said as she filled the last of the sugar caddies the following morning. "Jonathan has no claim on you."

"Well, of course he does! I've been loyal to him for eight years, Biddy!"

"But he hasn't been loyal to you," Biddy said reasonably. "You deserve better than Jonathan Crum, Cindy. You deserve someone who treats you like the princess you are. Someone who adores you." She picked up the tray full of caddies, carried it with both hands across the kitchen, and shouldered open the swinging door leading into the dining room.

"Someone," she said over her shoulder, "like Franklin Fitz." The door swung closed behind her.

"Wait!" Cindy dashed after Biddy, almost upsetting her tray of salt-and-pepper shakers in her hurry. "Just because Franklin *kissed* me doesn't mean he *adores* me, Biddy," she argued.

The whole idea made her nervous. The *word* made her nervous. It was the very word Franklin had used yesterday. Maybe the Jeep was bugged.

She shook her head crossly. Of course the Jeep wasn't bugged! She'd been very foolish to let Franklin kiss her in such a public place, that was all.

She shook her head again, frowning fiercely. What was she thinking? The public place wasn't the problem. She'd been very foolish to let Franklin kiss her, *period*.

"He adores you," Biddy said. "It's plain as the nose on his face."

By the time her shift was over, it was plain as the nose on *Cindy's* face that word about the Kiss had got around town in record time. No one seemed in the least surprised about it either. Moreover, everyone was as pleased as pigs in mud.

The Kitsch 'n' Caboodle crowd all agreed with Biddy's assessment of the situation and made no bones about voicing their joint opinion to Cindy: Franklin Cameron Fitz III was crazy about her.

"That young man is smitten, Cindy," Olga Pfefferkuchen said before she even sat down in her regular spot at her regular table. *"Smitten."*

Ina Rafferty agreed. "He's certainly taken a liking to you, Cindy. And well he should." She patted Cindy's hand affectionately.

"He *treasures* you, Cindy. You can see it in his eyes," said Suzie Wyatt Hunt, who dropped by during her lunch break from KinderKottage because Cindy hadn't returned her call the night before.

It wasn't just the women putting in their two-cents' worth either.

"The boy's been pinin' after you since the day you saved him from the chicken bone," Alf Mayer declared.

"Dotes on you, he does," Jonas Muncey agreed.

Harley Burns, after complaining Cindy had let his coffee cup run dry, allowed she did have some excuse for being "feather-brained" this morning: "Heard about that kiss by the side of the road last night. Heard you weren't walkin' straight afterward either . . ."

No one even brought up Jonathan. It was almost as if he'd never existed. As if she and Jonathan as a couple had never existed. Even though everyone in town knew about Cindy's self-improvement campaign — and knew it was for Jonathan's sake.

In fact, everyone was talking as if she and *Franklin* were an item. After one kiss! One kiss that they *knew* about anyhow. One

313

unplanned, spur-of-the-moment, road-
side kiss that didn't mean anything.

Didn't mean anything? a little voice nig-
gled. She ignored it.

She had an idea why Franklin was "in"
and Jonathan was "out" with the Kitsch 'n'
Caboodle regulars, of course. Pilchuck
didn't *know* Jonathan anymore. And since
the chicken-bone-choking incident, Pilchuck had adopted Franklin as a native
son.

Jonathan, after all, hadn't been around
much in the last six years. And he'd lived
in Pilchuck only three years in the first
place before trotting off to college in Seattle. His parents had since moved back to
California. His grandfather still lived outside town, but his grandfather tended to be
a bit standoffish.

Sure, Jonathan had made a name for
himself in high school. But that was then,
and this was now. Jonathan no longer
claimed Pilchuck, so Pilchuck no longer
claimed him.

Franklin Fitz, on the other hand, was
practically a town celebrity. Ever since his
picture had first appeared on the front
page of the *Pilchuck Post,* his name kept
popping up in this column or that news
item in the local paper — linked with

Cindy's name, more often than not. And whatever was in the *Post* was on the tip of everyone's tongue.

Cindy Reilly, local waitress and aspiring apparel designer, made her first major sale last week, thanks to a referral from Franklin Cameron Fitz III of the Strawbridge & Fitz department-store chain, whose life Miss Reilly recently saved. . . .

Tillicum County's own world-class pianist, Miniver Macready, and her nephew, Franklin Cameron Fitz III of Seattle, were visitors at the Pilchuck Church of Saints and Sinners last Sunday, where they shared a pew with Mrs. Joseph Reilly and her daughter Cindy. . . .

Strawbridge & Fitz department-store heir Franklin Cameron Fitz III bought a large bottle of Extra Strength Tums after dinner with the Reilly family last week, local pharmacy clerk Kimberlee Collins revealed. . . .

Carl Peabody had received some irate letters to the editor for that particular item. "Who cares?" "Your implication that Cait and Cindy Reilly are lousy cooks is an affront and totally untrue." "So the famous get tummyaches too. Big deal!"

Carl had printed the letters on the editorial page, but he hadn't promised to back off. The truth was, even if a few people objected, Franklin Cameron Fitz III sold newspapers. Poor Franklin, Cindy thought. Mini Mac would have been better off sending the twins to the pharmacy that day. What was so personal about a bottle of Tums anyhow?

Lon Shoemaker called just as Cindy's shift ended at Kitsch 'n' Caboodle and told her he'd modified a jigsaw over the weekend. Did she want to come over to the furniture factory with some fabric samples and try it out?

Cindy left Ruby Creek Woodworks several hours later in fine spirits. Lon hadn't mentioned Franklin once, bless him, and with a couple of minor adjustments, the jigsaw he'd come up with was going to work perfectly for cutting out her pattern pieces. She was going to get the Strawbridge & Fitz designer T-shirt order finished on time yet.

As for Franklin . . .

To be honest, she didn't know what to

think. She liked him, of course. And the Kiss . . .

Well, the Kiss had been quite wonderful. She probably wouldn't be feeling so guilty — so unfaithful to Jonathan, that is — if she hadn't enjoyed kissing Franklin so much.

But Jonathan was part and parcel of her history. More important, Jonathan was her future. Her fairy tale. Her dream.

She couldn't give up on the dream. Who would she be without it? And she couldn't let Franklin get in the way of it, either, no matter how much she liked him or how well he kissed. No matter how sweet and sensitive he was. No matter how much she wanted to call and tell him about Lon Shoemaker's innovation, and hear the delight in his voice, and bask in his encouragement.

So instead she called Jonathan when she got home, her throat tight with anxiety as she listened to the rings on his end of the line. She hadn't talked to him in more than three weeks, not even over the phone.

When he didn't answer, she was more relieved than sorry. She left a message on his machine that she'd see him at seven the following evening. After a long and awkward pause she added, hoping she didn't sound too desperate, "I really need to see you, Jonathan. I mean *really* . . ."

She spent the entire day on Tuesday primping, and by the time seven o'clock rolled around, she felt truly transformed. Truly glamorous. "Like a forties movie star!" the twins told her.

True Marie at the Belle o' the Ball Beauty Salon had copied a picture from one of Biddy's old movie magazines, sweeping Cindy's hair away from her face and off her neck in a thick roll that circled her head like a golden halo. And Narcissa's Personalized Carrie Mae Cosmetics Beauty Makeover was amazing. It didn't make sense, but by the time she'd worked her magic, Cindy looked exactly like herself — only ten times prettier.

With visions of Aubrey still in her head, Cindy had toyed with the idea of borrowing a scarlet dress from Nadine's dress shop, but scarlet really wasn't her color. Instead, she chose a robin's-egg blue silk slip dress with a matching jacket that her mother had made her for Suzie's wedding.

"Cindy Reilly," her mother said proudly as Cindy did a slow turn in the middle of the living room a few minutes before seven, "you look sensational. You *are* sensational. I hope you know that even without your self-improvement program, you had more class in your little *toe* than most people ever even dream of having. I hope you know how truly wonderful you are."

All well and good, Cindy thought, coming from her mother. The real question was, would Jonathan think she was sensational?

Do you care?

Of course she cared! She cared so much, she felt sick to her stomach.

But not as sick as she did a few minutes later. When promptly at seven, when the doorbell should have been ringing, the phone rang instead.

Franklin took Cookie to dinner at Fortunato's on Tuesday night to distract himself. The choice was unfortuitous, as Fortunato's reminded him not only of Cindy, but of the Crumb. Nonna Pippa didn't help matters out when she plopped down next to him during the appetizer and started grilling him about his *"innamorata."* She seemed to have forgotten Cindy wasn't his girlfriend.

The light on his answering machine was blinking when he let himself into his apartment shortly before ten. The caller had hung up without leaving a message, but the number displayed on his Caller ID box made his heart speed up.

Cindy. And she'd called around eight — awfully early to be back from dinner and dancing.

He tapped his fingers nervously against the table while he waited for her to pick up the phone.

But for the second time today, it was Cait Reilly who answered. When he'd called earlier to wish Cindy a happy birthday, she'd been gone to the beauty salon.

Now, however, Cait sounded distressed. "Cindy's gone to bed, Franklin."

"I'm returning her call," he said. "From earlier this evening."

"She called you?" Now Cait's voice sounded surprised.

"She didn't leave a message," he said. "My machine recorded the number. Is — is everything all right?"

Cait was silent for a moment. "Let me go see if she's awake," she finally said. "And if she wants to talk."

He waited for what seemed an eternity before Cindy's voice came over the line.

"It's been all for nothing, Franklin," she said without preamble. Her voice was so thick with sadness it hardly sounded like her. "My self-improvement campaign. My makeover."

He ached at the despair in her voice. "Jonathan's a fool, Cindy. If he can't see —"

"He didn't even give himself a chance to see," Cindy interrupted.

"What do you mean?"

"He didn't come."

"He stood you up?!"

"He called from Seattle at seven — when he was supposed to be at my door."

Franklin clenched his fist. The Creep! The Crumb! "And said what?" he asked, trying to keep his voice even.

"In so many words — he wasn't coming, he was never coming, and it wouldn't do me any good to think he was."

Franklin wanted to hit something. Or more specifically, some*one*.

"He said it was better not to drag out the inevitable. He said it was time for me to move on."

"The man's a fool," Franklin said again. And then, helplessly: "How could anyone ever let you go?"

"I looked beautiful," she sniffled.

"I'm sure you did."

"I could have knocked his socks off if he'd let me."

"Yes, you could."

"I could have hit him like a ton of bricks."

Franklin particularly liked that image. "I wish you had."

"I just can't believe he's *gone,* Franklin."

There wasn't much more to their conversation. By that time Cindy was crying as if there would be no tomorrow. Undoubtedly, that's how she felt.

"I'm here for you, Cindy," he said tenderly.

"Thank you," she said through her sobs. "I know —" She hiccuped. "I know you are."

Biddy tried to send Cindy back home the next morning when she showed up at the Kitsch 'n' Caboodle looking like "a cauliflower gone bad," as her employer so elegantly put it.

Biddy already knew about Jonathan's standing her up, of course. It was, after all, ten hours after the fact. If the news about Franklin's kiss had spread through Pilchuck as fast as it did, Cindy supposed she should have expected the news about Jonathan would move just as fast. She didn't know the origin of the news flash, and frankly, she didn't care to know.

When she insisted she was fine, she wasn't going to let a little thing like a broken heart get in the way of doing her job, Biddy insisted she at least lie down on her back on the break table with slices of cucumber over her eyelids till the doors opened for breakfast.

"I've got just one thing to say to you, Cindy Reilly," she said sternly as she removed the cucumbers and dabbed at the mascara she'd inadvertently smeared all over Cindy's face. "And that is that you never were in love with Jonathan Crum."

Cindy's cucumber-cooled eyelids flew open. "How can you say that?!"

"Because it's true, that's how. You were only in love with who you *thought* Jonathan was. And who you *thought* he was, was a figment of your imagination."

"Jonathan — a figment of my imagination!"

"That's what I said." She stood with her hands on her hips, fixing an unflinching eye on Cindy. "Seein' the good in people's not at *all* the same as seein' things that aren't there. Which in my opinion is what you've been doin' with Jonathan Crum for years."

"But —"

Biddy held up her hand. "He's not who

you've made him out to be in your head, Cindy. No matter how much you want him to be. He's not your fairy-tale prince, and you sure as *shootin'* aren't his idea of a fairy-tale princess — foolish man that he is."

Cindy was shocked at Biddy's take on the matter. "You've never said such things about Jonathan before," she protested.

"I'm sayin' as much about you as I am about Jonathan, Cindy."

Cindy was used to blunt from Biddy, but not this blunt. And she couldn't hide her hurt any more than she'd been able to hide her puffy eyes.

Biddy was immediately contrite. "I'm sorry, Cindy. Maybe it's not what you're needin' to hear just now. And I'm not sayin' you shouldn't grieve. Just know what it is you're grievin'."

Cindy stared at her, uncomprehending.

Biddy clarified: "Are you grievin' Jonathan? Or your dream?" When Cindy didn't respond, Biddy added with a sigh, "I just want you to be over him, Cindy. So's you can move on."

"That's what Jonathan said," Cindy sniffled.

"Believe him," said Biddy.

21

Cindy discovered as the day wore on that the Kitsch 'n' Caboodle crowd hadn't forgotten about Jonathan after all. They'd just been holding back their opinions.

Unless they were trying to make her feel better by saying they hadn't much liked Jonathan all along. If that was their intent, it wasn't working. Every comment made her feel more and more like a chump. A dupe. A fool.

"I seen it comin' a mile away."

"Always said Jonathan Crum was too handsome for his own good."

"Puffed up like a rooster thinkin' his crow is what brings up the sun in the mornin'."

"Selfish as old King Midas, he is."

"You're better off without the scoundrel, is my opinion, Cindy."

"He don't deserve you, honey."

"All show and no substance."

"What kind of man stands a gal up on her birthday?"

"He really *don't* deserve you, honey."

"You're not feelin' guilty about

smoochin' with Franklin Fitz *now,* are you?" Biddy asked her at the end of her shift. In private, thank goodness.

Cindy chewed on her lower lip for a moment before answering. "I can't help wondering if Jonathan sensed something was going on between me and Franklin," she finally said. "And if that's the reason he started to pull away . . ."

Biddy rolled her eyes in disbelief. "How long has it been since Jonathan's been to Pilchuck, Cindy?" she demanded.

"I don't know. Easter, I guess."

"And when was it Franklin choked on the chicken bone?"

"The week after Suzie and Harrison got back from their honeymoon . . . sometime in mid-June, I think."

"Ha!" Biddy crowed triumphantly. "You hadn't even met Franklin Fitz when Jonathan started to pull away! Oh, and by the way —"

Cindy held her breath. What now?

"I'm happy to hear you finally admittin' what you haven't so far — that something's goin' on between you and Franklin."

"I didn't mean *that* way," Cindy said, flustered.

Biddy raised her eyebrows. "Oh?"

"Franklin's my *mentor,* Biddy. A certain

. . . *intellectual* bond has grown up between us. That's what I meant."

"Sounds to me like that lip-lock everyone's talkin' about was intellectual, all right," Biddy said.

After everything else, Biddy's teasing was just too much for Cindy. "Good grief! What is all the excitement about one measly *kiss?*"

Biddy raised an eyebrow. "Testy."

But her point was made. The fact was, Franklin *wasn't* just her mentor.

Maybe the twins were right about what happened when someone saved another person's life — that it created a kind of bond between them, a knitting together of spirits that could never be unknit. She felt responsible for Franklin, in a way. Why else would she have helped him out at the Greater Seattle Combined Arts Council Most Eligible Bachelor Auction?

That and the fact that she genuinely liked him. What wasn't to like? He was such a nice man, and he was so good to her! The way he treated her was more than gratitude too. It was more than the fact that he was simply a very nice guy. It was more, even, than the fact that he was obviously attracted to her . . .

She'd always said that she and Jonathan

were kindred spirits. But in some ways —
in the ways that really counted most — she
felt as if she knew Franklin better than
she'd ever known Jonathan.

Which was ridiculous, of course, when she'd
met Franklin only a month ago and Jonathan
had been her boyfriend for eight years. You
couldn't know someone in one short month
the way she felt she knew Franklin.

"We do have more in common than I expected," she conceded to Biddy. "And we
do enjoy each other's company."

"Of course you do."

She thought about Franklin's telling her
she was the loveliest woman he'd ever
known, inside and out. She thought about
his saying that if he had the chance, he'd
find a hundred ways a day to tell her how
much he adored her. She thought about
Franklin's kiss by the side of the road. Lost
herself in the memory for a moment. And
the truth be told . . .

"Measly" was *not* the right description
for that kiss.

"Your face is red," said Biddy, unneces-
sarily. "And I'll bet you're not thinkin'
about Jonathan Crum."

Franklin had never in his life been in
such a quandary.

On the one hand, there was nothing he wanted more at the moment than to be in Pilchuck, holding Cindy in his arms. Exorcising the Crumb from her brain. Letting her know she was adored.

Something told him she might let him too. Something about the way she'd kissed him Sunday night. The way she'd called him for comfort on her birthday.

On the other hand . . .

He was pretty sure declaring himself to Cindy at the moment was a very bad idea.

If he'd been worried before about being her rebound fling, he was ten times more worried now. She was hurting. She needed comfort. She knew he liked her. It would be too easy.

Not that Cindy would purposely mislead him. But in her current state, she might very well delude herself. She might persuade herself she cared for Franklin in a special way. She might even convince herself she was in love with him — for a while.

The thing was — a while wasn't long enough. He couldn't bear the idea of just being her rebound fling or her transitional relationship. He knew now, beyond the shadow of a doubt, that he wanted to be The One.

But he also wanted to be in her life in the meantime.

In the end, he gave the whole ball of wax over to the Almighty. What Franklin couldn't do, the Lord of heaven could — if he so chose. And Franklin prayed fervently that he would so choose.

He called her Wednesday as soon as he thought she'd be home from work, but once again she wasn't in.

"I don't know if she got a chance to tell you," Cait said, "but one of her customers at the diner came up with a way to cut out her pattern pieces in bulk."

"The guy with the jigsaw?"

"Right. Lon Shoemaker. Anyhow, she's over there this afternoon to do the Larges. Figured it was safest to start out with the Larges so if anything went wrong she could trim them down to Mediums or Smalls."

As she had told him once herself, Cindy wasn't stupid. "So she's doing okay, Mrs. Reilly?"

"Better than she was last night. I'm glad she has the T-shirt project to keep her occupied. You know . . ."

"What?" Franklin prompted.

"She's so enjoyed the time you've spent together, Franklin. The dancing lessons and the dining out and the conversations about your readings. Church on Sunday mornings and Sunday dinners here. I wonder if it might not help her if you kept it up for a while."

Franklin's heart leapt. That was it. He'd stay in her life as her friend and her personal mentor while she got over Jonathan. That way he'd be around to catch her when she bounced off her rebound fling and fell out of her transitional romance. It wouldn't be easy, being with her but *not* being with her. Still, if that's what it took, if she needed the time —

He'd be as regular as the mail, he thought, warming to the idea. He'd call her every evening to review the Stuff of the Day, just the way he'd been doing the last three weeks. He'd spend every Saturday night on dancing lessons — help her polish her waltz, her fox trot, her West Coast swing, perhaps even teach her to rumba.

"You don't think she'd mind?" he asked cautiously, not wanting to get too excited for nothing.

"I think she'd welcome the diversion."

He'd go to church with her every Sunday and have dinner with her family and watch whatever Great Book video she'd borrowed from the library. If it meant more time with Cindy, he told himself, he'd even be willing to try out a sousaphone-flute duet!

"There is the Gallowglass Gala the end of next month. If she still wants to go."

"It would be so good for her, Franklin! And I've been thinking. If she wore a gown of her own design —"

"Yes! The Gallowglass could be the break she's been waiting for!" Franklin interrupted, suddenly excited. "You couldn't buy the kind of exposure the ball would give Glad Raggs!"

"You're a good man, Franklin. I'll have her call you as soon as she gets in."

Cindy was going to have her chance to prove herself to Jonathan after all, he told himself as he hung up the phone. Even if it was only in the "Scuttlebutt" column of the *Seattle Star* the morning after the Gallowglass. After all, wasn't success the best revenge?

Franklin might not be the outgoing, public personality type that Channel-Five joker at the bachelor auction was, but if it was for Cindy, he'd figure out how to get her the kind of attention that counted.

As if he'd even have to, he thought, thinking of the way she lit up a room when she walked into it. Thinking of the way she dazzled. She'd get attention at the Gallowglass Gala all right.

Till then — Franklin would continue to be her Henry Higgins. And maybe in time, like Eliza Doolittle, she'd fall in love with the professor.

"So you're going to keep seeing Franklin," Biddy said, eyeing Cindy with speculation.

"Don't get any ideas," said Cindy. "It's strictly friendly. He made *that* clear enough. Even said he got carried away last Sunday and it wouldn't happen again."

"And how do feel about *that?*"

Cindy considered for a moment. Closed her eyes and searched around inside her heart, beyond the pain of Jonathan's desertion. There was sweetness there, and hope. And fear. But mostly there was confusion.

"It's probably for the best," she said, opening her eyes again. "I admit — I liked it, Biddy. Franklin's kiss. But it wouldn't be fair, jumping into something with Franklin now."

"Wouldn't be fair for who?"

For whom, Cindy said to herself, remembering one of Franklin's gentle corrections. No sense in correcting Biddy though. It really didn't matter between friends. "It wouldn't be fair to Franklin," she said. "Or me, for that matter. Till I figure out my feelings."

"Just so's you're not worryin' about bein' fair to Jonathan — the pigheaded, cold-hearted, lily-livered goat."

It was ridiculous, really, with her broken heart and all — but Cindy couldn't help giggling.

"And as far as feelin' guilty goes — in case you haven't got over it yet," Biddy said, ignoring Cindy's giggles, "kissin' Franklin Fitz post-Jonathan — and it *was* post-Jonathan, Cindy, make no mistake — kissin' Franklin Fitz post-Jonathan is no comparison to Jonathan carryin' on with that snooty, sniffy, snobby woman whilst all the time leavin' you to believe *you* were his fairy-tale princess. *No* comparison."

"I thought you said I made up all that fairy-tale stuff."

"Well, Jonathan helped you along." Biddy sighed. "I don't blame you for believin' in fairy tales, Cindy. We all do, sometime in our lives. But like the Good Book says, when you're a child you think like a child, and when you're grown up, you put away childish things. Fairy tales — they're childish things. And that's all I'm goin' to say."

As the weeks of summer progressed, it seemed that Biddy must be right. Why, otherwise, would Cindy's life for the most part feel so unchanged? She didn't miss Jonathan — he hadn't been part of her daily life for so long, there was nothing to miss.

Except, as Biddy had said, the *idea* of Jonathan. The dream. The fantasy. The fairy tale. For that she did grieve, sometimes intensely.

But Jonathan himself — why, she didn't even know him anymore. She wondered if she ever had.

And despite the moments of sadness for the future she'd once believed in, Cindy's life at the moment felt rich. Full. A bit frenetic, but happy and hopeful for each new dawn.

Franklin called her every evening just as she was crawling into bed, to discuss their Stuff of the Day: lessons in history, politics, geography, the social sciences. But before they got to the big Stuff, they talked about their own, personal, little stuff.

She talked a lot about Jonathan that first week. About the whole fairy-tale thing, and how hard it was to let go of the dream. But after a week it felt like enough, and instead she found herself telling him about the characters at the Kitsch 'n' Caboodle and about what her mother and the twins were up to and about her progress on the T-shirts.

Within another week, she had the entire Ladies' Missionary Sewing Circle at the Pilchuck Church of Saints and Sinners in on the project. The little old ladies, most of them on meager pensions, were thrilled with the chance to make some extra spending money. "I explained I can't pay them till *I* get paid," she told Franklin. "But it doesn't seem to be a problem. Not if they get their money by Christmas."

"And that won't be a problem," he assured her.

Franklin, for his part, told Cindy about the characters in the John Philip Sousa Memorial Concert Band and about Cookie's adventures and Nonna Pippa's antics and about his work at Strawbridge & Fitz and his dream of someday starting a business of his own. He talked less about work and more about dreams as the days went by. She liked that.

Sometimes they didn't even get to the big Stuff, there was so much else to talk about that seemed interesting and important.

Most weekends, Franklin stayed at Mini Mac's. On Saturdays while Cindy worked, he spent time with his aunt or with Eustace, who was recovering nicely from his fractured metatarsal. On Friday and Saturday nights he took Cindy out — dining one night, dancing the other — but only so Cindy could practice her social graces and dance steps. Franklin was always the perfect gentleman, careful not to take "liberties," as Biddy called them. *Too* careful, Cindy found herself thinking once or twice.

She still hadn't forgotten that kiss.

One weekend in August she took the twins to Seafair in Seattle where, among other things, they listened to the Leschi Senior Center Sousa band — with Franklin on the sousaphone — play a rousing concert in the Food Court at Seattle Center.

And the last weekend before the Gallowglass Gala, Franklin brought his sousaphone to Pilchuck, and they really did play a sousaphone-flute duet for the Sunday-morning offertory at Cindy's church — accompanied by Miniver Macready on the piano, of course. Pastor Bob was so inspired by the music he threw his sermon notes out and led the congregation in readings from the Psalms for the entire rest of the hour. None that mentioned sousaphones — which wasn't surprising, as sousaphones hadn't been invented at the time — but plenty that talked about making a joyful noise.

"Let everything that has breath praise the Lord," Pastor Bob finished.

"Praise the Lord!" the congregation thundered in response.

Including Cindy. With an astonishingly joyful heart.

She was discovering every day, contrary to her fears, how much more there was to her life than the fairy-tale dream of a future with Jonathan.

Oh, that smile! Franklin thought as Cindy waved good-bye from her front porch later that afternoon.

And what a glorious thing it was to be in love! To see love blossom in the heart of his beloved, come to life in his beloved's eyes . . .

Not that Cindy had said anything out loud yet. But then, neither had he. And it was really up to him to make the first move, wasn't it?

The Gallowglass Gala, he decided. It was less than a week away. And the ball would be the perfect setting for Franklin to declare himself. Cindy might not believe in fairy tales anymore, but she'd find out she still believed in romance.

He was going to sweep her off her feet at the Gallowglass. He was going to convince her he could be her rebound fling, her transitional romance, and The One, all wrapped up together.

It wasn't that fairy tales didn't come true, he told himself. It was that Cindy Reilly had been stuck for too long in the wrong one.

And definitely with the wrong hero.

22

The Saturday of the Gallowglass Gala had an unreal quality from the moment Cindy woke up in the morning. For one thing, she didn't have to get up for work. She couldn't remember the last time she'd had a Saturday morning off, but Biddy had insisted.

"You oughtn't to be goin' to a fancy-dress ball smellin' like food — even food as good as Buster's," she'd said.

Biddy had a point. Sometimes even a shower and shampoo weren't enough to wash away the smells her skin and hair absorbed in the course of a day at the Kitsch 'n' Caboodle. Cindy knew from experience: One Saturday last spring, after serving the Grilled Dilled Mahimahi special all day long, she'd been asked to leave the Tillicum County Invitational Cat Show when she'd set the Abyssinians to prowling and the Siamese to yowling.

Buster had argued with Biddy — mostly for the sake of argument — that seeing as how the proverbial way to a man's heart was through his stomach, *eau de garlic* seemed an appropriate fragrance for a fancy-dress ball. But Biddy had prevailed, and Cindy had the day off.

She couldn't remember the last time she'd taken an entire day to indulge herself either. Even better, to allow herself to be indulged. After the luxury of two extra hours of unaccustomed sleep, Cindy opened her eyes to a pot of her favorite Tension Tamer Tea and the morning paper. Robin and Rosie followed their mother's soothing wake-up call with Cindy's favorite breakfast: half a ruby grapefruit, eggs Lorraine with pepper bacon, plus two slices on the side, and sourdough toast with real butter and honey.

After Cindy had soaked in a steaming bubble bath, Suzie Wyatt Hunt came over to give her a French manicure while Priscilla Cornwell Wyatt painted her toe-nails a glimmery gold-flecked pink. Thanks were due again to the twins, who watched Gordie and Gregor while their mother tended to Cindy's toes.

Later Cindy had appointments with True Marie and Narcissa, who once again worked their magic on her hair and face. Narcissa, after seeing the beautiful gold-glittered gown Cindy would be wearing to the ball, sold her a bottle of Carrie Mae

Gold-Glitter Spritzer to take with her. "Spray it on your hair and skin right before you put on your gown," she said. "You'll *glow*." And then, admiringly, "As if you didn't already."

Narcissa was going to make it big in sales.

Cindy did have an eerie moment of déjà vu when she reviewed the final results of all their work in her bedroom mirror. For the ride to Seattle she'd chosen a fluid rayon pants outfit, comfortable and easy to get into and out of without destroying True Marie and Narcissa's efforts. Unfortunately, it was the same robin's-egg blue as the dress she'd worn for the Disastrous Date That Didn't Happen.

But it wasn't her birthday, Cindy told herself, shaking the feeling. And Franklin wasn't Jonathan. Franklin was a warm, solid, dependable reality — not just a figment of her imagination. Amazingly, she trusted Franklin with her heart. Franklin, who was falling head over heels in love with her — the way she was with him. She was sure of it, even though they hadn't said the words.

Something was going to happen tonight between her and Franklin; she could feel it in her bones. Something important. Something that would forever change the course of their lives.

The phone rang just as she was packing away the gold-glittered pumps the twins had found last week at a funky little antique shop up the road in Hogg's Corner. *Sweet girls!* Cindy thought. Although shoes with straps would have been better for the kind of dancing she intended to do, the pumps fit well, and they did look perfect with her gown.

"Good," Franklin said when she answered the phone. "I caught you before Eustace got there."

She had another horrible moment of déjà vu, this time accompanied by a wildly fluttering heart. "Why? What's wrong?"

"Nothing. I just wanted to tell you I can't wait to see you."

The moment passed. Franklin would never stand her up. It wasn't in his nature.

"I can't wait to see you either," she said, wondering if she sounded as relieved as she felt. Wondering, too, if he was as excited and nervous as she was. Did he have the same premonition that something momentous was about to happen between them?

"Eustace is well enough to make this trip, isn't he?" she asked.

"He's been out of his cast for almost a month and driving Aunt Min since last weekend. They insisted, Cindy. I think they both have this vision of you as Cinderella going to the ball, and Eustace wants to be your coachman. Who am I to argue? It's my vision too."

Cindy laughed. "And mine, I'm afraid! And here I was bound and determined to give up on fairy tales. It's the dress, Franklin — it's just the perfect Cinderella gown. You won't believe how gorgeous it is."

"Did you design it?"

"I did."

"Did your mother make it?"

"She did."

"Then I already believe it," he said. "I can't wait to show you off, Cindy. I hope you don't mind."

"Show me off?"

"Your dress, your talent, your beauty, your brains, your charm —"

"Enough, already!" Cindy laughed. She'd never known anyone in all her life who gave as many compliments as Franklin did. "I'll think you're not sincere."

"I've never been so sincere. You're going to be the belle of the ball, Cindy Reilly.

Hands down. You'll probably have grown men swooning. You could make me swoon."

She laughed again. "Yeah, right."

"See you soon," he said.

"See you soon."

Unfortunately — as Franklin was reminded only moments after he hung up the phone with Cindy — the current fairy tale did include one particularly disagreeable stepmother.

Within half an hour, in fact, Franklin was ready to say his stepmother was downright evil.

He was surprised to see her standing on his doorstep in the first place. If she had something to say, she usually did it by phone — which was fine with Franklin. The less he had to deal with Filene in person, the better.

"Franklin." She ran her pale fingers, flashing with diamonds, through her black hair. Her black caftan and loose trousers fluttered around her. Her pale eyes, narrowed like a cat's, glittered with — what? Anger? Disdain? Triumph?

Franklin stared at her from the doorway, arms crossed, like a guard at the gates of a castle. "Filene." He wasn't about to invite her in, especially not with that look in her eyes. He recognized it now. It was the look she'd given Norman Meeks the day she fired him. It was anger, disdain, and triumph all rolled into one.

She wasn't going to fire her stepson. So what *was* she going to do?

"We need to talk," she said brusquely.

He didn't move. "So talk."

"Fine. If you won't show me the courtesy of asking me in, we'll have it out right here, Franklin."

He looked at her impassively. They both knew he was safer from her venom here on the stairs to his apartment, where all the world could see and hear, than he was inside. Sometimes his stepmother's sense of propriety worked to his advantage. Humiliating an employee in public was different from exposing family secrets — as if her displeasure with Franklin was a secret to anyone anyhow.

"What's it all about, Filene?"

"As if you didn't know," she spat. "*Cindy Reilly,* Franklin. *Cindy Reilly* is what it's all about."

His sudden sense of dread was so powerful it nearly knocked him off his feet. As if sensing his weakness, Filene pounced.

"Enough is enough, Franklin. You've

346

had your little fling. I'll give you tonight — which is generous, seeing as how Ms. Reilly didn't pay a single penny of the fifteen hundred dollars she bid for you at the bachelor auction."

"So you'd rather I was bringing Cookie then?" he asked innocently, hanging on to his composure with his fingernails.

She glared at him. And her expression didn't sweeten with his next words either: "It isn't a fling, Filene. I'm crazy about Cindy. I'm going to stay crazy about her the rest of my life."

"That's ridiculous!" she spat. "You're twenty-six years old, for heaven's sake. It's time you started thinking seriously about an *appropriate* mate."

"And how could anyone be more appropriate," he asked her calmly, "than the other half of my heart?"

"Heart, schmeart! Don't give me that sentimental slop!" Filene flung her hair away from her face, lifted her chin, and stared at Franklin down her patrician nose. "A coffee-shop waitress from a hick town like Pilchuck is certainly not a suitable partner for a Fitz."

The hair on the back of his neck stood on end. *If a salesclerk was good enough for my father,* the words popped into his head, *a coffee-shop waitress is good enough for me.*

But he held his tongue. No sense in stirring her up any more than she was already stirred, he told himself. Besides, he couldn't help but feel a little sorry for Filene. It wasn't just that his father had thrown her over for a shop girl; after all, Franklin Cameron Fitz Jr. had eventually married Filene.

It was the fact that Fitzy had never loved Filene the way he'd loved Molly.

Or the way Franklin loved Cindy.

No one had ever loved Filene that way.

How sad for her!

He didn't feel sad for long though. Not after Filene's next declaration. "You are going to stop seeing that girl," she said. "You are going to stop calling her. You are going to tell her good-bye, once and for all."

Every ingrained thought of keeping the peace suddenly fled Franklin's mind. Enough was enough, she'd said? Well, she was right.

Enough *was* enough.

"That's where you're wrong, Filene." He was surprised how calm and firm his voice was. How strong he felt. Not just strong . . . why, he felt absolutely exhilarated!

How could it be so easy, after so many

years of going along, to tell his stepmother he absolutely refused to go along anymore? "You've tried to control my life quite long enough," he said, his jaw set in a way he'd never before set his jaw in her presence. "No more, Filene. No more. You can't stop me from seeing Cindy. Or from marrying Cindy, for that matter. Any more than you could stop me from bringing Nonna Pippa to the Gallowglass Gala last year."

My, but it felt wonderful to stand up to her!

Filene, on the other hand, didn't seem the least bit impressed. Or intimidated. In fact, the look on her face was as close to a cartoon sneer as he'd ever seen in real life. "I'll tell you exactly what I can do," she said coldly. "If you don't stop seeing the Reilly girl, the junior-wear buyer at Strawbridge & Fitz is going to cancel her T-shirt order."

Franklin gasped. After all the time and effort Cindy had invested in the T-shirt project? All the money? He thought suddenly of all the little old ladies in the Ladies' Missionary Sewing Circle at the Pilchuck Church of Saints and Sinners who were expecting a Christmas bonus. "Filene — you can't do that!"

Her mouth twisted into an evil imitation of a smile. "Oh, but I can. And I will, Franklin. I will."

He stared at her open-mouthed, stunned into silence. He knew she wasn't bluffing — a threat from Filene was never empty.

And oh, was she enjoying this, he thought bitterly. He'd been so proud of his show of courage and independence — and all the time she'd been laughing at him. Playing with him, like a cat with a mouse that would soon be a meal.

"On the other hand . . ." Filene paused for dramatic effect. "If you do promise to give the girl up, Strawbridge & Fitz will indeed come through for her. *And* —"

Franklin waited.

"I will personally finance an expansion of her Glad Raggs evening-wear line."

Again he stared open-mouthed, but this time in disbelief. Filene would finance Glad Raggs?

"Close your mouth, Franklin," she said with irritation. "You look like a goof. I've been making inquiries since we ordered Ms. Reilly's T-shirts. I've seen her work. She may be plebeian, but she's talented, I'll give her that. Glad Raggs is a smart investment."

An investment! "So Cindy's good enough to be your business partner," he said slowly, "but *not* good enough to be my girlfriend."

"Business is business," she said coldly. "Family is family."

Family! As if Filene had any sense at all of what the word meant! Cindy Reilly and her mother and sisters — now, there was *family.* The way Franklin felt when he was with them — *that* was family. What he had with Cindy, what he *wanted* to have with Cindy . . .

How could he ever let it go?

But a chance for Cindy to realize her dream! He pressed his fingers against his temples, which were suddenly throbbing. "I need some time to think."

"I want a decision before she leaves tonight."

He felt sick to his stomach as he watched his stepmother march across the driveway to the mansion to direct the final preparations for the gala. The hired staff would be waiting, ready to bow and scrape.

Just the way Franklin always did.

"I want you to be available in the house an hour before the ball to manage the vendors," had been her parting shot.

"Filene — I have a date to escort."

"She isn't so helpless she can't make her way across the driveway by herself — is she?"

351

"She isn't helpless at all. She's —"

"An hour before, Franklin. If you really love Cindy Reilly as much as you say you do — well, you'd be wise to remember what's at stake, that's all."

Franklin narrowed his lips. She didn't know any more about love than she did about family. But he did.

"I'll be there," he said.

Cindy had been surprised and pleased when Eustace stopped off on the way to the ball to pick up Mini Mac in Bellingrath — but not nearly as surprised and pleased as Franklin seemed when they arrived at the Fitz estate. Especially when he found out Mini Mac had tickets to the Gallowglass and Eustace was her escort. For a moment, in fact, Franklin looked positively gleeful.

But he sobered abruptly, almost to the point of gloom, as he told them he was sorry, but Filene had him tied up with responsibilities in the mansion and he wouldn't be able to share the light supper Cookie was preparing in the cottage. "She wasn't expecting you, Aunt Min, but if I'm not there, there'll be plenty of food. You're not doing the cabbage soup thing this week, are you?"

Mini Mac sighed. "I never am by this time in the summer," she said.

"I'll try to sneak over at least to escort you to the door," he told Cindy.

"Don't worry about it," she said. "I'll come with Mini Mac and Eustace. But you will be available to dance with me?" she asked anxiously.

"Are you kiddin' me? I'm going to have a hard time giving you up even to Eustace, who'll want a dance or two with you, if I'm not mistaken."

Eustace's ears turned pink. "Eustace'd be honored, Miss Cindy. Dependin' on how the foot holds out."

"He's still wearing a wood-soled shoe," Mini Mac explained. "We may be doing more watching and conversing than dancing."

"Franklin?" a sharp voice called across the driveway. Filene, Cindy saw. Dressed in a slinky black sequined dress slit halfway up her thigh. "I need you in here. *Now.*" Not a word of greeting either to Cindy or Aunt Min. As for Eustace, Filene probably didn't even register chauffeurs as human beings.

"I'll see you at the ball," Franklin said, already on his way toward the house. "Cookie's all set up for you in the cottage . . ."

"Harrumph!" said Mini Mac, staring after him with her hands on her ample hips. "When is he ever going to grow up and start standing his ground with that woman?"

As if Filene's ultimatum wasn't enough for Franklin to deal with — that and directing the caterers and florists and musicians — almost the first guests to arrive for the Gallowglass Gala were Jonathan Crum and Aubrey du Puy. Jonathan and Aubrey! This wasn't going to be anything close to a fairy tale — it was going to be a *nightmare*. It already *was* a nightmare.

Aubrey disappeared immediately into the ladies' room upstairs, and Jonathan latched himself to Franklin like a tick to a dog. At the moment, they were standing at the foot of the grand staircase just outside the ballroom. Jonathan was talking, and Franklin was trying to listen politely.

But he doubted the Crumb could have carried on an interesting conversation if his life depended on it. Unless one considered torts and contracts interesting, of course, which he supposed some people did. But this was a *social* occasion, for Pete's sake — not a business meeting. No one was going to find Franklin talking about spreadsheets and market analyses.

What had Cindy ever seen in the Crumb anyhow?

What indeed? All he had to do to answer that question was see the way every woman who walked past them looked at Jonathan. At the moment, he was bestowing his movie-star smile on two dowagers at least three times his age, who were unabashedly ogling. They were dripping in diamonds, too, which Franklin guessed was the main attraction for Jonathan.

What if Cindy's not over him? he found himself worrying.

She was over him.

But what if she's not? And what if she sees Jonathan and the feelings all come flooding back and Jonathan realizes what a fool he's been —

"So how's it going with Aubrey?" Franklin asked, trying to sound casual.

Jonathan gave him a startled glance. "Going?"

"Yeah, I mean . . . are you two . . . ah . . . *serious?*"

"We've got a thing," Jonathan said nonchalantly.

Which told Franklin absolutely nothing, except that he wasn't going to leave Cindy alone for a minute with the Creep. He didn't trust the guy as far as he could throw him.

Where *was* Cindy anyhow? he wondered, glancing up the staircase for the umpteenth time.

He could hear the torch singer in the ballroom milking a tune he'd never heard before, its melody as haunting as its words:

The night we said good-bye
was sweet and sad and good and bad.
Sweet, and good, and sad . . .

His shoulders slumped as the words registered. He shoved his hands in the pockets of his new tuxedo trousers and stared unseeing at the floor. *Good-bye.* How could he tell her good-bye? How *could* he?

"I need a drink, old man," Jonathan interrupted his musings. "Bring you anything?"

"I'm fine."

He wasn't, of course, but his problem was nothing a drink could help. What was the cure for desperate confusion?

He loved Cindy Reilly. He couldn't give her up.

But to cause her to lose the Strawbridge & Fitz account!

But to leave her!

But to be able to give her Glad Raggs on a silver platter!

But to never see her again!

But to cause her to lose out on a *dream!*

He took a deep breath, trying to shut out the argument in his head. A pox on Filene! He didn't want to think about the choice she'd given him. He *couldn't* think about it. And he desperately needed to see Cindy.

Maybe he should try to sneak out and see what was keeping her. And what was keeping Aunt Min and Eustace, for that matter.

He smiled for the first time all evening at the thought of Aunt Min and Eustace attending the ball together — and relaxed just the tiniest bit to realize just how incensed Filene must be about it. It was galling enough, Franklin suspected, to have the sister of her husband's despised first wife attending the Gallowglass in the first place. But to have her bring along the chauffeur! It was the height of impropriety — even worse than Franklin's bringing Nonna Pippa to the ball last year. At least the Fortunatos had money.

Jonathan reappeared at his elbow, holding a drink in one hand.

"Aubrey can't still be in the ladies' room," Franklin said offhandedly.

"She's probably poking her nose where it doesn't belong," said Jonathan, sounding amused. "Aubrey adores your house, old man." He sipped at his drink, considering Franklin over the rim of the glass. "But a friendly warning," he said. "That doesn't mean she adores *you*. You're not her type, Fitz. Don't get yourself wrapped too tight over Aubrey."

"Jealous?" Franklin asked hopefully.

Jonathan's laugh was hollow. "Me? Jealous? As if —"

Franklin gave the Crumb a swift glance. It was as if he'd swallowed the rest of his sentence and then couldn't breathe around the words stuck in his throat. He was gazing up the stairs, his face drained of blood and his expression so shocked it was almost comical.

23

Franklin followed Jonathan's gaze up the staircase to the landing, where he spied Aunt Min and Eustace — an interesting Mutt-and-Jeff pair, as Aunt Min was nearly six feet tall and Eustace not much over five, but hardly cause for the astonishment on Jonathan's face.

Eustace was wearing a moth-eaten tuxedo and Aunt Min a royal-blue floor-length gown Franklin recognized instantly as one of Cindy's two-piece designs. The full skirt disguised Aunt Min's wide hips and heavy legs, while the boxy, short-sleeved jacket brought her tiny upper torso into balance. The color set off her dark eyes and her silver hair. She looked sensational, in fact. And she wouldn't be shy about telling people who'd designed her dress either.

How he did love his Aunt Min!

Then Miniver and Eustace stepped aside to greet someone, and Franklin saw why Jonathan was having trouble breathing. In fact, his own respiratory system failed him for a moment. For the first time in his life he understood exactly what *breathtaking* meant.

Cindy stood poised at the top of the staircase, golden and glowing against the purple light of evening that washed through the French doors behind her and the massive mullioned windows over the staircase. She was gazing upward with an expression of pure wonder on her face.

Talk about fairy tales. Talk about dreams!

Franklin knew the effect came from the great chandelier hanging over the staircase, but still she looked as if she were lit from within — as if her skin and hair were actually transparent and her golden glow came from a radiant inner light.

Her exquisite gown only added to the effect. Except for the glittery bodice, its pieced seams following the graceful curves of her body, it was indescribable as a garment — more like a cloud of gauzy golden light than a dress. It drifted around her shoulders and floated out from her slender waist like a swirling, white-gold mist.

All of this he took in at a glance, of course. In one time-stopping, earth-shaking, life-shattering instant.

To him, she was a fairy princess emerging from the mist.

But to Jonathan, she must have been a ghost.

Somewhere in the back of his mind, Franklin heard the sound of breaking glass, a strangled utterance, and a thud. It didn't matter. He couldn't take his eyes off Cindy.

Hadn't he told her she'd have grown men swooning?

It was the sound of breaking glass that drew Cindy's attention away from the string quartet playing in an upstairs alcove to the scene at the bottom of the stairs. The first thing she saw was Franklin — dear, sweet, loving and lovable Franklin. He was gazing up at her as if mesmerized.

The second thing she saw was the man laid out at Franklin's feet.

"Jonathan!"

She picked up her skirts and raced down the stairs, losing one of her high-heeled shoes as she ran and not even letting it slow her down. Jonathan — Franklin — surely not!

By the time she got there, Franklin was kneeling by Jonathan's side, loosening the white bow tie around his neck. The air was buzzing with excitement.

"What happened?" someone asked.

"He fainted dead away," someone else answered. "One minute he's standing, the next — kaput! Flat out on the floor!"

"Who is he, anyway?"

"I don't know, but *wow!* Is he *gorgeous!*"

So Franklin hadn't decked him, Cindy thought, breathing a sigh of relief as she jostled her way through the crowd. Not that Franklin was the type to go around hitting people, but she happened to know he had some issues with Jonathan. Especially since her birthday.

Jonathan stirred and groaned.

"He's coming to!"

His eyes fluttered open. "Cindy . . ."

He *was* gorgeous, Cindy thought. Even when he was groggy. Maybe too gorgeous for his own good. Maybe his looks had kept him from developing character.

"Cindy?"

Because, quite frankly, Jonathan Crum was a selfish, spoiled brat. Why had it taken her so long to figure that out?

She shifted her gaze to Franklin, who was lightly slapping Jonathan's face. She hadn't had anyone to compare him to, that was why. Until Franklin Fitz.

Until Franklin, she hadn't known what it meant to be treated like a princess. To be treasured, cherished, *adored.*

She shivered deliciously at the thought. He'd never said so, but she knew it was true. Franklin adored her!

And she adored him right back.

She knelt across from him. "Franklin Fitz, you are a dear, sweet man."

"Cindy . . ." Jonathan said again. His dark eyes focused on her face. He reached for her hand.

"I'm here, Jonathan."

"What a stunning couple!" Franklin heard someone whisper.

"Who *are* they?"

"Her gown is *exquisite!*"

"I'm sure I've seen their picture on the cover of *Roving Eye.* At the supermarket checkout stand, of course . . . I don't read the tabloids . . ."

"I heard the royal couple from that little country in Europe — oh, what's it called? — anyway, I heard they were coming to town this week."

"Think of it! Royalty . . . right here in the same room with us!"

It's for the best, Franklin told himself as he watched Cindy and Jonathan from across the room. They looked almost like an Old World painting, framed as they were in the large gilt mirror behind them, the reflection of the bronze-and-mahogany staircase adding depth and mystery to the portrait. They sat together on the walnut Victorian settee, Cindy's golden beauty a counterpoint to Jonathan's dark good looks as she leaned toward him in her diaphanous gown, retying his white bow tie in a gesture that seemed so intimate Franklin ached with longing.

"Is that her *shoe?*" he heard someone ask in an almost worshipful tone.

Franklin didn't even know he was holding Cindy's high-heeled slipper to his heart till he realized the question was directed to him. He looked down at the shoe in astonishment, then nodded numbly.

She'd be needing that shoe, he thought, if she was going to dazzle Jonathan on the dance floor. Jonathan and everyone else in the ballroom.

All she'd needed was a chance, he thought.

Not a beauty makeover.

Not a self-improvement program.

Not walking lessons or dancing lessons or etiquette lessons or Stuff Every Cultured American Really Should Know.

Just a chance to prove herself. To Jonathan Crum. To the social set he aspired to. To *herself.*

All she'd needed was a chance to wow the crowd who was going to make her a roaring success — the society women who'd clamor to lay down their credit cards just to be able to say they owned a Glad Raggs gown.

"A Woman to Watch," he imagined the widely read "Scuttlebutt" column would read in tomorrow's paper:

A rising star in the galaxy of high fashion, designer Cindy Reilly attended the Gallowglass Gala wearing a stunning gown from what just might be her premiere collection. Scuttlebutt has it that a partnership between Ms. Reilly and department-store tycoon Filene Downing Fitz is pending. . . .

Thank goodness he'd never got around to telling her how he felt about her. It would only have complicated matters.

Almost as if in a trance, he walked slowly toward the couple on the bench and knelt in front of them with Cindy's slipper. He reached for her foot beneath the hem of her gown, not saying a word.

"You've got to know you're the one I love," Jonathan was saying.

Franklin's hand connected with Cindy's foot.

"Oh!" Cindy's voice. Breathless.

I wanted to be the one to say those words, Franklin thought sadly. *To make you breathless . . .*

He slipped the shoe on her foot, his hand lingering just for a moment. He stood, still not speaking, lifted one of Cindy's hands, kissed it lightly, joined it with one of Jonathan's.

Only then did he speak: "Congratulations, Cindy. If anyone deserves to have her dreams come true, it's you."

Cindy was dumbfounded. She'd been dumbfounded during the entire Cinderella slipper scene. "Franklin!" she called after him as he walked away.

He stopped. Turned. Looked in her direction.

But not *at* her, Cindy thought, confused. He seemed so . . . distant. "It fits," she said, holding out her foot.

The words startled a direct look from him. Those wonderful dark-rimmed, summer-colored eyes! Eyes that said "I love you" as he held her gaze.

She smiled. "There wasn't a question you wanted to ask me?"

A brief flash of some strong emotion. And then nothing.

"No," he said, and turned away again.

Cindy stared after him. That expression on his face. Not the "I love you" in his eyes but that sudden flash . . .

Despair.

Despair?

She looked down at her hand, still joined with Jonathan's. Could it be —

It was! Franklin had misunderstood — that had to be it. And why wouldn't he? Cindy asked herself. Hadn't she first enlisted his help to get Jonathan back? Hadn't she asked him to be her Hegai so she could win the love of her chosen prince?

"Cindy? Did you hear me?" asked Jonathan. As if he hadn't even noticed Franklin's gesture, Cindy's response.

She pulled her hand away and looked over at Jonathan clear-eyed — as clear-eyed as she'd ever been with him.

"I heard you," she said calmly. "And the answer is no. I'm not the one you love. *You* are. You've never loved me, Jonathan. I can see that now. Now that I know what it really feels like to be loved."

"What it feels like to be —" He stopped, his expression actually alarmed. "You've met someone else?" His voice rose in a squeak like she'd never heard from Jonathan.

"Someone I love with all my heart," she said, standing and gathering her skirts to run up the stairs after Franklin.

It was the hardest thing Franklin had ever done. Especially after hearing Cindy say for the first time that she loved him. Especially when he wanted so badly to tell her he loved her too.

He almost did. But he knew it would only make things harder. "I know you have special feelings for me, Cindy."

"*Very* special. I love you, Franklin," she said again.

Oh, that smile! His heart ached from the warmth and beauty of it. And even here in a dim corner of the oak-paneled library, she had that incredible, transparent radiance about her. Maybe it hadn't been the chandelier.

Glad Raggs, he reminded himself. *Filene. Cindy's dream.*

"These feelings are common in situations like this," he tried again, fumbling for a kind but disinterested tone of voice.

Her smile faltered. "Situations like this?"

"It's the . . . the Henry Higgins phenomenon," he said. "You know, the student falling in love with the professor . . ."

Her smile failed completely. "Franklin —"

"The patient falling in love with the nurse, the client falling in love with the psychiatrist — it happens all the time."

She looked distressed. "You think I need a *psychiatrist?*"

"Oh no! I didn't mean that. I just . . ." He sighed in frustration. This wasn't going well.

Glad Raggs. Filene. Cindy's dream.

He decided to try a new tack. "You've been with Jonathan for eight years, Cindy. Don't you think he deserves another chance?"

She looked confused. "I can't believe you're saying that! After the way he's treated me!"

He couldn't believe he was saying it either. Handing her over like a lamb to a wolf. "Don't you see, Cindy? These feelings you have for me —"

He dug around in his brain furiously. What else could he say without lying to her? Because he could not, *would* not, tell her he didn't love her.

"It's natural when you've been rejected to . . . to latch on to the first person who comes along," he said.

"Latch on!"

"I've been your rebound fling, Cindy," he said, cringing as he heard himself say the words. "Your transitional relationship. Maybe it *isn't* Jonathan you should be with. I hope it isn't; you know I don't think he's good enough for you. But I know there's *someone* out there —"

Cindy drew herself up in her chair. She no longer looked either distressed or confused. She looked furious. "Why don't you just come right out and say it, Franklin?"

He blinked at the sudden change in her. "Say what?"

"Why don't you just come right out and say you don't love me?"

She didn't give him a chance to respond — not that he could have anyhow. She rose from her chair with the greatest of dignity, turned on her heel, and walked out the library door — head high, shoulders back, as regal as a queen.

Franklin slumped in his chair and closed his eyes. In the distance he could hear the buzz of endless conversations, the punch of laughter. Upstairs, in the third-floor alcove, the string quartet was playing Beethoven; downstairs, in the ballroom, Brown Derby Joe played Benny Goodman.

In his mind's eye he saw Cindy in Jonathan's arms, whirling around the dance floor. Wouldn't he be surprised at how well Cindy danced! Wouldn't she be pleased to show him!

This was the way things were meant to be, he tried to convince himself: Glad Raggs and Filene, Cindy and Jonathan.

Jonathan Crum. Self-seeking, self-serving, self-satisfied Jonathan Crum.

Franklin unconsciously tightened his jaw and clenched his fist. So help him, if the Crumb didn't start treating her the way she deserved to be treated . . .

"Well, well, if it isn't Franklin Fitz the Third."

Franklin opened his eyes to find Aubrey du Puy standing before him, hands on her sleek, scarlet-clad hips. Didn't she have anything in her closet but red? he wondered irritably.

"I wondered how I was going to get rid of my date, but it looks like you've done it for me," she said, sinking into the brocade chair Cindy had vacated. He guessed her wry half-smile was supposed to be flirtatious.

"I thought Jonathan was your boyfriend," he said coolly.

She laughed, but it wasn't a sound of delight, like Cindy's laugh. "*A* boyfriend," she said. "If you get my drift. I'm always open for new diversions."

"I'll bet you are."

How she could take the ironic words at face value he didn't know, but she did. In fact, she seemed to take them as some kind of invitation. She inclined her gleaming head toward him confidentially. "So what shall we do, now that the Big Bad Wolf and Little Miss Pollyanna have found each other again?"

And she laughed her mirthless laugh once more.

24

Aunt Min caught up with Franklin on the dance floor. In fact — to his great relief — she cut in on Aubrey, whom Franklin had asked to dance only in order to shut her up.

His relief was short-lived. Aunt Min had a bee in her bonnet. She wasn't a very good dancer either. Trying fancy footwork with Aunt Min was inviting serious damage to one's toes.

"I think you'd better tell me what's going on," she demanded.

"What do you mean?"

"Is Cindy Reilly your date for the evening or is she not?"

"Technically, yes."

"Have you danced with her?"

"Not yet. There was the thing with her old boyfriend, Jonathan —"

"Which you completely misinterpreted."

"Oh? They seem to be having a good time now." In fact, he'd been watching Cindy and Jonathan since the moment he walked into the ballroom. They did dance beautifully together. *Thanks to me,* he thought, disgruntled. When they weren't dancing, they were in the middle of a knot of admirers, Jonathan with a proprietary hand at Cindy's elbow.

Franklin wasn't the only one watching them either. Or talking about them. From the remarks he'd overheard, it appeared that Jonathan and Cindy had a full-blown mythology swirling around them, of which Cindy was probably completely unaware and Jonathan was probably milking for all he was worth. The Crumb.

"I can't believe you're letting some petty jealousy get in the way of your happiness," his aunt said.

He sighed. She read him so well. "Aunt Min, you don't know anything about it."

"I know you love her. I know you told her her feelings were 'common.' Which hurt her to no end, and besides is the silliest thing I ever heard. There's nothing common about that girl, Franklin, and *certainly* nothing common about her feelings."

So Cindy had already talked to Aunt Min.

"Does she hate me?" he asked.

"Of course she doesn't hate you. She's mad as a hornet though. And I don't blame her. What's it all about, Franklin?"

It took another two dance tunes and several stomped toes, but eventually Aunt Min wore him down. Maybe it was the stomped toes that did it. He told her everything.

Expecting some understanding. Expecting some sympathy. Which his aunt did not provide.

"So what you're telling me," she said, her tone sharp, "is that once again you allowed your stepmother to manipulate you into something patently against your best interests."

"It's not about my best interests. It's about Cindy's best interests."

"Oh, is it now? You don't think Cindy ought to have a say where her interests are concerned? You don't think you're being a wee bit presumptuous, arranging her entire life without even asking her?"

"You're the one to talk! Aunt Min, you've been trying to arrange my life since the first day I met Cindy! And I certainly don't remember asking!"

His aunt sniffed. "That's different. You were as googly-eyed as that inflatable cartoon character on the roof of the Kitsch 'n' Caboodle from the first time I saw you with Cindy."

"She'd just saved my *life*," he said.

"Exactly. As you may have noticed,

Cindy Reilly isn't exactly a damsel in distress waiting to be rescued by a knight in shining armor. If she were, you wouldn't have fallen in love with her."

"What's that got to do with anything?"

Aunt Min rolled her eyes as if he were the slowest thing since Christmas coming. "Are you kidding me? Making this decision without getting her input? It doesn't show her an *ounce* of respect, Franklin! Cindy doesn't want a savior, not besides the One she's already got anyhow. She wants a partner! An equal! And to tell the truth, Franklin, I'm not so sure you *are* equals."

Franklin jumped immediately to Cindy's defense. "What are you talking about? She's every bit my —"

"You're misinterpreting again," Aunt Min interrupted. "I mean I'm not so sure Cindy hasn't outgrown *you*. Oh sure, you taught her a few things. Just look at her out there on that dance floor! Just listen to the way folks are talking about her! But where are the lessons *she* taught *you*, son? About standing up for yourself? About going after what you really want?"

Trust Aunt Min to lay it on the line.

Franklin scanned the room and zeroed in on Cindy. He set his jaw.

It wasn't going to be easy, facing her

now. It wasn't going to be easy, standing up to Filene. But when a man was in love —

Well, a man had to do what a man had to do.

One minute Cindy was dancing with Jonathan. The next minute she was in Franklin's arms and Jonathan was looking at her over Mini Mac's shoulder, his expression quite comically helpless. Mini Mac might not be exactly graceful on the dance floor, but she was *strong*.

"I think I'd like to sit this one out," Cindy said, struggling to keep her composure. She never wanted to dance with Franklin Fitz again. After tonight, she never wanted to *see* him again. Him *or* Jonathan. In fact, Cindy Reilly was through with romance. Through with *men*. A *pox* on men!

"Fine," he said. "To tell the truth, Aunt Min's worn me out, and I'd just as soon sit for a while."

She followed Franklin to the spacious hall outside the ballroom. To the Victorian settee where she'd earlier sat with Jonathan.

The only reason she was still here and not at Cookie's, drowning her sorrows in root beer and Swiss Almond ice cream, was the attention her gown was getting.

Franklin had been right about one thing: She couldn't buy the kind of exposure the Gallowglass Gala was giving Glad Raggs.

She was glad she'd had that crash course on business and finance from her Kitsch 'n' Caboodle regulars too. Everyone she'd talked to around here wanted to talk business. In fact, they were much more interested in Stuff about Business than Stuff Every Cultured American Really Should Know. That and high fashion, which she hadn't needed a crash course to know about, as it was her business to be in the know. These high-society types were so surprising!

"A drink?" Franklin asked.

"In the absence of Pepto-Bismol — do you think you could find me a ginger ale?"

"Are you all right?"

Oh, he was so solicitous *now*, she thought peevishly. "It's been a rather unnerving evening," she said.

He started to get up, then hesitated. "Will you still be here when I get back?"

She considered him for a moment. "Only because I'm curious," she said, lifting her chin and trying for Aubrey's haughty tone. It must have worked — he looked miserable as he turned away. Which only made her feel miserable too.

What was wrong with her? Here she was at the Gallowglass Gala, with no one questioning that she belonged — well, maybe Aubrey, but frankly she didn't care about Aubrey anymore, not when Jonathan was begging Cindy to give him another chance. And on top of everything else, she even had tentative appointments with a couple of venture capitalists who wanted to see her business plan and portfolio!

Her self-improvement campaign had been a smashing success, and her dreams for Glad Raggs looked as if they might finally come true. So why wasn't her heart tripping all over itself with excitement? Why wasn't she floating around the room for joy?

Because, the truth be told, none of it meant u thing to her. Not without Franklin.

She closed her eyes and leaned against the mirror behind her. The truth was — she was only furious with Franklin because she was also madly, hopelessly, crazy in love with the man.

"What would you say to my stepmother's financing Glad Raggs?"

Cindy opened her eyes. Franklin stood before her, holding out a glass of ginger ale. "She'll have to stand in line," she said, reaching for the glass.

Franklin looked startled. "I beg your pardon?"

"I have other interested parties."

He stood with his mouth open, his face growing increasingly pale as she told him about the contacts she'd made earlier in the evening. He sank down on the settee next to her as if his legs couldn't support him.

"Franklin? *You're* not going to faint on me, too, are you?"

"You mean you . . . you mean I . . ." he sputtered.

"I don't know why you're so surprised. You're the one who said it would be good advertising for me to be here."

He shook his head, making a sound that was halfway between a sob and a laugh. He took her hands in his, and it felt so good she decided not to object. And then he told her the most incredible story of manipulation, control, and deviousness she'd ever heard outside of the movies.

"Wow," she said when he was done, overwhelmed at the idea that someone she knew in real life could do something so underhanded. "You're not making this up, Franklin?"

"I'm not making this up."

"So that's why you were such a jerk to me."

"You do see that I did it for you, Cindy?" he asked anxiously. "I know how much effort and money you've put into those designer T-shirts. Besides, to be able to see your dream come true for Glad Raggs . . . what can I say? I wanted you to have it."

"But Franklin, I've got *years* ahead of me to build my business. And sure, it's scary to think about losing the T-shirt order. But if *your* junior-wear buyer wanted them, why not Saks Fifth Avenue? Why not Bergdorf Goodman?"

"Why not Cinderella's Closet?"

Cindy smiled. Cinderella's Closet was the chain of formal-wear specialty stores Franklin had been talking about opening after he came into his inheritance. "I'd like to earn my money back before the end of the decade, Franklin. But the point is . . . Strawbridge & Fitz isn't the only game in town. Is it?"

"You're right. I don't know what I was thinking. I *wasn't* thinking. I just wanted so badly to make your dreams come true."

"You're so much more important to me than any dream, Franklin. Don't you know?"

He squeezed her hands and gazed at her

with such love and tenderness, the last of her hurt and anger dissolved into nothing.

"So you'll be okay if Filene cancels the order?"

"I'll be okay. I don't want success so badly I'm willing to sell my soul for it. Thank you anyhow, but I'll find someone else to buy my T-shirts."

Franklin sighed a most satisfying sigh and smiled a smile a hundred times more gorgeous than Jonathan Crum's movie-star grin. A thousand *thousand* times more gorgeous. Because Franklin was the man Cindy Reilly really loved.

Suddenly the gorgeous smile wavered and disappeared. When Franklin spoke, his voice had an edge of anxiety. "Cindy, would you —"

He stopped.

"What is it, Franklin?" Cindy asked, her pulse quickening.

"Would you ever consider a boyfriend who's unemployed?"

She looked at him blankly. "Unemployed?"

"I'd rather quit Strawbridge & Fitz before Filene fires me."

"Ahh," she said, trying to hold back her smile. Her pulse had returned to normal, but after everything he'd put her through,

382

Franklin deserved a few more moments of worry. "Well, that depends, doesn't it?"

She could feel his palms sweating against her own. "Depends? On what?"

"On how long he plans to be unemployed —"

"He's eminently employable."

"— and whether he ever gets around to saying he loves me."

"I haven't said I love you?"

"You have not."

His smile was back in place. "I love you, Cindy Reilly. I love you, I love you, I love you —"

"I'll believe it when you kiss me."

He did. Soundly.

Then they went to find Filene, who was so shocked when she realized Franklin was finally standing up to her that she choked on the olive in her martini.

"I've got it covered!" Cindy cried, and jumped to the rescue — thinking, in the seconds before she started her abdominal thrusts, that the Kitsch 'n' Caboodle crowd was *never* going to believe this one.

Postscript

And so, Gentle Reader, a storybook romance began. And except for a few lean years before Glad Raggs and Cinderella's Closet got off the ground, one terrible year when both sets of twins had measles, mumps, and chicken pox one after the other, and an occasional visit from Filene, who felt obligated after the olive-choking incident . . .

THEY LIVED HAPPILY EVER AFTER!